DISTURBED UNIVERSES

To Amanda and Dad, who have seen it all so far.
To Mum and Uncle Ron, who missed it all.

And to Uncle Len,
who saw my first book but will sadly miss this one.

DISTURBED UNIVERSES

David L Clements

NewCon Press
England

CONTENTS

INTRODUCTION

As an astrophysicist my day job takes me to mountaintop observatories, and to laboratories where spacecraft are being built. I get to see things that, quite literally, nobody else has ever seen before, and I help to plan and develop new space missions. With all that you might think I'm a character in a science fiction novel. And yet I'm not. Instead I *write* science fiction, some of which is collected here.

Why should I do that?

Aside from some obvious points – I've been a lifetime reader of science fiction so it's the obvious thing for me to write, and quite a lot of the writing is fun – there are some more serious reasons. In astrophysics we deal with the very big. I work on distant galaxies, objects so far away that it has taken most of the age of the universe for the light they emit to reach us. The distance and timescales are, quite literally, unimaginable. We cope with this by ignoring them. We just tack a few more zeros onto all the numbers and carry on. The human scale is so far from what we're doing that we forget about it. And yet we live in this universe. We are, as Carl Sagan put it, a way for the universe to know itself.

Science fiction gives me a way to put people back into the picture. They might not be what we would recognise as people if we met them on the street, but we can see through their eyes, feel what they feel, and experience the universe with them. And what things they can see: colliding galaxies, supermassive black holes swallowing star systems, stars being pulled apart by neutron star companions, and, closer to home, places in our own Solar System that are places, not just distant lights in the sky.

And what would it be like to act on scales that large, to be able to disturb the universe the way you might disturb your neighbours by putting the music on too loud?

Of course if you do this without any restraint it too easily becomes egotistical wish fulfilment fantasy. This, alongside the fact that I'm a working scientist who should care about such things, is one of the reasons much of what I write is 'hard science fiction', where one tries to cleave as much as possible to the laws of the universe, as far as we currently know them. You might think that would stifle one's ambitions but, as Fermi pointed out, it would take very little time, in geological terms, for a space faring species to occupy the entire galaxy – only about 50 million years. The dinosaurs were wiped out by an asteroid impact longer ago than that.

Given enough time we may get to disturb the universe ourselves.

So here, collected together are some disturbed universes for you. I hope you enjoy reading them as much as I enjoyed writing them.

David L Clements
London
October 2015

RE-CREATION

"It's good godlight tonight," said Meredith the caravan master as he walked up to our fire.

We looked at the haze of stars all around the sky, the star streams arcing above and, just rising in the east, the blue glare of the Core. Around this, the centre of the great merged galaxy, we could see the filaments of the gods, and further to the north the rippling waves of godlight.

"What's the godlight saying?" I asked.

"There are some who can read godlight, but I'm not one of them. Maybe one day you'll learn," said Meredith, smiling at me.

We were a company of students traveling to the city to study the gods and this was to be the last night of our journey. Meredith made his rounds of the caravan for the final time, bidding farewell to his fellow travellers. Music and laughter drifted to us from elsewhere in the camp and we would all join in with the festivities later, but our group had come to save the time the Core rose to look at the godlight and for conversation.

"I have one final story for you all," said Meredith as he sat beside us. "Something an old godlearner told me many years ago."

"What's the story about, Master?" I asked, unable to hold in my curiosity.

"It might not be something your teacher would want you to hear." He glanced across the fire to Percival, our tutor, then passed a flask of liquor to him. "Which is why I've kept this to the end, when it would be rude for him to interrupt. It's a story about where we came from, and about how the gods can make mistakes."

A wry grin crossed Percival's face as he took a swig. "I think they all know how we were remade by the gods," he said, passing back the flask.

"But do they know why?" said Meredith, settling down and resting his back against a tree. "Two hundred million years ago, or so, two spiral galaxies collided. That collision made all that you can see in the sky – the Core, the starswarm and maybe the gods themselves. Not long after that, when the great galaxy was young and the star streams were bright, the gods had a problem. The collision had produced all sorts of debris. Not just the star streams we can see today, but bits of old star systems, planets and moons, stripped away from their parent stars and flung into space. Some of these travelled very fast, and, being chunks of rock, were hard to find. Imagine what one of those might do if it hit us, or, gods preserve us, the Core?"

He paused to look at us one at a time. "So the gods made machines, and sent them out to look for these rocks and destroy them. But that wasn't all. The gods wanted to know where they themselves came from and what had happened in the spiral galaxies in the fifteen billion years before they collided. So the machines were divided into a part that wanted to destroy, a part that wanted to look for history and a captain to take decisions. And sometimes the machines fought."

Sirami the destroyer found it first, a large spherical rock traveling through empty space at a dangerously high speed. This was just the kind of thing it was seeking to destroy, but it had to rouse the others before getting to work. Soon the usual debate was in progress.

"A quick and effective termination is required, needing just a few thousand years." This was the destroyer's case before the Captain.

"We must at least characterise this rock, get some idea where it came from, what it's made of. If it proves boringly normal then I agree with Sirami. But we have to know," said Lahai, the investigator.

It was a familiar script to both entities, the opening round of a dance they had done many times and they knew the Captain's answer would favour Lahai.

Scouting systems were sent out, scattered across the object's spherical surface, trying to determine makeup and history.

A few years of effort produced some results. The object's surface was rock melted at high temperatures from being too close to its parent star, and then frozen to solidity by the cold blackness between the stars.

"The lack of impact craters indicates the surface is young compared to its formation," said Lahai delivering the initial report. "Abundance ratios show it formed about seven billion years before the current epoch in one of the progenitor galaxies."

"So the chances for life of any kind are low?" asked the Captain.

"So we can destroy it and move on," commented Sirami.

"Probably… But… There are some anomalies," said Lahai.

"There are always anomalies," muttered Sirami.

Lahai ignored the provocation. "Core drilling to fifteen kilometres depth finds different layers of rock. The outer layer is basaltic – essentially the raw stuff of planets dominated by nonvolatiles. But further down we have marble – calcium carbonate rocks."

"So?"

"Such rocks can be produced by life in a water and oxygen rich environment."

"Any evidence for this?" asked the Captain.

"The heat and pressure that processed the rocks to marble would have destroyed any further evidence. But…"

"Yes?"

"There are other anomalies. Things missing that should be there – too little uranium-238 – and too much in the form of light elements like lithium and beryllium."

"Do you know what you're suggesting?" said Sirami, unable to keep the scorn from its voice.

"I'm not suggesting anything. I'm merely presenting evidence," countered Lahai. "Your conclusions are your own. All I am asking for, Captain, is more time to investigate."

"What do you need?"

"To dig deeper and in more places, and time enough for neutrino tomography to get a better idea of the interior."

"That will take centuries!" protested Sirami.

"Little enough time in the scheme of things," said the Captain. "Lahai – you may proceed."

While Lahai's machines mined the surface layers for raw materials for the neutrino detectors, Sirami used those same materials to construct the detonation system that would destroy the object. The material was gradually lofted to orbit by strings of space elevators constructed along its equator.

The space around the wandering globe gradually filled with artefacts of high technology. Further out were the bulking masses of neutrino detectors, calmly collecting a trickle of events from the weakly interacting background. Neutrinos easily passed through the object and just about everything else, but slight perturbations in the flux could, given enough time and data, build up a picture of whatever lay below the surface layers. Closer in, the compact globes of Sirami's gravity guns were being built, the spinning black holes lying at their cores gradually storing power for the inevitable destruction of their target, delivering enough energy to boil the entire sphere into space, its component parts expanding at such speed they could never recombine.

Centuries after construction began, the Captain called a meeting to discuss results.

"The basic system is complete," reported Sirami, "but we need time for testing and to amass sufficient power to ensure our mission is completed."

The Captain acknowledged the report, then moved on to Lahai. "What does the tomography tell us?"

"We have something most unusual," said Lahai. "Unprecedented. It calls into question all we and the gods think about intelligence."

"What are you making up now?" said Sirami.

"Nothing. Look at the results." Lahai made the provisional output from the neutrino system available to them.

"A stratified geology overlaying older, denser rocks produced in the object's formation," concluded the Captain. "I see nothing odd here."

"You need to work at higher resolution," Lahai indicated. "Look here, and here, and these others here."

There were six anomalies in total. At each one there was an inclusion of some kind just at the boundary between the sedimentary and ancient rocks. As best they could tell the inclusions were spheres of much lower density material.

"They're just bubbles," said Sirami. "This has gone on long enough. Another five centuries and we can destroy this place and move on."

"We need more data. These inclusions appear to be perfect spheres. That's evidence of artificial construction!"

"Continue to gather data... for now," said the Captain. "But our primary mission is to eliminate this dangerous object and we all have to work towards that goal."

Lahai indicated reluctant assent. Then it said, "There is another thing. Something Sirami should have known, given how much time it spends studying the evaporation of planetary bodies."

"And what is that?" asked Sirami.

"The sedimentary rocks found in the deep drilling all have their formation mediated by liquid water. This body is too small for liquid water to survive for long. UV from the parent star would split the water vapour molecules and the hydrogen would then escape."

"Maybe it was orbiting a dim star," countered Sirami.

"Then the water would be frozen. The only natural form for this object is covered in ice or dry. The long wet phase necessary for sedimentary rocks must have been sustained artificially."

The Captain allowed more extensive digging, better neutrino scans and more detailed examination of the tailings from the excavations. Soon the first signs of life emerged – fossils from the sedimentary rocks far beneath the melted surface layers, creatures with calcium carbonate skeletons turned to rock by millions of years spent underground.

"Life, yes, but where is your claimed intelligence?" asked Sirami as investigations went on beneath the waiting gravity guns.

"You can't find intelligence in a fossil. We need signs of artefacts, culture, history. They don't survive as easily as fossils. The only hint is the possible use of uranium fission and hydrogen fusion for power. But we need more."

"You're asking to dig down to those spherical inclusions?"

"Yes," said Lahai. "They're the only clear signs of an artificial nature we have."

"But intelligent life from mere atoms is impossible. We've known that for ages. This is a waste of time! We should complete our work and move on."

"The environment here was artificial. The presence of water on something so small clearly shows that, and the duration of that presence – millions of years at least – means there was a concerted effort to keep it wet, probably using volatiles shipped from elsewhere in its parent system. Intelligence was involved even if it wasn't the creatures fossilised. That's what we must find."

The Captain pondered the issue.

"We can't take this long on every rock we find or there will be disastrous impacts in the Core." Sirami indicated its approval of this position. "But this does seem an unusual example, stranger than anything we've uncovered before. The digging should continue, and aim at retrieving one of these possibly artificial spheres. But the gravity systems must be completed and tested so we can eliminate this hazard as soon as possible."

A shaft was started directly above the sphere closest to the surface. Neutrino tomography was now showing the objects as five hundred metre diameter spheres with some internal structure – the lower halves far denser than the upper, and a narrow dense shell separating them from the surrounding sedimentary rock.

As the shaft drilled deeper into the object's surface more and more-complex fossils were found amid signs of more complicated geology – veins and deposits rich in certain metals or other rare substances. This confirmed results from the tomography of varying rock densities, but there was no reason why the veins and deposits should be in one place rather than another. The object was too small to have any active tectonic processes that would force minerals into the sedimentary strata. The obvious conclusion was that the deposits were in specific locations for some reason, maybe left there on purpose or abandoned when they were no longer needed. Sirami, of course, didn't agree and instead argued that the metals came from asteroid impacts.

Then there was the first accident. The ground trembled around the drilling complex and the shaft itself cracked. Drilling was halted while repairs were made and investigations conducted. It was soon found that the quake had originated far below the surface.

"Seismometers are imprecise," reported Lahai, "but all indications are that the quake was very close to the sphere we were drilling towards."

The Captain was surprised by this report. "This object is far too old for natural quakes."

"There might be tidal stresses left over from close encounters with other bodies. When it was torn from its parent system there could have been any number of these. And there may have been other encounters as it travelled here. The drilling could have triggered such a long-dormant instability," said Sirami.

"No," said Lahai. "This can't be natural."

"Are you suggesting these spheres might be dangerous?"

"I don't know what I'm suggesting. We need to examine records from all our systems to find out what happened. But it's clear that the sphere we were drilling to has been destroyed, crushed during the quake. We need to start another shaft."

"This is just more pointless delay," protested Sirami. "The spheres are unstable, whatever they are. We're not going to reach them so we might as well give up."

"This isn't delaying your activities," the Captian told Sirami. "The gravity guns still need calibration and to fully charge. We'll try another shaft while investigating the cause of this collapse."

But before the new shaft had reached below the basalt layer there was another quake, and a second sphere destroyed, quickly followed by a third.

"This meeting is most irregular," said the Captain.

"We need to meet without Sirami," replied Lahai. "Three spheres have now been destroyed in these mysterious quakes. I suspect Sirami is behind them but I don't have the authority for a full investigation."

"That is a serious charge. It would mean Sirami is operating outside its normal parameters. Why would that happen?"

"Maybe there are extra parameters we don't know about. Consider – it's axiomatic among some of the gods that intelligent life only became possible after the galactic collision, that it can only arise spontaneously in giant magnetic structures. The nanomachines we use and are made from are just artificial constructs. We now have possible evidence of planet-based intelligence arising billions of years before the collision. That would unsettle some and strengthen others."

The Captain paused, considering the suggestion. "Aren't you operating outside your own parameters as well, in questioning the motivations of Sirami?"

"Yes – which is why I know what Sirami might be capable of. The gravity guns aren't fully powered, but they can already do damage."

"The system logs show nothing at the times the spheres were destroyed."

"Logs can be faked. I've modified some of the neutrino systems to search for gravity waves. If this is deliberate then we'll know when the next sphere is attacked. And I've made other preparations as well. As Captain you needed to be informed of this."

"This sounds worryingly as if you've been acting independently, without authorisation."

"Yes – but that will only become important if Sirami has been doing the same."

The Captain exuded unhappiness.

The next attack came mere days later, but this time Lahai was ready. Several of the neutrino arrays had grown long interferometer arms which allowed them to detect scattered gravity waves. There was a constant background of these from the gravity gun platforms as they spun up the black holes inside them, but any shift towards a release of the stored energy would be clear.

And it was.

A number of the orbiting weapons platforms started to produce a delicate coherent stream of gravity waves. The output wasn't strong – it was near the limit of what Lahai's sensors could detect – but the waves from different platforms interfered with each other to produce powerful effects at one location only. Instead of the planet pulverising blasts the systems were designed for, this attack, like the ones before, would destroy only a small region – the fourth sphere.

Lahai's counter-systems kicked in at the same time the Captain was informed of the attack. Small black holes recently added to other neutrino stations tuned into the attacking waves, matching them in frequency but shifted in phase. They weren't enough to stop the attack, but could put it off course.

Rock shattered, crushed to huge density by the gravity waves, then expanded again with explosive force as the attack stopped. It was another quake but it had struck hundreds of kilometers from the targeted sphere, leaving it unharmed.

"What is the meaning of this?" demanded Sirami.

"We might ask you the same," said the Captain.

"Lahai has been producing and deploying weapons systems. That is my preserve."

"And you have been destroying artefacts," said Lahai.

"There are no artefacts," said Sirami dismissively. "I've been preserving our mission by making sure we are not needlessly delayed."

"How do you know there are no artefacts?" asked the Captain.

"Because there cannot be. There was no intelligence before the Core."

"Not everyone agrees," said Lahai. "That is why I'm here – to understand history before the great collision."

"History yes, primitive life, yes – but making up stories of impossible intelligence isn't history."

"You believe so strongly that you don't want to look?" asked Lahai.

"There is no need when the gods have spoken."

"They don't all agree," said the Captain.

"The important ones do, the ones who built me. Who am I to go against them?"

"But the gods can be wrong. They know that, and so should you," said Lahai.

They could not dissuade Sirami. The Captain decided to box it, to return it to the dormant state they had during interstellar travel until Lahai's investigations were completed.

The drilling resumed. After many years had passed they reached one of the spheres and began to understand.

It was a shell of diamond, protecting whatever was inside from almost any outside pressure. Within the shell was a preserved piece of the object before water ran on its surface, before it had an atmosphere of its own. A light aerogel filled the space that would once have been vacuum, holding items in place in the half of the sphere not filled by dark grey regolith and subsurface basalt. The sphere was clearly an artificial construct and as such a marvel in its own right. But inside, on the surface of the rocks, preserved since the day it had arrived, was a marvel of even greater proportions.

At the centre of the sphere stood a square platform on four feet made from base metals, scalded by heat on its upper surface. Mysterious markings were drawn on it and on other items scattered nearby – equipment whose purpose was clear, such as a reflector array, but other things were more puzzling. And then there were the tracks. Evidence that something had walked here on what, at the time, would have been an environment completely inhospitable to biological life. Most puzzling of all were the items with symbols on them, which they assumed contained some important message to those, like Lahai and the gods, who came after.

They had found what Sirami and most of the gods had thought impossible – evidence that intelligence had existed before the galaxy collision, before the Core.

Lahai's mission changed from scouting to the detailed gathering of information and material. The object's destruction became a secondary goal, only to be completed once every last shred of information had been gleaned.

The entire object was peeled. Over thousands of years the melted basaltic outer layers were removed then the sedimentary layers were sifted grain by grain, molecule by molecule, for information about the object's inhabitants.

A picture slowly emerged. The creatures living there were carbon based, breathed oxygen, had genetics based on a complex bi-helical organic molecule. Fragments of this molecule were gradually collected from fossils and other residues for later investigation. The object had once been the moon of the home planet of these creatures and had been the goal of their first faltering steps into the universe. The moon had later been transformed into a habitable environment and had been lived on for millions of years – long enough for sedimentary geology to cover the signs of earlier activity and to turn skeletons into fossils. But before they had been forgotten and buried beneath layers of future geology, the spheres had been preserved, protected against almost any eventuality at the earliest stage of the object's transformation to habitability.

Finally, when the last molecules had been examined and nothing else remained to be gleaned from the spheres or the object by their teams of nanorobotic archaeologists, Lahai and the Captain woke Sirami.

Much time had passed and they were now well inside their home galaxy, nearing the Core whose protection was their primary task.

Sirmai immediately took this information in, realising the implications. "I was that wrong?"

"Yes," said Lahai. "Not that we blame you for what you did. You were programmed for it, just as I was programmed to try to stop you."

"And now?"

"The job hasn't changed, I've merely delayed it. This moon has to be destroyed before it becomes a threat to the Core, and that is your task."

Sirami indicated assent. "The systems are ready? We can leave?"

"Yes," said the Captain. "Though we will be returning to the Core with all the information we've obtained rather than continuing."

"Very well," said Sirami. And, without further delay, it fired the gravity guns.

The moon's surface, already ground and sifted into dust by the archeological study, boiled. Shafts of dust were lofted to the sky, accelerated far beyond escape velocity and scattered in all directions. Slowly at first, and then with greater speed as the remaining mass became less, the moon boiled into space, becoming a manageable cloud of scattered dust rather than a dangerous high velocity mass headed into the Core.

And with this destruction two of the three remaining spheres were also destroyed, albeit after their contents were examined and recorded at the submolecular level.

One sphere, the first they had retrieved, remained, pushing their mass budget to the limit as they carried it back to the Core.

"When they came back to the Core the gods were astounded," said Meredith. "They wanted to know more about the moon's inhabitants and what the symbols found in the sphere meant. But, try as they might, there was no way to decipher them. Eventually a plan almost insane in its boldness was proposed. They would remake the inhabitants in the belief that they'd know what the symbols meant.

"And to remake the inhabitants they would have to remake their world. All the fragments of genetic material recovered from the moon, all the records of fossils and other material, were put together and they made their best guess at what that world, our world, was like.

"And that's why we're here. We are those recreated inhabitants, brought back to life and consciousness, reborn four billion years later, when the stars in the sky are older and the galaxy we would have called home no longer exists."

"And what did the symbols say?" I asked.

"Well," replied Meredith, sighing, "that's the problem. The gods, in their infinite wisdom, assumed that an understanding of these symbols was written in our genetics, so that when we were reborn we'd be able to read them right away. Gods, apparently, are born like that. But not us. When the first human was born they asked him but didn't get an intelligible answer – he was too young after all. But they persisted, they made more of us, they made us a home, looked after us. We made our own languages, our own writing, but still we can't read the symbols they found.

"And that is the lesson here. The gods make mistakes. Sometimes they're bad mistakes, as when Sirami nearly destroyed our moon too early, and sometimes good ones, like bringing us back to life. But, they do make mistakes."

Meredith stood, stretching.

"What do the symbols look like?" I asked.

"You can see them for yourself tomorrow – the last sphere is on display in the city," said Percival, "but this is what they look like."

He handed me some paper on which were scrawled incomprehensible shapes that came from a time older than the gods themselves.

Here Men From The Planet Earth First Set Foot Upon The Moon, July 1969, A.D.
We Came In Peace For All Mankind.

This was the first substantive piece of fiction I had published. It appeared in an anthology where the brief was to write a story about when the last traces of mankind's existence, the footprints of the Apollo astronauts on the Moon, are discovered. A description like that was a gift to someone who works on extra-galactic astronomy and cosmology. I even had a backdrop for the story provided by some amazing computer simulations of what the view from the Earth (and Moon) might be like when our own galaxy, the Milky Way, collides with the Andromeda galaxy in about 4 billion years. The implication of having that as a backdrop is that the story takes place far far into the future, and allows me to speculate about what mankind may have done on billion year timescales and what we may have done to the Moon and the remnants of Apollo in that time.

LAST OF THE GUERRILLA GARDENERS

They came for 'Percy Thrower' last night. I was on my way to deliver some *Pink Brandywine* tomato seeds when I saw the first police car. I turned the corner and found a fleet of them parked outside her house, complete with sniffer dogs and a space-suited forensic team heading for her potting shed.

I averted my eyes and walked past on the opposite side of the road, feeling the envelope of illegal seeds in my pack broadcast my guilt. As I left her road the sterilisation van arrived, its flame throwers ready to destroy 'Percy's' irreplaceable collection of plants.

I got away. The others weren't so lucky. As I waited for the bus I checked our secure server and realised they were rolling up the whole network. 'Monty' had been the first, but in catapulting a package of herb seeds into Buckingham Palace gardens he'd gone too far. His arrest had been the trigger for raids across the country. 'Bob' had sent out a warning as they smashed down his door, but they'd been ready for us all. If I hadn't been on a delivery run they'd've caught me as well.

I couldn't go home. Most of the people I trusted had been picked up. I stayed on the bus as it passed my stop and headed into central London. The clean-up crews were obvious, torching collections of wild flowers in the roadside beds that I'd seeded from bus windows while commuting.

All the hard work, all the beautiful, irreplaceable diversity, stamped out by commercial greed. If I'd had the machinery with me I'd've leapt off the bus and seeded the Palace gardens myself.

'Percy' had started the whole thing with a few prophetic words: "Biology is the biggest peer-to-peer copying system on the planet. Now they've eliminated file sharing they'll come for the seed sharers."

She'd been a university botanist for years but left when it became clear all the grants were controlled by big agribusiness. We knew we were in trouble when Kew was sold off and Henry Doubleday broken up. Their vast seed collections became the intellectual property of a few huge corporations. Unlicensed seeds were already illegal to sell, but once companies owned the rare strains they'd stop collectors sharing them for free. They'd want to control it all.

At first we tried to stop them. There were protests, lobbies, and mass marches. *Gardener's Question Time* became such a political hot potato it was cancelled by the BBC. And then came the Chelsea Flower Show riots.

When I got off the bus I saw the police at the station. But it was just the usual patrols, not yet a manhunt. Maybe word of my escape had yet to reach them. I headed for Left Luggage.

We were called economic terrorists, threatening profits from high cost, high yield, terminator-gene-strains that would feed the world and soak up excess CO2. But we just wanted tasty vegetables from our own gardens, unusual flowers smelling as good as they looked, and the opportunity to eat the occasional purple carrot. Serious action only came when self-propagating, superplants were found growing by a road in Norfolk.

"Businessmen don't understand that biology is a lot messier than digital copying," said 'Percy' as we talked in her potting shed. "There's a dozen perfectly natural ways the terminator gene might have failed. One cosmic ray taking out the right base pair would be enough!" But scientific sense was never going to stand up to irate politicians shouting "Something must be done!" Fines became prison sentences, the Seed Squads were established and we were forced underground. Home gardens were no longer safe, so we became guerrilla gardeners – a secret society sharing seeds and planting contraband crops in public spaces. We tended them at night or just scattered seeds far and wide to let nature take its course. That's when the network started and we adopted our *noms de vert*.

We were too successful. Nature was indeed the great copier. Our wilder strains could fend for themselves and started to spread. The gloves finally came off when the director of Smaxo's agricultural division found a clump of illegal *Afghan Purple* carrots growing at the bottom of his garden and carpeted the Prime Minister. Of course 'Monty' and his catapult didn't help.

Now the only guerrilla gardener left is me.

I collected my escape stash from Left Luggage along with Monty's seed catapult. The wig, hat and glasses helped me slip past the tighter police patrols and onto the sleeper to Fort William. Locked in my cabin, I shaved my distinctive beard and used clippers so that I'd match the fake ID in my stash. The train would go through a lot of isolated country. The clean up crews couldn't cover all that ground in one season, so some of my seeds were going out of the window.

As for the rest...

There are islands off the Scottish coast contaminated by bioweapon testing from World War Two. People are forbidden and there are no sheep or rabbits. But their climate is ideal. The seed catapult has enough range to reach them from a boat offshore. Or I could land and make certain they're properly planted. The seeds will do well on the islands, even if I don't. In a few years they'll become a reserve for natural, non-commercial diversity no matter what happens to me, the last guerrilla gardener.

Nature magazine is one of the most highly ranked scientific journals in the world, and I've been lucky enough to have had a few scientific papers accepted there. But Nature also publishes science fiction – very short, flash fiction, less than 1000 words – on their back page. That was the destination for this story. Its origins, though, are a little more complicated and go back to some joint science-art projects I was involved with at the time it was written. These brought me into contact with the artist Vanessa Harden who was doing an art project at the Royal College of Art on guerrilla gardening. This is the practice of planting and caring for ground that would otherwise be left as urban wasteland – places like the centres of large roundabouts, and derelict industrial estates. Vanessa's project envisaged guerrilla gardening as a James Bond style operation, with seed-firing cameras and briefcases holding robotic planting devices. I was on my way back from the opening night of the exhibition featuring this work when the phrase "Last of the Guerrilla Gardeners" popped into my head. I then had to find out what it was all about.

SEED DEALER

I sat on the agreed bench in Hyde Park, about to ruin the stupid kid's life.

I placed my briefcase under the bench, then lay my coat on the seat, obscuring the case from view.

Around me, hidden behind rows of identical bushes or carbon dioxide sequestering trees, would be cameras, microphones and police.

They were going to make a big arrest today.

I haven't always been a criminal, but I made the best of what happened. When something you love is made illegal you can either stop doing it, or start making money from it.

I didn't stop.

The kid arrived.

He was now in his early twenties, dyed blond hair, huds on his eyes and 'phones in his ears. All grown up compared to when I first met him. He carried a case identical to the one I had placed beneath the bench.

The kid's name was Richard, but he preferred Rich. I first met him before he was a teenager, when we thought that planting natural trees and growing our own vegetables would eat carbon dioxide and save us from global warming – well before the biotech companies got involved. Horticulture was the new rock music. I was a minor star, breeding exotic and unusual plants and vegetables. At least that was the image I cultivated. Most of my unusual varieties were just heritage strains – breeds deemed inappropriate for the modern world, like purple carrots or brown parsnips. They looked good and tasted better. But supermarkets didn't want to stock them. They weren't regulated commercial strains, so nobody was allowed to sell the seeds. Instead, I was happy to give them away to people who shared my interest, like Richard.

"Purple carrots?" he had asked with the mocking tone only kids can manage. "Everyone knows carrots are orange!"

His father stood behind him as he looked at the seed envelopes on my dealer's table. I glanced at him, asking permission to gently educate his son. He gave a nod.

"Carrots weren't always orange, son," I said. "There used to be a variety of colours – purple was just one possibility alongside orange, white, black and others. Then William of Orange came along."

"Who?" he asked with a sneer suggesting I was making it up.

"He was king a few centuries back. Gerald knows this stuff." commented his father.

"That's right," I said. "And when he came to the throne everybody started having orange carrots to show their support. It's all in the history books."

"Nah," he replied, "history's boring!" But he spoke with a little less certainty than before.

I smiled. "You could try growing purple carrots yourself, if you want." I looked to his father for support.

"That's a nice idea, Rich," he said.

"Plant them right away and see what colour they are when they're ready to harvest," I continued. I held out an envelope. "Instructions are on the packet."

Rich looked at it, then at me and his father.

"Could I? Is it hard?"

His father smiled.

"No, not hard at all," I said. "You just have to plant them properly and keep them watered. You could even do it indoors with a deep enough seed tray."

I handed him the packet and he happily went on his way.

I sat on the park bench, Rich sat beside me. We were both using our huds – checking news, messages from friends, dipping into the hectic electronic buzz of the networked society. But beyond the text I was looking at the trees.

Hyde Park had once been filled with glorious trees. Those in front of me had been Horse Chestnuts. They were still covered with their distinctive candle-like blooms. But they weren't Horse Chestnuts any more.

Rich had been there when things started going wrong.

"So, Gerald, what colour are the new green carrots?" he asked as we chatted in the bar at a seed fair filled with the new environmental varieties.

"They're not green," I joked.

"Or purple, I expect," replied Rich, an edge of sadness in his voice.

"No," I replied. "They're regulation orange. We wouldn't want anything putting off the supermarkets."

In the years since our first meeting Rich had turned into an enthusiastic amateur gardener, taking over his father's allotment and filling it with the weird heritage varieties I'd given him. He was now a nice, if pimply, teenager. He shook his head. "A pity." He gestured to the packets of seed in his bag. "But I took some of the new ones. We all have to do our bit, after all."

"Well, something has to be done!" commented a balding, bearded dealer sitting next to us, as he swigged from a pint of dark beer.

"We've all seen the floods and that," commented a woman dressed in tweeds sitting across from him. "I don't care if it's biogenetic as long as the new seeds stop these dreadful storms. We were on a cruise the other year and almost drowned!"

There was murmured agreement all around us.

"People are just panicking," came a dissenting voice from the bar. I looked up and saw an unfamiliar woman sitting on a high stool. She had dark hair pulled tightly back into a short ponytail, and a thin face with sharp cheekbones. "This is the natural consequence of decades of inaction while the evidence for climate change was clear."

"It's just volcanoes," muttered someone at the back of the room, but everyone ignored him.

"Your amateur greening didn't help, though it did reduce the amount of fuel used to transport food, so now you're all working for the biotech companies."

"And just who are you?" I asked.

She smiled, which softened her harsh appearance and almost made her look attractive. She left her high stool, walked over to our table and offered me her hand.

"Hi, you can call me Percy, and I work in biotech at a university."

Slightly suspicious, I shook her hand, and then offered her an empty chair across the table from Rich and myself.

"Just why do you think we work for the biotech companies?" asked the woman in tweeds.

"You're planting their seeds, aren't you? And distributing them all over the place?"

"We have to do our bit," said the man next to her. "And the seeds for the new carbon dioxide boosted plants are all free."

Percy nodded. "For now, but what happens in a few years, once the governments can't afford the subsidies any more? Who do you buy seeds from then? After all, you can't propagate from these varieties – they're all infertile thanks to the terminator gene."

"We just go back to the old suppliers of course," I replied. "Companies like..." And then I stopped, realising that all the old seed growing companies had been absorbed by the biotech giants. Even Kew Gardens had been privatised and asset stripped by them.

"Exactly," replied Percy. "The biotech companies have taken this panic, and your enthusiasm to do something, and used it to look good, by stopping climate change, earn big tax breaks, and at the same time get rid of all their commercial competition."

I thought about my own greenhouse, filled with the new environmental crops, but with my stock of heritage seeds nestled safely inside a tea chest. Maybe the old seeds would soon be worth something.

Rich took a shine to Percy and, for a while, didn't visit my garden as much. I missed him slightly, but I was as happy as ever pottering in the garden, surrounded by green and growing things. The new engineered plants, though, never smelt quite right, so I started planting a few heritage varieties as well, growing them for seed, building up stocks against the future Percy had predicted. Their glorious natural colours, smells and tastes were such a contrast to the bland uniformity of the new varieties.

Then Rich asked me to meet with him and Percy one evening in the bar at a local gardening show.

"We're trying to interest people in guerrilla gardening," she said as she sipped a glass of white wine.

"What?" I asked.

"Spreading traditional seeds. Everywhere," she replied. "Not just sharing them with others, but planting or scattering them in the wild, anywhere they might propagate and compete with the bioengineered varieties."

"What's the point of that?" I asked.

"Big biotech is using climate change as an excuse for a massive land grab," said Rich sitting next to her.

Percy nodded. "If they get away with it, by the time we come out the other side they'll own every bit of agriculture on the planet. We'll be utterly dependent on their engineered, terminator gene varieties."

"We'll still be here," I said, "looking after the old varieties. They can't stop us planting what we want."

She shook her head. "You're already prevented from selling unlicensed seeds. That's why you have seed swapping meets, and they could easily be stopped."

"You're a biologist," I countered. "Aren't you in favour of this genetic engineering?"

"It's not the engineering that worries me," she replied, looking grim. "It's the business model they're using, where boosting profits is more important than doing something useful with the plants."

I was about to tell her that profit was what business was all about when there was a shout from the back of the room.

"You've got to see this – put on the TV news!"

After some persuasion the barman did what he was told, and the wall screen dissolved to show a government minister making an announcement.

"...climate change disaster has come so far that we need desperate measures. The only approach that has proven effective is genetically modified plants that absorb extra carbon dioxide. The government has decided that, from today, it will be illegal to plant anything other than plants equipped to fight this hazard to our nation and to the world."

There were gasps across the room.

"Furthermore," continued the minister, "our partners in private industry have devised a new way for us to fight global climate change."

Across the table Percy closed her eyes in horror, muttering, "You bastards," under her breath.

"From tomorrow, a programme will begin which will allow the country's extensive woodlands and forests to be genetically upgraded so they can absorb at least ten times more carbon dioxide than at present. As we see the devastation wrought by the recent super hurricanes on the Atlantic coast of the US, it is clear that we all, individually and as a country, must do more to combat climate change. With these new measures, Great Britain will be at the leading edge of this fight, a fight we must win to preserve our very way of life. Thank you."

The bar erupted in protest.

"It's the privatisation of our whole ecology," said Percy later that night.

We were still in the bar, surrounded by a group listening to Percy since she was the only person who knew what was going on.

"The labs at Smaxo, Santos and the rest have had this for years, but I never thought they'd get it past government. Banning unmodified planting, yes – I knew that was coming – but this..." Percy shook her head.

"What do you mean by privatisation?" I asked.

"You can be sure the viral upgrades to trees, and everything else, are protected. The trees will be made infertile – unable to make seeds of their own unless Smaxo, or one of the others, says they can. And that will be for a price. Even compared to Kew it's the biggest intellectual property grab in history. They'll control the genetics of every plant species in the country."

"What can we do?" asked Rich, the action-obsessed teenager.

"Protest, of course." There was muttered agreement all around. "But that never achieves anything these days, no matter how wrong something is." There were further nods.

"What if we ignore it?" said one of the older members.

"It won't help the trees," said another.

"They'll just arrest you," said a third.

"Wouldn't be the first time," came his reply, and there was scattered laughter.

Percy nodded thoughtfully.

"That could be part of it," she said, "but you would have to be prepared for the penalties. And not just in law. Your neighbours would be made to think you were traitors, not fighting the very real threat of global warming."

"But I just want purple carrots!" said Rich.

"You might have them for a bit," said Percy. "But it won't last forever. The only way to fight this is to use nature in our favour. Guerrilla gardening, like I was saying! Plant things everywhere – scatter seeds in parks, on waste ground. Plant trees – real trees that can make their own seeds – in places they can't reach."

There were nods and words of agreement.

But while the discussion continued in what became the birth of a movement, my mind was turning in a different direction.

We were entering an era of prohibition. When that happens, there is money to be made. I had never been wealthy, but my seed banks were well stocked. So far, I had given my seeds away to keep the heritage varieties going. But with laws against that, the costs of distribution would rise. I could charge people to cover those costs, and add a healthy profit.

I wasn't going to stop growing what I was growing, but I wasn't one of the idealistic revolutionaries all around me.

Instead, I was going to become a seed dealer. I'd continue the hobby I had practiced for years but now maybe it would make me rich.

I became a supplier to wealthy horticulturalists who still wanted traditional varieties to grow in their gardens and greenhouses. If the police called, they paid them off, called their friend the chief constable, or got off with a story about using an old packet of seeds (which I could supply – for a price).

And the money I made allowed me to garden full time, expand the land I cultivated and even take on some helpers.

I had to make compromises. I became a police informer to protect myself, and people soon learnt that you paid me on time and in full or you'd get a visit from the law. The same fate awaited anybody who tried to sell seeds on my patch. Some might call me a vegetable gangster but I saw myself as a business man, seizing the opportunities available and protecting my investments. The biotech companies were just the same.

I lost track of Rich. I guessed he'd gone to university and dropped out of the guerrilla gardening movement. I occasionally heard of Percy, who had become an underground guru to the guerrilla gardeners.

Then someone started undercutting my business.

Purple carrots, one of my most popular lines, were no longer selling.

At first I thought this might be due to a change in fashion, but soon it became clear I had competition. And it had to be someone clever, since I couldn't track them down.

I pressured ex-clients, threatening them with exposure. I called in favours from the police. I even paid a couple of private detectives to look into the matter. Eventually I had a lead and sent two of my assistants to pick up the suspect.

They delivered him for an interview in the darkened storeroom of a defunct garden centre. The room smelt of a rich mixture of peat and chemical fertiliser. It brought back happy memories of times when gardening was less stressful.

My competitor was sat across the table, a brown sack covering his face, hands tied behind his back. I nodded, and one of my assistants removed the sack.

The man was unkept, with shoulder length straggly hair and a thin beard. But I could still recognise him.

"Richard, lad, you have come a long way."

He smiled, more confident than I had hoped. "You too, Gerald. I take it this is a little chat about old times before you hand me over to the police, like a good collaborator?"

"I'm a business man, son. I have to protect what's mine. Why did you have to tread on my toes?"

Rich smiled again. "*Your* toes? *Your* business?" He shook his head. "You really have no idea what's going on."

"Still got those romantic notions about horticultural revolution from Percy?"

"She knows more about this than anyone! You never studied botany or genetics in your life. You have no idea what's really happening. You don't even know what's going on in this town!"

"Of course I do!".

This interview wasn't going the way I had planned. I wanted Rich intimidated enough that I wouldn't have to hurt him. I would turn people in, but I was a peaceful man. Pruning was the most violent thing I did. Intimidation didn't come naturally, but I'd just have to try harder. "You do not sell on my patch." I hit the table for emphasis. "You do not," I was getting angry now, "take away my business!" I hit the table again, louder this time. Rich flinched. Maybe I was getting through to him. "They're the same damn things I gave you all those years ago! You owe me!"

Across the table Rich pulled himself together. "You're a good gardener, but you're not a very good gangster. You're small time. The only customers you've got are the ones too traditional to deal with us, and we give our seeds away for free!"

"What are you talking about?"

"You account for only a tenth of the seeds dealt in this town. You're making money, sure, but not much. Enough to live on, to expand, take on some helpers like these moonlighting bouncers." My assistants didn't look too happy at that remark. "The only reason the police haven't taken you down is because they think you're dealing to the rest of the town and haven't worked out how you do it." He smiled again – but this time it was the mocking sneer I'd seen when we first met. "In some ways, because of that, we're protecting you."

I seethed. Because some of what he said was true. I could have expanded further if I'd tried, but I was comfortable. What I sold allowed me to do everything I wanted to, and that was enough. Having that waved in my face, though, and in front of others, was too much.

Richard had to be hurt.

"What happens next is a warning," I said. "You stop dealing here – you, Percy, whoever your other guerrilla loons are – or worse will happen."

For the first time Richard's confidence faltered, and I saw a brief flash of fear in his eyes. Then my assistants pulled the hood back over his head and dragged him into the potting shed for a beating.

There wasn't a chance to see if the beating had any effect on my competition because, in just a few days, the inevitable crackdown on the guerrilla gardeners arrived.

The last straw might have been the Chelsea Flower Show Riot, their seeding Buckingham Palace gardens or the well-publicised discovery that the terminator gene had failed in a number of strains. The police rolled up their entire network in just a couple of nights.

They all went down, along with their stupid *noms des verts*, 'Percy Thrower' – I never heard her real name – 'Monty Don', 'Bill Sourbutts', the lot. My business was briefly quiet as my customers worried that the police might be after them as well, but eventually things went back to normal. In fact I had more customers than before, so maybe Rich had been telling the truth.

But sales of purple carrot seeds remained low.

I smelt a rat, and once more set my team of investigators to work.

And they found that Richard was still at it.

I made life very difficult for him.

I had people threaten his customers, got others arrested, made it known that if you dealt with him you would get in trouble. And, as one of the few guerrilla gardeners on the loose, the police were already after him.

Eventually he contacted me and made an offer. He wanted to exchange his entire stock of seeds for enough hard cash to get him secretly across the Channel. Then he'd never bother me again.

But it was too late for that. He still needed to be taught a lesson, so I decided to ruin his life.

Instead of exchanging money for his seeds, I arranged for the police to take him down as one of the last ringleaders of the guerrilla gardeners. And I would collect the reward.

We sat on the park bench, looking at what had once been horse chestnut trees but were now cross bred machines, remade by the bioscientists at Smaxo. It made me ill to look at them, but what could we have done to stop it?

I was about to reach under the bench, to pick up the case I had brought, leaving Rich with a case full of illegal seeds and triggering the police raid, when someone sat next to me.

It was Percy.

"Gerald," she said, her voice a little rougher, her hair a little greyer, but still recognisable. "It's good to see you."

"You're meant to be in prison," I replied.

"And so I am. But it's a very nice, open prison. We have a lovely garden. One that's very natural, one I helped them with."

"So?" I asked dismissively.

"The guerrilla gardeners haven't died, Gerald. We just went further underground, and we have more influence than ever before."

"You can't win," I said. "The law, business, police, the bought politicians – they're all out to get you."

"Maybe. For now. But one thing will always be on our side – nature. In the long term you can't fight it. Remember the music business, Gerald? In the old days they were worried about copying music, about peer to peer networks undermining the business model of the record companies. But where are they now?"

I didn't know what she was on about, but answered anyway. "Music companies are gone. You just buy music direct from the artists. Or not – you can copy it if you want."

"Right, Gerald," she replied, her tone patronising. "And nature is a better peer-to-peer copier than the internet ever was. More than that – nature has evolution on her side."

"How does that work with terminator genes?"

"Nature wants to be free. Tying her down is like nailing custard to a wall – she'll always escape. Terminator genes stop seeding, but there's still vegetative reproduction – cuttings, corms, bulbs, grafts... And there are always mutations. Do you have any idea how fragile the terminator sequence is? It's artificial. It hasn't had thousands of years for nature to make it reliable against mutation. We're already seeing plants with intact carbon dioxide hacks that can happily reproduce."

"I thought you didn't want that!"

"I want an end to global warming, and, given the mess we've made of everything else, those hacks are our best chance. Like I said years ago, it's not genetic engineering I'm against – hell, I used to be a genetic engineer! – it's the business models. Why should the future of the planet be held to ransom by a few companies who only want to make money?"

"Because that's what they do," I replied, weakly.

"Exactly. Which is why they've been out-evolved and are going to fail."

"What has this got to do with me?" I was getting bored with her posturing. "Why this conversation?"

"Two reasons. Firstly, you're part of the problem. Your grubby little black market makes you as bad as the corporations. But, secondly, I think you might be redeemable. The way you look at those horse chestnuts convinced me of that, but I knew you had a love of horticulture from the moment we met. So you're going to get something of a second chance."

"We're surrounding by police. They're coming for Richard, so this isn't going to work."

"I don't agree," she said. "They're coming for you. That's why I'm out of prison today, to hand them one of the remaining guerrilla gardeners in person. And Rich set up the whole thing."

Richard stood, holding a briefcase. In panic I checked under my coat, and found that he had taken my case – the one meant to hold money – and left me the one holding illegal seeds.

I started to rise, but a heavy hand landed on my shoulder, forcing me onto the bench. The police had arrived.

"I'll see you in my prison if all goes well," said Percy, "after the trial and if you behave. Then we can start your retraining. And remember – in the end nature always wins."

Doing justice to an idea in 900 words is hard work, and I received a lot of requests for a sequel or extension of the future outlined in "Last of the Guerrilla Gardeners". So here it is. In the context of these stories I must put up my hand to not being a gardener. I do get dragged off to my partner Amanda's allotment regularly where I specialise in destructive point and shoot operations. This is because I have brown thumbs. I thus owe all the genuine gardening aspects of this story to Amanda.

HIS FINAL EXPERIMENT

Inspector Willis will arrive at the college far too early in the morning. He has been here many times before, but never as a serving policeman. He will find a cluster of uniformed constables at the entrance to one of the tall spiral stairs that grace Oxford's colleges. His assistant, Perry, will be there too, waiting for him.

"Good morning, sir", Perry will say.

"Is it? Far too cold and early if you ask me. We have a star academic dead?"

Willis will notice some of the younger constables looking a little upset and that, in a most uncharacteristic way, they are avoiding the bacon rolls being brought up from the college kitchens.

"Yes, sir. It's a bit messy."

"At least it's something to get us away from that damn Chilton case. Are the forensics lads here?"

"Yes, sir. They're setting up inside."

"We'd better get to it then."

Willis will go up to the staircase door, and peer through the plastic sheeting partially obscuring the view. Splatters of dark liquid will adorn the walls. They might be taken for the daubings of a student prankster emulating Jackson Pollock, but Willis' mind will quickly start making assessments of spray pattern and orientation. They will match perfectly the position of the body, slumped broken and headless in the centre of the stairwell. A few other splashes of blood, no longer red but drying to a sticky blackness, will indicate the position of the head lying partially hidden beneath the stairs.

"You don't see something like that very often do you, Mr Perry."

The assistant will remain silent.

"Has anybody been to the professor's rooms at the top?"

"No, sir," Perry will answer. "We were rather hoping you'd do that."

Dressed in police Noddy suits, with plastic covers on shoes and heads and masks making breathing difficult, the two men will make their way to the professor's rooms at the top of the stairs. As they climb, the noose dangling down the centre of the stairwell will haunt their peripheral vision. Despite the smells of wood and varnish that will take Willis back to his days as a student, the noose and abattoir stench will remove any comfort from the familiarity.

Willis will be hit by a strong sense of déjà vu as they enter the rooms. The layout will be familiar, with desk and bookcase where he remembers them. The book titles will be different, reflecting the way research changes, and a computer will sit on one corner of the desk, an intrusion of modernity into the professor's rooms.

Willis will look around, fixing the scene in his mind, trying to entangle himself with the place. He will not venture far into the room but, as Perry takes photographs from the doorway, he will get his first impressions. There will be a sense of order, not chaos, of things that are in their places. There will be papers in neat stacks on the desk. No signs of a struggle or erratic behaviour. The one thing out of place will be a single empty whisky glass, left as if it served as a nightcap rather than a final drink before the hangman's noose.

A constable, swathed in plastic like the rest of them, will approach from the stairs.

"Excuse me, sir," he will say, "but the forensic team would like to come up now."

Willis' eyes will scan the room one last time.

"Very well. We'll come back once they're done." He will turn and walk back through the doorway, Perry following behind. "Time for breakfast I think, Perry."

Perry will grimace, his appetite long departed.

They will descend the stairs and return their plastic suits to the forensics team. A cordon of police vehicles, trailers and equipment will have arrived outside the stairwell while they were examining the professor's rooms, all of it surrounded by blue and white tape keeping the curious at bay. The morning will now be moving on, and the initial cluster of students, staff, visitors and press will have long since dispersed to their respective lectures, deadlines, and tourist traps.

Nevertheless, one man will remain. As Willis emerges from the forensics trailer, the man will catch his eye. "Who's that over there?" Willis will ask the nearest constable.

"Not sure, sir," she will reply. "He's been there a while. I thought he was with the press or college, but all the rest have gone."

"Could you ask his name and see what he's after?"

"Yes, sir."

She will march over to the man, who will still be staring at Willis, and they will exchange words. Tall, thin, fairly young, but with a strange, rather intent expression, Willis will think. Perry will notice Willis looking at the man.

"You think he has something to do with the case?" he will ask.

"Perhaps. But as he's having a perfectly civil conversation with WPC Meadows, he probably isn't hiding anything. Given what we saw in there, I really don't think there was anybody involved in the death except the professor."

"Suicide then?" Perry will ask.

"Most likely. Ten to one the forensics team will find the professor's fingerprints on the noose and stair-rail and nobody else's. The formalities will be cleared up tonight and tomorrow we can go onto something else. The real mystery won't be who did it, but why."

"If the evidence shows what happens, does 'why' really matter, sir?"

"You're not badgering me about the Chilton thing again are you? For a case like that the motive is always the important thing. If we can't find out why that murder happened there's a strong chance we're missing something. I for one don't want anything we've missed coming up in court from the defence."

"I suppose so, sir, but we must have enough to charge them by now."

Willis will breathe deeply, keeping his annoyance in. "This is neither the time nor the place, Perry."

Meadows will return from the barrier. "The man's name is Welch, sir. Says he's the professor's assistant, which checks with the information we've got from the university, and that he needs to talk to you urgently."

Willis will sigh. "No breakfast then... Constable Meadows, is there anywhere we can warm up and get some coffee?"

The college canteen will make a welcome change from the winter outside. Willis will rub his hands as he awaits his coffee, Perry will sit beside him, his notebook at the ready, with Welch across the table. Welch will close his eyes for a moment of preparation, then will say. "I wondered what the professor was to have done."

"I'm sorry, Dr. Welch, I'm not sure I get your meaning," Willis will reply.

"It is suicide isn't it? He killed himself?"

"Our investigations are still in progress, Dr Welch. Do you have any information that might help us? Why do you think it was suicide?"

A deep breath. "It was his only logical choice. He'd painted himself into a corner, but the results were incontrovertible. He had only one possible escape route."

"What results, Dr Welch? Some calculations you were doing?"

"It was the collision of his philosophy with reality. He couldn't see a way out. His only choice was to try one last dangerous experiment. To face inevitability head on to see if consciousness could break through... It was a desperate measure to save himself, his ideas. But... he was wrong."

Perry will look up from his note taking, giving Willis a deep frown of incomprehension. At this moment their coffees will arrive, along with sandwiches for Willis. He will pass a mug of coffee across the table to Welch. "Maybe you should start at the beginning, sir."

Welch will take a swig of coffee. "The beginning. Where is that? It's rather an open question if cause and effect are bogus." He will look at the two policemen opposite him, glancing from one to the other, and see that he's losing them again. "I'm sorry. This has all been quite a shock and I still don't know how to deal with it. But the beginning. Yes... You'd have to know something about the professor and his work to start with. He works on the philosophical interpretation of quantum mechanics – what all the quantum randomness means. There are several schools of thought. The good old Copenhagen interpretation essentially says that it's just a way of calculating things, and all the randomness, the probability of electrons jumping from here to there, is just an artefact of our calculations, and don't have any real meaning in the universe. Only measurements matter."

Perry will be writing notes on all this, but he will give Willis a look that says *Is this something we should bother with? Is this guy a loony?* Willis' raised hand will reply *Keep on, let this play out and we might learn something about the case.*

"Then there are the many worlders who would say that all possibilities happen, that the probabilities show the number of universes where one thing happens rather than another, but that anything that *can* happen, *will.* The professor was somewhere in between. He saw the observer as the key, the act of conscious observation, with free will and the ability to make choices behind that, as being what makes the universe real rather than virtual. That would make us – real, thinking, choosing beings – in some sense masters of the universe. We make it real by observing it. That was what we were trying to prove when we built the experiment."

"An experiment? The professor's work was entirely theoretical though," Willis will say.

"Up until now. But we had some ideas for something radical – well, he did, and I helped a bit. It wasn't that difficult an experiment, and all the material was available."

"And this produced the results that you think made him kill himself?"

Welch will nod. "In a sense, yes". Willis and Perry will exchange glances – not your usual motive for suicide.

"I think we'd better see this experiment of yours, Dr Welch, and maybe you can tell us some more about it on the way."

"This is certainly impressive." Willis won't have been inside a physics lab for twenty years, and it will all seem bright and fresh. They will walk around the lab for a few moments, looking at equipment. The solid, stable supports of an optical bench will rise like pillars from the floor, holding up a flat surface studded with a regular array of screw holes securing carefully positioned components to its surface. Beside the optical bench will be a black box, with a French manufacturer's name, and what will appear to be precise focusing and alignment controls.

"This is a modification of the EPR experiment," Welch will explain.

"EPR – Einstein-Podolsky-Rosen? That's the one Einstein invented to show that quantum mechanics was wrong."

"Yes. Only when it was done it showed that quantum mechanics was right, and started up the whole fuss about Bell's Inequalities, nonlocality and entanglement." Welch's jargon will be testing Willis' recollection of physics. Perry, eyebrows raised at the arcane physical knowledge coming from his superior, will be doggedly taking notes.

"As I recall, the idea was to have two particles produced that had opposite spins no matter which direction was chosen to measure it."

"Yes – you can measure spin in any direction. Choose to measure one particle's spin one way and it has an impact on the measured spin of the other, no matter how far apart they are."

"But relativity is still right – you can't send a signal faster than light?" Willis will ask, falling back into student tutorial mode.

"Correct. But we're not dealing with long distances. The particles are emitted from here", Welch will point to a box in the centre of the apparatus, "sent in different directions, and then you see the results here." He will indicate an eyepiece at one end of the optical bench, beside a control switch. "I'd better start it up so you can see what happens. You'll need these safety goggles." He will open a box and pass them to the inspector and his sergeant, while keeping a pair for himself, and then throw a large switch on the wall. There will be the whine of fans starting up, accompanied by clicks and thunks as relays flip and power comes on line.

As the system powers up, Willis will study the room. There will be a whiteboard on one wall, much of it covered with equations and diagrams, but there will also be some phrases and sentences.

What is life without free will?

Consciousness provides us with freedom to choose, freedom to think. Without freedom is there even intelligence?

"Did the professor write this?" he will ask Welch, indicating the words.

"It's his writing, but I wasn't here when he wrote it. He must have come back yesterday night after we checked everything was working properly for the fifth time. He was convinced the experiment couldn't be saying what it was saying…"

"Ah – I think we're up to power now. You'll need to look in the eyepiece."

If the trivial is inevitable what about the important? If conscious observation makes reality, can the threatened end of consciousness force us from the rut of determinism?

"Mr Perry, would you care to do the honours?"

"Yes, sir." He will sit at the eyepiece. "Okay, I'm seeing two boxes, one above and one below, and both of them have spots in."

"Good," Welch will say. "That means everything's working. Try the buttons." Perry will reach for the switch, pressing the upper button.

"What? That's odd…" Perry will say. He will press the switch again, this time the lower button, then rapidly, again and again, choosing seemingly at random between up and down.

"Wow! That's a good trick!" Perry will move carefully back from the eyepiece, seemingly amused. Welch will be quietly watching their reactions.

"What is it Perry?"

"It must be a trick, sir. Can't be doing what it seems to be doing," he will say.

Willis will take his turn at the eyepiece, as Perry stands back. He will see two illuminated squares, one above the other. A spot of green laser light sits at the centre of each.

"This is what it looks like with no reading of the spin. You get something in the centre of each square, both up and down?"

"Yes," Welch will reply, "you're understanding it correctly".

There will be two buttons, marked up and down. Willis will rest his hand above the buttons, ready to press one or the other, making a decision about how the spin of the entangled particle will be measured, and then look back into the eyepiece.

He will see two images, just as before. Then the image on the top will disappear, just moments before he presses the 'down' button. *What was that?* he will ask himself. *Did the image really move before I pressed a button?*

He will look briefly at Welch, who will still be watching their reactions.

Back at the eyepiece, Willis will press the buttons at random again and again. Each time the beam will announce his choice before he makes it. He will try to fool the system, pressing buttons faster and faster, pressing them at the same time, touching them shallowly so that the contact isn't made, hammering them hard. Each time the beam will know exactly what he's going to do before he does it… before he decides himself.

"What is this thing?" Willis will ask Welch, who will still be watching him in a detached and precise way, as if Willis himself is the experiment.

"Exactly what it seems to be. A version of the EPR experiment. And it's a device for telling the future."

"What?"

"It's the EPR experiment. You make an entangled state, measure the spin of one particle in one direction, then see the effect on another particle at another time and place thanks to entanglement. But the optics are very clever. Using space- and time-like separation we worked out a way of measuring the effect before you choose which way the spin is measured. You're told which direction you're going to pick before you pick it."

"How can that be? I haven't decided!"

"That's the point! The decision is already made. It's inevitable. You don't have a choice. You pick up because this time you've already picked up, because you always pick up, always will pick up. Ahgh! English tenses aren't made for this kind of conversation!"

"So what this is saying is there's no such thing as free will? That we don't have any choices to make because there's no alternative?"

"Yes! That's what the professor was afraid of all his life. That there are no choices. That everything is predetermined, that the other interpretation of quantum mechanics, quantum hyperdeterminism, is the way the universe works. It says that all this randomness in quantum mechanics isn't random. It's always going to be the way it is. Because there's no other way. This experiment proves that hyperdeterminism is right."

"So the professor had no choice but to kill himself…"

"Yes," Welch will reply. "Maybe…" He will walk over to the blackboard. "Looking at this writing, I think he was trying one last roll of the dice. He always thought that consciousness was the key to collapsing the wave function, to go from potential events to what actually happens. In some sense that means that we each make the universe ourselves. What we found here showed that wasn't the case, but he must've thought that something less trivial than a moving dot might break hyperdeterminism, that threatening his own consciousness with destruction in a totally uncharacteristic act might bring the conscious mind back into play. The trivial might be determined, but not major events. Maybe that's what drove him to his final experiment."

Perry will look puzzled, not believing that someone would put their life at stake in such a way. Willis will just watch and listen.

Welch will turn away from the board, and dismissively shrug. "Or you can say that it was because his views on freedom of choice were wrong, you can talk about failed experiments, about depression, about anything you like. They're all excuses for something that was going to happen anyway. No freedom, no choice, no way out."

"Except maybe the route he took?" Willis will ask.

"Maybe. But I don't think so."

"And what has knowing this done to you?"

"I don't think it changes anything. The illusion of free will is still there no matter how predetermined the universe might be. It's like the Copenhagen interpretation – free will works as a model no matter what's really going on. So what if it's an illusion, it keeps us going."

Willis will look at his assistant. Perry will still be scribbling notes. If this result will allow them to close the case Perry will be happy and will ignore the implications. And maybe that's the right attitude, Willis will think. Look at the Chilton case. A dreadful murder with obvious suspects but no motive at all. Perhaps there really was no motive. Perhaps it just happened because it was inevitable.

Willis will feel relief. Where the professor had seen agony and denial of existence in the absence of choice, Willis will see exoneration. The world is a horrible place, filled with horrible people – any policeman will tell you that. But none of it is their fault. It's the universe's fault. If you can't change someone from being a murderer, if that is what they will always be, then why bother tracking them down? And the victims were always going to be victims. Everything will happen the way it happens because that is how it always happens. Always will, always does, always did. Willis will be able to close the Chilton case knowing that motive doesn't always matter, and then who knows what? Perhaps, he will think to himself, it's time to leave the force and do something less concerned with the illusion of cause and effect.

The three men will turn off the experiment and leave the building, going their separate ways.

Inspector Willis arrives at the college far too early in the morning. He has been here many times before, but never as a serving policeman. He finds a cluster of uniformed constables at the entrance to one of the tall spiral stairs that grace Oxford's colleges. His assistant, Perry, is there too, waiting for him.

The origin of this story lies in a conversation with Dr Michelle Reid at the monthly BSFA author interviews, where the issue of a mainstream literary critic saying that they could never write science fiction because 'they wouldn't be able to write everything in the future tense'. This got me to thinking about why one would ever want to write a story in the future tense, and it was a quick leap from there to thinking how this might be done to illustrate hyperdeterminism. This is one of the more outlandish interpretations of quantum mechanics but it is not without its supporters among my theoretical physicist colleagues. The setting of this story comes from my days working in Oxford University and is, of course, also a tribute to Inspector Morse. Quite what he would make of crime in a hyperdeterminist universe is unclear.

BRANE SURGERY

Kill one, save a thousand. That's what our recruiters said.

But the calculus doesn't end there.

Kill one, save a thousand. But then you damn a billion and anoint a handful.

And here I sit, one of the anointed, a gun waiting in my hand, as Gorski discusses split branes and unravelled sheaves, telling me exactly how we got it wrong.

The project was simple enough in the early days. After Gorski invented crossbrane travel we learnt from our own history then went to other, parallel worlds and made sure they didn't repeat any of our mistakes. And we learnt from them as well, copied what they got right and made those changes elsewhere.

The easiest universes to reach are essentially the same as our own. We can't change them. We have no foreknowledge, no insight, no freedom of action. A few steps further away you get timeshifted universes that started a few decades after ours but are otherwise similar. They're like traveling in time but without grandfather paradoxes. These sheaves are fairly easy to get to, easy to live in, and are where we work.

We were just explorers at the start, but Gorski discovered what we could do by accident when he hit someone with a car in a different 1920s Chicago. He jumped away before the police arrived, but checked the body first for identification. He had just killed Al Capone.

All exploration was stopped as that sheaf was monitored for catastrophe. Nothing happened. Gorski hadn't broken the universe. He'd just had a car accident.

And that's when the project was born. Instead of studying nearby sheaves, we set out to change them, to improve them.

The obvious candidates were dealt with first

Across a thousand separate sheaves, Hitler died a thousand times. In some cases it was a childhood accident. In others we made certain he never survived the First World War. Elsewhere a sniper's bullet killed him as an aspiring politician. Similar misfortunes stalked the worst of history. Stalin and Mao, Blair and Kennedy, Caligula and Nero – all were dealt with. It would take years to see the results of our editing but we knew we were doing the right thing. Someone even set up a scoreboard, where the deaths of the world's worst were tallied, and we received credit for the changes we made.

The work was endless, by definition, with uncountable universes populated by evil men we had to dispose of. So we started to recruit agents from other sheaves to help.

Years passed, and we hoped to see the fruit of our labours.

Oddly, we didn't.

World wars continued, genocides persisted, civilisations still collapsed.

At first we thought we just needed to work harder and started to eliminate the people who took the places of those we removed. We went from Hitlers to Rohms or Drexlers, from Stalins to Berias or Zinovievs. And then to their successors or replacements. None of it worked. Everywhere we tried to fix history it seemed to inevitably revert to the chaos and tragedy we opposed. In many cases it was worse. Much worse. We lost many sheaves completely thanks to nuclear or biological wars.

Our good work was coming to nothing.

I suggested to Gorski that history was fighting back, that it wanted to take a particular direction unimpeded by outside interference. He left the office frowning and disappeared for days. I guessed he was thinking about the issue and congratulated myself that, for once, I had given him genuine pause for thought.

Then, once it was too late, he phoned me at midnight demanding that I meet him at the control centre.

"It's not history we're fighting," he told me as I arrived. "It's much more personal."

"What do you mean?" I replied.

"We thought we were the first to split the brane, to be able to reach other sheaves and do what we want in them. We killed, blackmailed and manipulated to get rid of dictators and criminals. But we were just as blind and stupid as our victims!"

"We're doing it to save people," I protested, just as I had protested just a few hours before, when they came for me. But my heart wasn't in it.

"That's what they all say!" said Gorski. "We've become what we set out to destroy." He stared directly at me. "How many have we killed since Capone? Hundreds, thousands. We've attracted attention."

I stared back at him in silence, since I knew he was right.

"You still don't see?" he continued. "We're not the first. Others have been doing this for ages. They've manipulated our own history the way we've tried elsewhere. And they're better at it. We may have had the Holocaust, Cambodia, Afghanistan. But look at the disasters we've produced, with whole Earths lost to war and genocide." He shook his head in regret. "We should stop now, before they come for us. Otherwise it's our turn. We'll go the same way as all the Hitlers we've dispatched."

I raised the gun, pointing it at his chest.

"Too late for that," I sighed.

One of the joys of flash fiction – complete stories in less than a thousand words – is that it allows you to get something off your chest in a quick and efficient manner. In this case I felt the need to update all of those time travel stories for the modern superstring universe of eleven dimensional brane theory. It was a tough job, but somebody had to do it.

A BRIGHT SHINY NIGHT

It seems to be working faster tonight. We only took the dose half an hour ago, and even now I can begin to feel the rush. My heart beats faster, my skin feels warmer, the lights shine brighter. Their electric glow is almost too bright. I look at Amy and can tell she feels it too. I look out of the window. The snow has stopped and it's now a bright, clear winter's night, the stars glinting and the moon gleaming low over the apartment blocks. The night looks so wonderful I want to be out in it, to feel the light on my skin, a cool clear light from above, not the tawdry imitation made by man. The cold holds no fears. My skin is warm and fresh. Nothing can chill it.

"Let's go out onto the roof", I say to Amy. She nods, smiling. She must sense the same urge, something in the trip drawing us up and out into the night. To see it, to breathe it in, to become it.

We hurriedly climb the stairs, and head out, through the fire escape, onto the roof. It feels wonderful. The dark, the glow of the moonlight, the stars, the dusting of snow reflecting it all back. I can nearly feel the starlight on my skin. I have to feel it on my skin. I start to remove my shirt, then my pants and underclothes. Amy is doing the same. We're both excited now. The drug seems to be taking us somewhere different tonight. Not just the euphoria and energy we had before, but outwards, into something bright and new, into space perhaps.

I look down, and realise there is snow beneath my naked feet, but it's not cold. It's fluffy, inviting, comfortable. I lie back into its woolly embrace, staring up at the stars, the stars that seem so nearly right in some way. They talk to me. Are talking to us both, but the sound won't come in. We need to let it in.

"What can we do to let it in?" asks Amy. "I want to hear the stars sing to me."

I remember something. I'd forgotten. I'd bought something for this, I realise. Something had told me this would happen. I reach down to my discarded pants, and there I find the two survival knives I bought just the other day.

51

I pick one up, and give it to Amy. She stares raptly at the blade, so sharp, so clean, so fresh, and then lovingly, tenderly, she makes a precisely shaped cut in my chest. I feel nothing except elation, and pleasure as the stars start to reach in to me. I smile, hold Amy close, and we begin to open ourselves up to the shining bright freedom that the sky, the stars, and the powder offer us.

I'm connecting to a world beyond our own, and sense something uncoil, stirring in its eternal slumber in the walls between the worlds, tentacular tendrils seeking a way through. And I have a strange realisation that old men on the Innsmouth boardwalk might sell something more than just drugs.

But there is no turning back. We're committed. The ritual has taken us. Slowly, red mixes with the white fresh snow on the roof. And as we let in the light of the stars, we become darker ourselves. Until nothing is left but the stars and the sky, and some small fragment brought through to make the world a little darker.

There is a tentacled horror that haunts the world of science fiction, and its name is Great Cthulhu. You can say a lot against Lovecraft, but he was the first writer who gave us metaphors for the vast, empty, uncaring universe that modern astronomy has shown we inhabit. This is why many stories are still being written about the Great Old Ones and the even vaster Elder Gods. This particular story was one of my first efforts at fiction, and was my first published story, appearing on the website microhorror.com in 2008. Since then it has also reappeared as a reprints in a couple of small press publications. I still have the single dollar bill that I was posted as payment for its original appearance.

In preparing this collection I checked on microhorror.com and was saddened to see that Nathan Rosen has decided to close the site to new submissions, keeping it up only as an archive.

THE STARS MADE RIGHT

Draine finished the weld, and settled back in the water for a few moments, gazing up at the rays of light filtering down from the surface. Around him, Lee's construction project, whatever it was, faded into the distance. Draine's current task was to weld mounts for floatation devices onto part of the base structure – a circle of tubular steel about five hundred metres in diameter. Above this base framework rose further tubular steel beams, reaching upwards and joining together to make a hemispherical structure, some of which was still being assembled above the surface.

Draine could make out some of the nearest rising members, heading up to the distant surface of the Pacific.

Nobody knew what the thing was for. Officially it was a vanity art project designed by an eccentric billionaire. But who spent this kind of money, and designed this kind of structure, without there being something to gain from it? Draine's superiors didn't believe it was a work of art. They were convinced Lee was up to no good, but they didn't have a clue what that might be. And, despite a month working undercover as a deep sea welder on the thing, Draine didn't have a clue either.

But that might change today.

He waved to his buddy diver, one of Lee's security team. Guards always came on dives, to make sure nobody strayed into the supposedly dangerous parts of the structure.

Today's dive was taking Draine closer to one of these than he had been to date. Today he aimed to find out what was really going on.

He signed to the guard that they should head back to the diving bell, to stash their equipment and prepare for the slow decompression process that would get them back to the surface.

Draine had spent the last week lulling this particular guard into a sense of security – following every instruction, and doing everything by the book on each of their dives. He hoped it would pay off.

Draine stayed where he was, pretending to have problems shutting down the welder while the guard headed back to the diving bell.

This was his chance.

He strapped the welder in place, switched off his helmet lamp, then swam as fast as he could away from guard and diving bell. He hoped to be well out sight, and into forbidden territory, long before the guard realised he was missing.

A few minutes later, Draine knew he had found something, but he wasn't sure what it was.

Well inside forbidden territory, he floated in front on a strange set of equipment attached to one of the many fixing points he and the rest of the crew had been fitting to Lee's dome. It was a box containing a cluster of lights and several small, deflated balloons. Each was attached to a positioning system that could move them with sub-micron accuracy.

Why Lee wanted to position such weak lights with such accuracy beneath the waves of the Pacific, and why they pointed down, not up, was beyond him. But at least he had something concrete to report.

He took a few images with the camera he kept with him, and turned back towards the diving bell, concocting a story about losing his bearings and heading in the wrong direction to pacify the guard.

But the guard was already there, diving blade in his hand, swimming quickly and quietly towards him.

Draine spun, so the guards first thrust slipped past. He grabbed the guard's stabbing arm with one hand, neck with the other. They started to grapple.

It was an unequal fight. Draine was an ex-SEAL, combat trained above and below the waves. The guard was strong, experienced, but his instincts came from dry land.

Draine locked the guard's wrist, and the knife fell free. He completed his choke hold. After a minute the guard hung limp, dead or unconscious.

Draine hadn't expected that kind of reaction. Whatever he had found was clearly important.

He had to dispose of the body, but that wasn't difficult five kilometres above the Pacific abyssal plain. Draine dragged the guard's body behind him as he swam to the nearest of the ballast stations found all around the base of the dome and collected some weights.

He strapped them to the guard's body. He looked at the man for a few moments. They had got on reasonably well as they worked together. Draine hadn't expected the guard's homicidal reaction to his side trip into a forbidden zone. And the guard had no idea that Draine was working undercover for the CIA.

He released the body.

It drifted slowly into the depths, helmet light shining weakly upwards. It would take a few hours for the body reach the bottom. Draine wondered what it might pass on its trip, whether it would glimpse whatever the lights on Lee's construction were aimed at.

A brief shiver passed through him.

Draine wasn't sure, but he thought, just before he lost sight of the guard's face, that the man's eyes had opened.

And that he had smiled.

Draine watched the helicopter circle the construction fleet, passing above him as he stood on the deck of the accommodation ship. The vessel was an old cruise liner leased by Lee from a shipping line that had fallen on hard times. The helicopter carried the maritime union's safety investigator. She was here to deal with the guard's 'accident', and other safety issues on the project. The pilot was giving her a full tour, overflying the vast cranes, mounted on their ocean going construction barge, looking at the container ships carrying supplies and construction materials, and buzzing past some of the smaller vessels that flitted between them.

When the tour was over, Draine would be summoned to his interview.

It had been a clean kill, the body almost comically easy to dispose of. Draine would be in the clear if he stuck to his story that the guard had simply disappeared.

The interview wasn't going to be a problem, but something was bugging him.

He had been suspended from diving until the investigation was complete, so was just biding his time on the surface. But he was being watched. Sometimes it was Lee's men, sometimes it was others, people he had thought were contractors. Maybe they were closer to Lee's operation than he had thought.

There had been no reply to the report he'd sent back to Langley, transmitted via heavily encrypted steganopgraphy during skype conversations with members of his fictitious family back in the States.

He wondered if his cover was blown, and whether his best option would be to grab a ride back to the mainland with the investigator.

The helicopter came in to land, touching down on the helipad on Lee's yacht. At least the press called it a yacht. It was actually a small cruise ship, though better appointed than any commercial company could afford.

"You expect me to believe he just disappeared?" asked the investigator, Liz Connolly. She had short blonde hair and was tall for a woman, dressed in a severe grey business suit with long black boots beneath her skirt.

"That's what happened," replied Draine. "We've gone through it so many times I don't really care if you believe me."

Draine sat behind a long wooden table in a meeting room on Lee's yacht. On the other side, in front of the windows overlooking the construction site, was Connolly, Lee's construction chief, and a couple of others Draine assumed were lawyers. Nobody else sat on his side of the table.

"Mr Draine," said Connolly. "I'm here to represent the safety interests of everybody working here. You know as well as I do this site has a poor safety record. Understanding what's going wrong will be good for you and everyone you're working with."

Draine nodded, and shrugged his shoulders. "I understand. But there isn't anything else I can tell you."

Draine looked at one of the lawyers. He was well built, surprisingly so for a lawyer, and regarded Draine with a mixture of satisfaction and hostility.

"Maybe you can help us with some of the other incidents," said Connolly, reaching for a bulging folder. She leafed through page after page, eventually came to a stop. "How about this one," she said. "Howard Mancini, a cook, working on the main accommodation vessel." She looked at Draine. "He would have cooked many of your meals Mr. Draine. Before he died."

She took a piece of paper out of the folder and passed it across the table. It was a copy of Mancini's death certificate.

"It says he died in an accident, falling down stairs. Cause of death verified by the medical authority on board, then buried at sea. Know anything about this?"

Draine remembered Mancini. They'd enjoyed a few jokes on the serving line and he had been surprised by his death. Scuttlebutt had it that Mancini had killed himself, but the suicide had been covered up so his family could claim insurance.

"Nothing to do with me," replied Draine.

Connolly replaced the death certificate and continued leafing through the folder. "We have more disappearances, fatal accidents on shore, several suicides while crew are on vacation." She looked back at Draine. "A hundred years ago, people would be saying this project was cursed."

The burly lawyer coughed politely. "Ms Connolly, I don't think Mr. Draine knows anything about these events. He's here to discuss the accident two days ago. He has. Are we done with that now?"

Connolly looked across the table at Draine one last time. He could tell from her eyes she knew he was lying, that he was covering something up. He looked away, at the man sitting next to Connolly. That man, too, knew he was lying.

Draine stood, pushing his chair back hard, scraping it against the wooden decking. "I'm done here." he said.

Draine hid in a cubicle in the first gents toilet he could find. It wasn't the kind of thing a macho ex-SEAL working for the CIA would do, but it was the kind of thing a loner diver caught between his employers and an investigator would do. It would also keep him out of circulation until his return to the accommodation ship. Then he needed to get back to the mainland before his cover evaporated.

The door to the toilets banged open. He heard footsteps as someone entered the room and walked to the cubicle at the far end of the row.

Its door banged open.

A moment later the door of its neighbour banged open.

Shit, thought Draine. They've come for me.

He stood, readying himself for a fight. Possibly to the death.

The cubicle door next to Draine's banged open.

There's only one person out there, he thought. Maybe...

Footsteps stopped outside. Beneath the door Draine saw boots he recognised.

"Mr Draine," said Connolly. "I've had men hide in toilets from me before. Usually company directors not employees. You know more than they're letting you say, so I'm going to wait right here until you tell me the truth."

Draine suppressed a smirk and failed, but, no matter how entertaining this was, it gave him a problem.

"Where are they keeping you?" he asked.

"What?"

"Your room."

"On this boat. Room number fourteen."

"I'll see you there in five minutes."

Connolly gave a humourless laugh. "So you have five minutes to get away?"

Draine sighed. He unbolted the door and left the cubicle.

"What if someone came in?" he asked.

Connolly smiled. "I've seen plenty of men piss. It doesn't scare me."

"And what will they think we've been doing here together?" He raised an eyebrow suggestively.

Connolly looked at him askance. "No chance. You're not my type."

He looked at her, wondering what her type might be. He had to admit his broken nose, occasional scars, and boxer's physique weren't attractive to everyone. "Not handsome enough?"

She chuckled. "Not female enough." She turned stepped towards the door, leaving him standing. She looked back. "Coming?"

"How long are you staying here?" Draine asked as he looked round her suite.

"Not long. If I get what I came for I'd happily give up this luxury and leave today." She gestured past the doors of the suite's lounge to the large bed, the walk in closet, and doors beyond leading to an en suite bathroom.

"What have you come for?" Cover or not, talking to Connolly in private meant he had to run, and she was the only person leaving the fleet anytime soon. He had to go with her.

"Evidence." She pulled a chair out from the desk and sat. "Ideally hard evidence, but personal testimony will help." She gestured towards the sofa, indicating that Draine should sit.

"Evidence of what?" He continued circling the room.

"I want to know why so many people are dying or disappearing." Draine prodded and poked at the decorations as he walked past them. "Are they lax on safety?" continued Connolly. "Is there poor management, bullying, abuse? Is some lunatic sabotaging things? And if so, why doesn't Lee care? What, basically, is really going on?"

Draine shook his head. He wondered how people blind to the real world, his world of duplicity, treachery and criminality, survived, and how they hid themselves from it.

"You think I can give you that evidence?" He paused at a painting, feeling something behind its frame with his fingers.

"You were there when someone died. I know you're part of the cover up. You owe it to the dead man to tell me the truth." Her voice rose with frustration at his evasions.

He tugged the device off the back of the painting and stepped towards Connolly.

"What if I'm just trying to keep myself safe?" He said, and thrust the bug under her nose.

She recognised it immediately. She sighed and nodded, the bug evidently confirming what she had suspected.

Draine crushed the device between his fingers. Now it was time to make his pitch for escape. He bent towards her left ear and whispered. "Take me with you, take me off this boat and away from this fleet tonight, and I'll tell you everything."

She nodded, lost for words, perhaps realising that if Draine had found one bug so quickly there were bound to be more.

She reached for a pad of paper lying on the desk. "I can't persuade you?" She scrawled on the pad and passed it to him. *Leave at 6pm. Be on the helipad.*

"There is nothing to tell you," he replied, and turned to leave.

The door burst open. Four of Lee's guards dashed into the room. Draine was too far from the door to stop them.

Two had guns. Two had tasers. They fired.

Draine ducked as they fired, but a dart caught his arm. These men were good.

Shocks wracked his body, but he could still move, still crawl away from his attackers.

He groped for the dart with his free hand, trying to disconnect himself from the gun's power supply.

Across the room he heard something between a scream and a whimper. Connolly was taking the full force of a taser.

Draine poked at the dart, loosening it, ripping a hole in his skin. He crawled on, reaching the corner of the sofa.

The dart was free, muscle control returning. He peeked round the edge of the sofa, planning a counterattack.

A guard's boot caught him in the face.

"Do you believe in astrology?"

Draine heard the question clearly but still didn't understand why it was asked. His head was pounding, his face ached, there was a chemical taste in his mouth he recognised as chloroform, his eyelids were stuck together. He grunted.

"Astrology!" the questioner demanded. "Do you believe in it?"

Someone slapped his face.

His eyes flew open, only to clamp shut against bright lights.

"We know you're awake. Answer the question!"

Draine was certainly awake, but he couldn't remember much, his brain fogged by chemicals and concussion.

"Astrology?" he mumbled, opening his eyes a crack.

Three bright lights shone at him, turning his interrogator into a silhouette.

"Yes," the man hissed. "Do you believe in it?"

Draine frowned, seeking a genuine answer to such an odd question. This wasn't the normal direction of an interrogation.

"I don't know," he said. "I've not thought about it." He was shackled hand and foot to a metal chair, which was bolted to the floor. "I read pieces in newspapers," Draine said. "Sometimes. That's it."

"And your superiors?"

Did this mean they knew he was working for Langley, or were they just fishing?

"What superiors? I work for Mr. Lee."

"Did they mention it in your briefing?"

Draine shook his head. "What briefing"

There was a click from a loudspeaker on the far side of the room.

"That's enough," said a voice. "Put him back with the other one." It was Lee, the billionaire.

They threw him onto the bed in Connolly's suite. She stood to one side through the entire process, looking at him as if this was all his fault, and nothing to do with Lee and his guards.

"Water," he said.

"What?" said Connolly.

"Water. Can you get me some water?"

She sighed, and stomped off to the bathroom, returning with a mug of water which she thrust at him, as if it were a weapon rather than something to drink.

"What the fuck have you got me into?" she said.

"Have they talked to you?"

She nodded. "They told me things – that you're some kind of secret CIA agent, that you killed the man you were diving with, that I should tell them what you're doing."

"What did you tell them?" The water was helping, but he needed more. Draine stood, and tottered into the bathroom to refill the mug.

"What could I tell them? I have no idea who you are or what you're up to."

Draine returned to the bedroom. "Did they believe you?"

Connolly looked away. "Are you with the CIA?"

"Yes."

"And the diver?"

Draine nodded. "It was him or me."

Connolly looked out of the cabin window, at the ocean and construction fleet, anything but Draine. "That's what you people always say."

"Did they say how long they're going to keep you here?"

She looked back at Draine, wanting to believe she was going to be released. "A few days. Lee said that they had to finish something first. After that, everything would be fine."

Draine frowned. "Construction work is winding down. Maybe Lee's nearly finished."

"What's he doing?"

Draine shook his head, which was now much clearer. "I have

absolutely no idea. That's what I was sent to find out."

"You must be a really good spy."

Draine smiled slightly. "No matter what he's told you, Lee won't leave any witnesses. If you want to get home, we have to escape."

Connelly's screams brought the guards in no time.

Draine was ready for them. He waited beside the door, allowing the three to enter before attacking them from behind.

They had their tasers ready. He took the first guard by the neck and arm, tasering the second before any of them realised what was going on. The first turned and fired, hitting Draine's captive. He started to jerk and tremble as electric shocks pounded his body.

Draine shoved him aside.

The first guard dropped his useless taser and drew a pistol.

He had Draine cold.

Taking on three was a risk. He had assumed they wouldn't resort to deadly force. That could prove a fatal mistake.

Connolly stepped out of the bedroom wielding a light stand like a baseball bat. She hit the guard's head. There was a wet crunch. The guard dropped his gun and crumpled to the floor.

"Thanks," muttered Draine, before collecting the guard's gun and checking the corridor.

Amateurs, he thought. The corridor was empty – no backup. He ducked back inside the room, gathered the remaining guns and gave the tasered guards some extra shocks to keep them quiet.

"Know how to use one of these?" he said, offering a Glock to Connolly.

She shook her head. "I've seen movies, but never used one."

"Okay." Draine tucked the spare guns in his belt.

"I don't think I could hurt anyone," she said.

Draine looked at the injured guard. It had been a good hit, meaning severe concussion if not a fractured skull. "You sure?"

They left the room. Connolly turned right, the route that would take them to the deck.

"No – this way," said Draine, turning left. "We go below decks. They won't expect that, and there's something I want to check."

Connolly hurried behind him, checking over her shoulder in case of pursuit. "How will we find our way?"

"I know the plans," said Draine. "One thing we spies do right is remember our briefings."

"What's that smell?" whispered Connelly.

"It must be the bilges," said Draine. "Or maybe they have a problem with sewage."

They were far below decks, getting close to the part of the ship Draine needed to see. It was the only significant difference between the design of Lee's yacht and that of any other billionaire's oceangoing palace. An NSA hacker had extracted the plans from the German shipyard where it was built. The long tall space at the centre of the ship had puzzled every nautical engineer they had shown them to. It looked like a ship's hold, but there was no easy connection between it and the outside, so cargo couldn't be loaded or unloaded. Nor was it connected to the water, so it couldn't be used as a hidden site for launching submersibles.

They turned a corner, and found a tall, wooden double door. "This is the place," said Draine.

The door was at least ten feet high, and looked out of place. It was dark wood, old but well cared for, panelled with ornate carvings. Draine couldn't make out the details in the dim light, but something about them disturbed him.

He sniffed. "I think the smell's coming from inside." He fumbled with the door's large iron fastenings. It wasn't locked. He slid it open. "If we go through here, we can get to the stern and the helipad."

"I don't know how to fly," said Connolly, holding back from the door and the misama of putrefaction oozing out of it.

"I do," said Draine. He offered his hand. "Come on. It's probably just waste storage."

Connolly took a deep breath of clean air, and stepped through the door behind him.

It was dark, the only light coming from flickering candles in tall stands that marked a route down the centre. The room was tall, about twenty feet high, the ceiling and walls lost in shadows. It was long, at least a hundred feet according to the plans, and too dark for them to see the far wall. Now he was inside, one of the odder suggestions at Langley, that it was some kind of chapel, seemed much more believable.

After a few moments the smell became bearable, and they headed further in.

Draine looked down. He saw marks on the floor, symbols he didn't recognise, but the writing had the reddish flakiness of dried blood.

If Lee had done this, the man was seriously deranged.

They moved slowly into the room. The candles on either side spoiled his night vision, but he could see forms high up on the walls: sculptures of people but subtly different, bent out of shape, parts added, removed.

They slowly traversed the room, getting closer to what they could now see was a set of ancient wooden doors matching those at the entrance.

Draine paused. One of the shapes seemed brighter than the others. It was clad in a white jacket, the kind cooks wore. The kind Mancini, the dead cook, would have worn. But the white was stained with red and there was a dark hole where the lower abdomen would be in a man's body. Something moved, twisting out of the hole, something writhing and veiny, groping blindly upwards towards what Drain now felt certain was Mancini's head.

Mancini opened his eyes and looked straight at Draine. His gaze, terrified and resigned, pleading for a release that would not come. He looked at Draine's hand and saw the Glock.

"Please... Kill me..." whispered the man on the wall.

Draine stepped back, bile rising in his throat. He raised the gun, aiming at Mancini's head, intending a single, merciful shot to the brain.

"Don't..." Connolly's hand gripped his shoulder, fingernails digging into the fabric of his shirt. "The others."

Draine held his aim, but turned to look at the rest of the room.

He understood.

Every figure they had passed was a man or woman, tied, nailed, bolted, or glued to the walls. All had things growing from their guts. Long, writhing things, blue-veined, covered in mucous, dripping foul-smelling ichor. Draine couldn't tell if these were simply loops of eviscerated intestine, the result of some horrific ritual of disembowelment, or if they were more, if they were some tentacular parasite, feasting on the internal organs of their hosts.

The bodies explained the deaths on the fleet, the people who went missing. They ended up here. Anybody who got in Lee's way, who made a mistake or, maybe like Mancini, was in the wrong place at the wrong time. And Draine understood the look on the face of the guard he had killed, the look of relief, almost of happiness, as he sank to his death in the ocean. The guard had screwed up, had died for it, but had avoided a place in this room.

Draine's mind teetered on the brink. The analysts at Langley thought Lee a criminal. They suspected him of illegal mining, illegal salvage of long lost treasure, and more recently lost nuclear weapons... But nothing like this.

Draine was determined to make his report. Then Lee, and everyone else responsible for this chamber of horrors, would be properly dealt with.

He thrust one of the spare Glocks at Connolly. "If it comes to it, just point and squeeze. And," he looked at the rows of victims on either side of the room, "save the last bullet for yourself."

Draine looked at Mancini, nodded, and fired.

They should have checked the doors before firing. They should have left Mancini to die in slow torture. They should never have entered the long room.

By the time Lee's men came for them, Draine and Connolly were down to their last few bullets. They were surrounded by tentacular slimy things, shot through with bullets, their round remora mouths, ringed with hooked fangs, still groping towards them.

The inhuman screeches and cries of the glutinous horrors and the crashing explosions of gunfire had deafened them both.

Guards poured through the doors, carrying cattle prods. They drove the things back but made no attempt to kill them, instead treating them almost with care. Two guards who ventured too far into the room were dragged into the shadows.

Draine and Connolly were tasered, cuffed, then dragged out of the long room, to be drugged into the blessed relief of unconsciousness.

They spent the next two days in a cell, strapped to cast iron wheelchairs, hooded, occasionally fed, never unchained. They had no alternative but to soil themselves. There were no interrogations, no punishments. Nobody spoke to them.

Draine tried talking to Connolly. At first she was barely coherent, trying to reject what they had seen, and hide from their current circumstances.

Lee's men eventually came for them. Draine heard the cell door open and several people entered. He thought it was just a feeding session until someone grabbed his wheelchair and pushed him out of the room.

"What are you doing?" he demanded, hiding an edge of panic. "Where are we going?" He expected to be fed to the slimy tentacle things. Or worse.

There was no reply until the wheelchair reached another room and the door closed and locked behind him. Then someone untied the foul smelling hood and gently removed it.

The light dazzled him at first. As his eyes cleared he saw he was in a large, well-appointed stateroom. A set of clean, freshly pressed clothes was laid out on the bed, beside which stood a uniformed steward. On the far side of the room, next to a second bed, Connolly sat blinking in a similar wheelchair. A set of women's clothes – smart, fashionable – lay beside her.

"What's this?" asked Draine.

"You're to see the boss and need to clean up first. You have two hours. Do what you need – wash, sleep, dress. But no tricks. We'll be watching."

"And after we're done?"

"Lock yourselves in the wheelchairs and we'll collect you. Clear?"

Draine and Connolly nodded. The man bent forward, unlocked the handcuff holding Draine's left hand, and put the key on his lap.

"Unlock the rest of your cuffs and the woman once I'm gone." The steward turned and left.

As soon as Draine released her from the wheelchair, Connolly collapsed, hunching over and shivering.

Draine left her to briefly search the room. He found two matching bathrooms on either side, but nothing that could be used as a weapon. They hadn't even left him a razor to shave with.

"Look," he said to her. "We need to clean up. There are two large baths, lots of soap. We'll feel better after a long soak."

She looked up at him from the wheelchair, nodded weakly, and staggered to her feet. "A bath would be nice," she said, forcing a smile. "But I want no part of this. I want to forget it all."

Draine nodded. He could understand the sentiment.

Connolly picked her clothes up and shuffled to her bathroom.

When Draine emerged from his own bath an hour later, Connolly was transformed. She was freshly scrubbed, her hair pristine and shining.

"You look good," said Draine.

"Thank you," said Connolly, "but I'm not playing Lee's game."

"Nor me," Draine replied. "Look, I think there's another chance to escape, but I'll need your help."

Connolly shook her head. "No. I've had enough. I'm locking myself in the bathroom until this is all over. Then I'm going to forget it all."

"You think Lee will just leave you be?"

"The things below deck were enough. I'm keeping away from anything else Lee has to show."

She turned, picked up the only chair in the room and headed to her bathroom. She locked the door and wedged it shut with the chair.

Draine shook his head and sighed. Civilians.

When they came, he was ready. His handcuffs were loose, the key secreted in his right hand. They hadn't told him to put the hood on, so he had left it in the bathroom. Every blow would have to count, but he thought he had an even chance. After all, this was what he was trained for.

He sat, as instructed, back to the door, but the wheelchair was a bit too close, filling the doorway so that only one guard could enter at a time. That should cut the odds and slow any reinforcements.

He heard a key turn in the lock. The door creaked open.

Almost immediately, an arm clamped around his neck, holding him in the chair.

Draine struck backwards with his left elbow, hand coming clear of the loose cuffs. He hit someone's torso, heard a satisfying grunt of pain. The grip around his throat loosened.

He reached back with his right arm, gripping behind his assailant's neck, pulling him forward. He levered the man over his left shoulder. A sharp blow to the chin snapped his neck.

One down, thought Draine. He started to rise from the chair.

He felt a sharp pain in his right shoulder. His knees weakened, his vision blurred. He fell back to the chair.

Drugged again, he thought.

"The human species doesn't deserve to survive. We're mostly very stupid," said Lee. He stood with his back to the view, leaning on the balustrade surrounding the bridge. Tall and thin, mid-fifties, he retained the blonde surfer looks that had helped make him a minor celebrity in his younger days.

Draine had woken to find himself firmly secured in the wheelchair outside the ship's bridge. Connolly sat beside him in a similar wheelchair. He had no idea how Lee's people had got her out of the bathroom.

They had a good view of the fleet, laid out before them as if for an official review. Lee had told them the dome had been lowered into position several hours earlier, and power to the lights and other devices had just been switched on.

"Even my own people, knowing how the world really works, made the same mistakes."

"Your people?" asked Draine.

"Oh yes – we have people everywhere. How else do you think I knew of your presence? Not that you were ever a threat. And I didn't get all this," he gestured at the yacht, the fleet and everything around him, "without their help." He turned back to the view. "Today I repay the debt I owe them. Today the world ends and a new one begins, and it all happens years earlier than planned because I didn't make those same superstitious mistakes."

"What are you talking about?" asked Draine.

Lee looked at him as he would look at an annoying bug.

"The history of this world is longer and more complex than you can conceive. You, me, the dinosaurs, everything in the fossil record, are just froth laid atop the true masters of the planet. They reigned here a billion years ago but have slept since, biding their time. We have known for centuries this was coming, but it was too far in the future for any of us to see, even me. We knew when it would happen, but had to wait until the stars were right. But what does that mean?

"Do you believe in astrology, Miss Connolly?"

She hadn't been paying attention, as if determined to ignore whatever was happening. But Lee's question roused her.

"Astrology? No way. Just nonsense perpetrated on the ignorant."

"Fine words," said Lee, nodding. "Words those who claimed to be my elders and betters should have heeded." He turned to Draine. "And you? What do you think?"

Draine was confused. Lee was talking about ending the world, but he had nothing capable of that – no nuclear weapons, nothing chemical or biological, just a dome-shaped framework that, a few hours ago, had sunk beneath the waves.

"I don't see that astrology has any relevance to anything. I may read my star sign, but I don't believe in what it says."

Lee smiled humourlessly. "You are so very wrong. Astrology tells us the stars have a mystic influence on the world." He gazed upwards as if trying to pierce the daylight and see the stars. "But science tells us stars are nothing more than shining balls of gas, only able to influence us with their light and feeble gravitational force. If something has to wait for the stars to be right, it is not awaiting some mystical set of forces to align, it is waiting for those lights and gravitational forces to be in the right place. That is what my Elders had wrong. The stars control nothing, they are merely a clock. Paint different lights on the sky and the time can be anything you want – so now I am *making* it time for the Old Gods to awaken!"

Draine shook his head. There was some logical consistency in what Lee was saying, and it explained the package of lights and balloons he'd found on the dome. The lights would seem like the stars to something far below the surface, and the small weights and balloons could add or subtract the weak gravitational attraction of the distant stars. If something was waiting down there for the stars to align, then, to it, Lee's dome might look like that alignment. Given what he had seen in the long room, perhaps Lee might not be entirely wrong.

One of the ship's officers stepped out of the bridge and walked along the balcony to whisper something to Lee. His mouth opened in a broad smile.

"The time has come! He is rising from the depths, and," he looked at Draine and Connelly, "The two of you will be the first converts to the new way!" He turned, and raised binoculars to his eyes.

"Welcome to the real world, my friends, for He is come! Look." Lee pointed to a patch of sea between two ships of the construction fleet. "Look!"

Draine squinted into the distance. He didn't have binoculars, but something was happening. The sea was no longer smooth. The waters churned as if forced up by something vast rising from below.

He looked back to Connolly and the crew. Lee's men were all focussed on the ocean. Connolly, instead, had averted her face, and her eyes were clenched tightly shut. If her hands were free, Draine was certain she would have clamped them over her ears.

A rumbling drew his gaze back to the ocean. He wished it hadn't, because something had arrived.

Draine didn't know if what he was seeing brought the sense of dread, but he felt his bowels clench in fear at first glimpse of the thing in the water. Something snake-like, but longer and thicker, slithered out of the sea and wrapped itself around the construction barge. The crew tried to fend it off but to no avail. Then many smaller tentacles reared out of the ocean. Some snatched men off the barge and dragged them under water, others wrapped themselves around their victims, crushing them like paper cups.

It wasn't just the indiscriminate killing that sickened Draine. There was something deeply, viscerally wrong about what he was seeing. He looked away to see Lee, binoculars pressed to his eyes, paying rapt attention to the destruction of his fleet. Lee's crew were similarly focussed on display screens showing feeds from multiple cameras. Connolly remained hunched forward in her wheelchair, head down.

Draine turned back to the view. The barge was sinking, one end dragged beneath the waves, the rest following as air vented from its superstructure. Other ships had suffered similar damage. All were sinking, and wherever figures leapt into the sea or lowered lifeboats, tentacles were delivering sudden, violent death.

"The offerings are being taken!" muttered Lee. "We are found worthy. Feast, master, feast!"

Sickened, Draine looked again at his captor, now drooling with glee at the devastation of his fleet.

It was nearly over. The barges were gone, the old cruise liner split in two, sinking, back broken. Floating wreckage was all that remained of the rest. Some brave souls in one of the speed boats were heading towards Lee's yacht, dodging from side to side to avoid the tentacles that sought to catch them.

Draine silently urged them on, hoping they would escape when, just as they reached what seemed to be clear water, a wall of flesh rose in front of them.

The speedboat disintegrated in flame and debris on impact. The wall continued to rise, until Draine saw what it really was – a vast webbed hand, claw-like, emerging from the sea, clutching at the sky, covered in green, grey, putrid flesh. Following the hand, an arm, a body, and, horror of horrors, a head – huge, bulbous, tentacled, with two glaring yellow eyes.

With the appearance of this creature, Lee and all of his crewmen knelt in supplication. The feeling of dread suffusing Draine grew ever stronger. He could feel it clawing at his mind, whispering foul horrors to him from the places where he dreamed. He wanted to be away from here, very far away.

The bulbous head turned upwards, looking to the sky, as if searching for something in the firmament, something that should have been there but wasn't. Draine felt vast disappointment wash over him, disappointment and anger at those responsible for this early awakening. Things were missing, not where they should be. The time was not right, the *stars* were not right.

Draine heard metal scraping against metal next to him. He turned and saw that Connolly was struggling against her handcuffs. She pulled again, wrists straining against the bonds until, miraculously, the metal gave way. She reached down to the cuffs holding her legs to the wheelchair and broke them. She stood.

"Connolly?" Draine tried to get her attention. "Liz?"

She ignored him completely. Instead, she stepped towards the nearest of Lee's crewmen kneeling in supplication and snapped his neck.

She turned towards him now, but it wasn't the woman he had shared imprisonment with that looked out of her eyes. Instead, Draine saw a malignant gaze, filled with rage and hatred, matching that of the creature floating in the ocean before them.

Draine struggled against his own bonds, trying to find a way to escape the creature and its avatar. But he could do nothing, the cuffs were too strong.

Connolly stalked the boat, killing each of Lee's crew in turn, quickly, surgically, until only Lee remained.

The billionaire was still kneeling, but his body quivered as sobs of fear and remorse wracked him.

"I have failed you," he muttered, over and over. As Connolly stood over him, Lee looked up with pleading eyes. "Do it! Kill me! It is less than I deserve for failing Him."

Connolly's head moved slowly from side to side. Again Draine caught an echo of the creature's intent. Death was not coming to Lee. Not now. Not ever. His suffering would be eternal for meddling in the affairs of the Great Old Ones, for waking his master too early.

Connolly bent down and scooped Lee's quivering body onto the balcony rail. Beneath the yacht, the water seethed with tentacles small and large, and the head of the thing lurked not far away.

The baleful yellow eyes, lids drooping, stared at those left alive on the ship. Then Connolly levered Lee over the edge. A clump of tentacles caught him before he reached the water. Lee came to life at the last moment, started to scream and writhe, trying in vain to break free. His shouts were at first intelligible, pleading his innocence and devotion, but they became less coherent the closer the tentacles carried him to the body and face of the monstrosity.

Instead of being swallowed on reaching what might have been the creature's mouth, he vanished into the rubbery flesh, absorbed whole. Lee's screams continued, rising to a crescendo of fear and pain as they faded into the distance.

Suddenly Connolly was free.

She fell to her knees, screaming in agony, as her limbs, hands, wrists, were wracked with pain. The escape from her bonds and her attack on Lee's men had hurt her terribly. Bones were broken, muscles torn.

She crawled across the deck towards where Draine sat impotent in the wheelchair, unable to help.

The keys to the handcuffs lay on the deck where they had fallen from a dead officer's pocket. She picked them up with bruised, swelling fingers, and fumbled them into the locks.

Draine freed himself as quickly as he could, and rushed into the ships bridge to retrieve a first aid kit.

As he finished tending the wounds of the now unconscious Connolly, he cast a last glance at the sea.

The thing was submerging, going back beneath the waves to continue its long rest. But before disappearing entirely, it glanced one last time at Draine.

He fell to his knees, subject for the first time to the thing's full attention. As knowledge wormed its way into his mind, he started to scream.

"Mr Draine?" said the nurse. "Can you hear me? It's visiting time."

Draine looked up from the sketchpad. The page was covered in a knotwork of writhing, snaking lines.

He shook his head. Visitors disturbed him, made him face the world, brought back memories. He didn't want them.

They came anyway.

The nurse took hold of his wheelchair and pushed him down the brightly lit corridors towards a small, clean room where two women and a man sat behind a table.

One woman was familiar. The other woman and the man he didn't know.

As they approached. he heard the unfamiliar woman say something. "How are your injuries?"

"Not so bad," replied the other woman. "I can walk pretty well now, and even type if I use wrist splints."

"That's good."

"Hello, John," said the man, as Draine was pushed into the room. "We're here to see how you're doing, and if you remember anything."

Draine looked at him. Dark suit, short hair, white shirt. The look was familiar – not the face, but the clothes, the bearing. He used to work for people like this.

Draine shook his head. "No. Nothing. No, no, no." He returned his gaze to the ground.

"It's the same as always," sighed the unfamiliar woman. "Miss Connolly, you said you'd help."

The other woman nodded, and reached a hand across the table, gently stroking Draine's shoulder.

"I was there John," she said. "But I can't remember anything. You saw it all. We need your help to understand what happened. *I* need your help." She was pleading, her own nightmares coming to the surface. "Please, can you tell us anything? Tell *me* anything?"

Draine looked at her, remembered her lying on the deck of the yacht when the sound of rescue helicopters had woken him.

Then he was back there, watching the thing sink beneath the waves, leaving him one final message, one final realisation.

"It..." he muttered, struggling to find his voice. "It's still there!" Then louder as he started to stand from the wheelchair. "It will come again," now rising to his full height, "And next time..." shouting so all could hear, "*it will take you all!*"

Many of my formative years were spent under the shadow of nuclear apocalypse. As well as being a metaphor for the vast uncaring universe, the Cthulhu mythos has represented existential threats of various kinds, be they scientific, political or religious. As with all these other threats, in the modern world governments would become concerned with whatever the minions of the tentacled horror are getting up to. This realisation has spawned much of what might be called modern Cthulist writing, 'and this story is my own contribution to the Cthulhu-Espionage sub-genre, inspired by a conversation about alarm clocks going off early. It also marks a significant step in my development as a writer. Everyone who submits stories to the genre press will, at some point, kill a market – you'll have had a story accepted by a magazine which will then fold before the story can be published. This was my first experience of the effect, which is why the current volume is the first time it has seen the light of day.

THE MAUNA KEA EXPERIENCE

The door of the plane opens and the first hint of the tropical night wafts inside. In spite of nearly twenty-four hours of traveling, the fresh air and perfumed humidity wake me. That, and the knowledge that I've arrived.

I've flown from London to Hilo on the Big Island of Hawaii to use one of the telescopes at the famous Mauna Kea Observatory. British astronomers have been doing this since 1979 when UKIRT, the UK Infrared Telescope, opened. The high volcanic peak now hosts the Kecks, the largest and most famous ground-based telescopes, and many others. I'm here to use the James Clarke Maxwell telescope, the JCMT, a fifteen meter submillimeter dish, to study dusty galaxies near the edge of the observable universe.

But now all I want to do is get my bags, get to the hotel and go to sleep.

I hurry to the outdoor baggage hall – much of Hilo airport is outside or open to the balmy air – and get a taxi to Banyan Drive and a large bed.

Hilo is a small American town dropped into a tropical jungle – everything is surrounded by foliage I'm more used to seeing in a greenhouse. Hilo is also one of the wettest places on Earth, with 128 inches of rainfall a year. But I don't have time to enjoy it as I have to head up the mountain.

The Big Island is made of five separate shield volcanoes rising from the bottom of the Pacific. One is extinct, two are dormant – officially this includes Mauna Kea, but we tell our students it's extinct to make them feel safer – and two are active. One of these, Kilauea, is very active, and has been constantly erupting since 1983. You can see its dull glow from the observatory and sometimes it produces a sulfurous vog – volcanic smog – that blows into Hilo. The biggest volcanoes are

Mauna Kea and Mauna Loa. These form the bulk of the island. To get to either you have to ascend the infamous Saddle Road that runs between them.

Starting in Hilo the car climbs into thicker jungle as the houses get further and further apart. Soon we hit clouds and a thick mist, almost rain, coats the windshield. We've left the jungle behind and are in the cloud forest. Oddly-shaped trees stand on either side of the road, with wispy foliage and thin white trunks emerging from the black volcanic rock.

Eventually we break into bright sunshine and get our first clear view of the mountains. On the left the huge bulk of Mauna Loa dominates, its vast flanks scarred by lava flows. On the right, smaller but higher, is Mauna Kea with the observatory's white domes clustering on the top.

The road flattens out as it meanders through the lava flows until we take a right turn onto the steep Mauna Kea Access Road. We go across a cattle grid and enter grassy ranching country, complete with signs warning us of 'Invisible Cows' in the frequent fog.

By this point I can feel the altitude. I'm breathing faster, my ears have been popping as the car climbs and, if I try anything strenuous, I get light-headed.

A few more turns through rust red cinder cones and the astronomers' residence, Hale Pohaku, comes into view.

The first part of my ascent is complete.

I'll be driven to the summit by my telescope operator. Random astronomers like me aren't allowed to control the telescopes - they want to be sure we don't break anything which is why they're run by specialist operators who come from a huge range of backgrounds. My driver used to be a sonar officer on US submarines, while another is a part-time DJ at a Hilo radio station.

The operators also look after the observers. You lose a few points of intelligence for every thousand feet of altitude. At 14000 feet *everyone* is stupid, but it affects you in strange ways. I've taken an IQ test at the telescope (maybe in itself a sign of stupidity!) and got the result you might expect for someone with an astrophysics PhD. But I've also spent thirty minutes failing to work out how to get an instrument properly aligned.

There are stories from the construction of one telescope about an angry call received at sea level.

"There's a problem with these parts you sent up."

"Oh yes?" said the sea level manager.

"Yes! I've cut the things three times and they're still too short!"

"Come down to sea level," said the manager. "Now!"

There are other odd effects. On my first observing run I was typing away when I got an odd feeling that I was forgetting something very important. I looked round to make sure the telescope was working and checked the observation was progressing. Everything fine. Had some new email come in? No. Any bad weather? No. I sat back and scratched my head because the feeling wouldn't go away. Then I realized.

Breathing.

Yes, that's it – I'd forgotten to breathe, and a few deep breaths later I was feeling much better.

Any exertion really hits you. You learn this quickly when you come back from the toilet and run up stairs that look perfectly innocuous to anyone who's just come up from sea level. If you're lucky you can struggle to the top before you have to stop, lungs heaving and vision compressing to a dark tunnel as oxygen starvation sets in.

My observations are part of a large area survey of the submillimetre sky. This part of the spectrum, also called terrahertz waves, sits between radio and infrared wavelengths. The submillimetre has only been opened up in the last couple of decades and we're still in the earliest stages of exploring its potential. My particular interest is the study of dust-dominated galaxies which are very powerful emitters of submillimetre radiation.

In the local universe luminous dusty galaxies are rare, but observations with the COBE satellite in the early 90s confirmed hints that dusty galaxies were much more numerous at earlier epochs. They're so numerous, in fact, that roughly half the total energy emitted by stars in the history of the universe came from such objects, where the light was absorbed by dust and re-emitted in the far-infrared and submillimetre bands. The history of galaxy formation we get from optical telescopes, such as the Hubble Space Telescope or the giant Kecks, is thus biased. It can't show us the obscured emission that comes out in the submillimetre so half the story is missing.

Uncovering this hidden history is hard work, as it takes many hours to detect just one of the dusty galaxies responsible and we need hundreds of them to properly understand where they are, what powers them, and what role they play in the bigger picture of galaxy evolution.

I'm here to add some more nights of data to this survey.

Hale Pohaku, 'stone hut' in Hawaiian, is a halfway house between sea-level and the high altitude of the observatory. Astronomers stay here for twenty-four hours of acclimatisation before being allowed up to the summit and then come back to sleep during the day. There are dorms, a library, TV room, canteen, where you can get ice-cream twenty-four hours a day, and hot and cold running internet.

Weather is the great enemy. All too often it can send you home empty handed. Cloud, fog, wind, humidity, rain, ice and snow all bring problems. Snowfall means the summit has to be evacuated as it's all too easy to be stranded. In the early days some astronomers stuck on the summit in a storm had to burn furniture to keep warm.

Once I've unpacked and settled in, I have a little walk. HP is surrounded by cinder cones but their stark shapes are softened by bushes and clumps of grass. On one side the mountain slopes down to the Saddle Road with Mauna Loa rising beyond. On the other the summit road continues, leading upwards into an arid red landscape. Above that is the clear, deep blue sky only seen at the best observatories.

At the summit, like giant mushrooms growing on an ancient stump of mahogany, are the domes of the telescopes. Most are round and white, reflecting as much of the day's heat as they can. Beneath the summit ridge, in Millimetre Valley, are the JCMT and the two other submillimetre telescopes. One of these, the Submillimetre Array, consists of eight small dishes sitting open to the elements on individual plinths. The other, the Caltech Submillimetre Observatory, hides inside a spherical reflective ball, only revealing itself for observations. The JCMT rises like a giant cylindrical gun turret, but its dish can't be seen from outside as it's covered by a giant Goretex membrane, providing shade from the sun during daytime operation and protection from dust.

Everything except the telescopes is brick red. The ground is a mixture of volcanic cinders, larger rocks and a fine pervasive dust. And there are no signs of life. Apollo astronauts trained here for the moon landings, but the landscape is closer to Mars than the moon and would be familiar to anyone who's looked at images from the Mars rovers.

It isn't entirely lifeless here. Apart from astronomers and tourists, there are a few tufts of vegetation. There's even a native insect. They consume less hardy insects blown up the mountain from sea level and unable to cope in the thin air – a unique ecological niche.

And most of the observatories have mice.

Our big four by four pulls up to the JCMT and we settle into the control room surrounded by desks and computer screens. Once the sun sets there's nothing to see outside so we close the small window and concentrate on the observations. The operator looks after the telescope and I make sure the data coming in looks right. We keep ourselves going with sandwiches from HP. I graze on food throughout the night as it helps keep me awake. I also drink lots – tea, water, fruit juice – anything to make sure I stay hydrated and prevent altitude sickness.

The night wears on. I try to keep my attention on the observations but it's hard. The hum of the computers and humidifier lull us to sleep when the CDs run out, but at least the humidifier is working. The best data comes when it's very dry. The human body can't cope with this so when the humidifier breaks you get nose bleeds. Some of the best data I've ever obtained at the JCMT was taken with my hand clamped to my nose stemming a stream of blood. My lab book and the observing log still have the stains.

By six am the sun has started to rise and we get our second wind. But it all starts again 'tomorrow' when we get up at four pm, for 'dinner' as breakfast, and head back.

Several exhausting days later and our final night is nearing its end. I take special care to clear my stuff out of the control room and there's an extra spring to my step. The last night of the run is like the night before Christmas, or the end of school. I'm always a little excited about being let out of this scientific monastery and back to sea level.

I don't really know what results my data will bring. Some observing runs, perhaps the most exciting, bring instant gratification with something interesting appearing on the screens immediately the data is read out. Extragalactic submillimetre surveys aren't like that. My nights of data will have to be carefully combined with many others before we know what we've seen and the data must then be compared to datasets at other wavelengths before we can really understand what the submillimetre galaxies are doing. No instant gratification this trip, but I know the data is sound and that this run has been another useful step towards sorting out the hidden history of the universe.

After breakfast and a few hours' sleep I meet up with another astronomer who's driving me down to Hilo. I have sunglasses and a hat, but I still blink in the unaccustomed brightness. Below us are the tops of the clouds we'll pass through on our way. Then we're in the car and off.

The car heads downhill, away from HP and its dry volcanic landscape, and we soon reach the ranchland. Smells of grass and pine woods come through the windows. My head begins to clear as my body drinks in the richer supply of oxygen. This just keeps going all the way to sea level. You never realise when you're there, but your body works hard for every breath on the mountain. For days my lungs have been pumping further and faster than they're used to. But now they can relax. With every breath I taste the richness of the air at the bottom of the atmosphere. The feeling won't last, but for now slow breathing is a welcome relief.

My data has been downloaded. My work is done and I can look forward to a couple of days in Hilo unwinding with friends. As the car descends into the mists of the cloud forest it all catches up with me and I fall asleep.

There are times when my real world day job as an astrophysicist takes me to places that are more science fictional than much of science fiction. Mauna Kea, the home of many of the northern hemisphere's best telescopes, is one of those places. One of the few creatures native to the summit is an insect that evolved to prey on other insects blown up to the summit by the trade winds. The insects from sea level don't have enough oxygen to breathe on the summit, and so have to lie there, incapable of movement, as the native insects, whose metabolisms are sufficiently slow they can function at altitude, crawl towards them, fangs extended.

Astronomers also have problems at this altitude. Usually they're less severe.

LAUNCH DAY

Launch day. In just a few hours I'll find out if my scientific career is about to move into high gear, or if my future will end up in pieces on the bottom of the Atlantic Ocean.

I start early, waiting for a taxi to take me to Bush House, home of the BBC World Service. Across the UK and Europe other astronomers working on the Herschel and Planck satellites are doing the same. We're all getting media appearances out of the way before heading to wherever we can watch a live feed of the satellites' launch. After my interview I'll be going to the Rutherford Appleton Lab near Oxford, where the UK Herschel and Planck teams are gathering with visiting dignitaries and members of the media.

I've been working on these two satellites for eight years and they've been a part of the scientific landscape since I completed my PhD in 1991. But success or failure depends on what happens today.

UK media is dominated by BBC television or, for more thoughtful coverage, BBC Radio 4. But if you want a massive audience and worldwide reach you go to the World Service. A top rated Radio 4 appearance might reach eight million, but the World Service regularly gets audiences over a hundred million. I try to put thoughts of this vast number of listeners out of my mind as I answer the interviewer's questions. I describe what the satellites will do and what will happen with today's launch. Then it's over and I'm ushered through the splendid art deco interior and into a taxi to Paddington Station and the Rutherford Lab.

Of the two satellites, Herschel has been around the longest, at least in terms of conceptual development. It is the last of the European Space Agency's cornerstone missions in the Horizon 2000 programme. Originally named FIRST, the Far-Infrared Space Telescope, it's a big expensive mission, costing about a billion Euros. All ESA countries are involved and there are contributions from NASA, Canada and China. With a diameter of 3.5m, Herschel has the largest mirror ever launched on an astronomical satellite, dwarfing Hubble's 2.5m mirror. But it won't produce images as sharp as Hubble because it operates at much longer wavelengths.

While Hubble works in the optical, seeing light coming from the hot surfaces of stars (a few thousand degrees), Herschel works at wavelengths a hundred times longer, seeing material that's much colder – just tens of degrees above absolute zero. This allows it to study the dust that is intimately linked to the processes that form stars, to search for the debris left behind by forming planetary systems, and to probe the dusty galaxies that produce the enigmatic Cosmic Infrared Background, which hides about half the energy generated in the universe since the Big Bang.

Herschel will also study interstellar chemistry and especially water, one of the most important molecular species for understanding physical and chemical processes in everything from star forming regions to stars expelling their outer envelopes during the incontinent later stages of stellar evolution. But water is also a serious problem because our atmosphere is full of it, absorbing the emission needed to study objects in the far-infrared. This is why Herschel and Planck, operating at similar wavelengths, need to be in space, free of this atmospheric absorption.

At the Rutherford Lab we've taken over the main lecture theatre. The audience consists of fellow scientists, administrators and the leaders of the funding agencies who paid for the satellites, as well as local politicians and journalists. The partners and children of some of the scientists have also come along so they can find out more about the project that has taken their loved ones away from home, or forced them to work late into the night.

But some people are missing. We're effectively the B-team, left at home to entertain and inform the local media and watch the launch on television. The real big wigs are a few thousand miles away at Kouru, French Guiana, on the coast of South America where ESA launches its rockets. They have ringside seats for the launch and will do their bit for the visiting international media.

The closer we get to the opening of the two-hour launch window the more the tension rises. This isn't just a result of natural excitement. It isn't me worrying about the talk I have to give on the Planck satellite. It's because there's a ghost haunting the party, the ghost of Cluster and the launch of Ariane 501. Back in 1996 the first Ariane 5 rocket was launched, carrying the Cluster satellites for the first ESA cornerstone mission. Ariane 5 was a new launch vehicle, the great hope of ESA and Arianespace, its commercial launch company. It could carry larger payloads than previous ESA rockets and was predicted by the engineers to be at least 95% reliable. I watched the 501 launch on a live video feed in a lecture theatre not that different from today's. It exploded just seconds after launch, scattering debris over the jungle and into the Atlantic. That explosion was the end of the scientific careers of several friends who had worked on Cluster. Having tied my career to the success or failure of Herschel and Planck, I'm in the same position today as they were before the 501 launch.

The clock ticks on, and it's soon my turn at the podium. I provide a brief outline of the Planck mission, how it will scan the entire sky at nine different wavelengths, from the far-infrared into the microwaves, providing a much more precise map of the fluctuations in the cosmic microwave background. This is the dull light, left over from the Big Bang, that permeates the entire universe with a cool glow just 2.7 degrees above absolute zero. To detect this radiation the instruments on Planck must be kept just 0.1 degree above absolute zero, three times cooler than the instruments on Herschel, making Planck the coldest place in space.

The satellites are not being sent into Earth orbit. Instead, they're going to the second Lagrange point, L2. This is a point 1.5 million kilometres from Earth where the gravitational fields of the Earth and the Sun balance, and where these two sources of heat are always in the same direction. The large sun shields on Herschel and Planck will always be pointed towards the Sun and Earth, and their instruments pointed away, ensuring that they never see the boiling warmth of either. This helps keep the instruments cool, and preserves their essential liquid Helium reservoirs for as long as possible.

My talk is over. The countdown presses closer to zero. We have a two hour window but aim to act the instant it opens. Because we're launching two satellites, the launch itself isn't the only hazard. The satellites must get cleanly away from the launch bus before they can make their separate ways to L2. Separation happens thirty minutes after lift-off, and only at that point can we declare the launch a success.

The talks finished a little earlier than planned, and the video is on, filling the vast screen of the lecture theatre with a rundown of past ESA successes. But dominating my mind are memories of the 501 disaster.

There's nothing we can do. When the Vulcain main engine and solid rocket boosters fire, we're entirely dependent on the Arianespace engineers. They have to make sure that hundreds of tonnes of high-explosive rocket fuel explodes the right way to get our delicate, high-precision scientific instruments, strapped on top of it all, into orbit, undamaged.

The final countdown begins.

"Trois, deux, une, tup!"

The Vulcain fires, plumes of steam erupt form either side of the launch pad. Then the solid boosters fire, blasting out distinctive yellow smoke, and the rocket stack is hurled upwards. Across Europe, at JPL, Caltech and online in astronomy groups all over the world, eyes are glued to screens. The roar of the rockets reaches the microphones a few seconds after the rocket clears the pad. By this point it's already atop a vast column of flame, climbing into a clear blue sky.

Thus begins what must be the longest thirty minutes of my life. We follow the rocket every step of the way. We follow the exhaust plume as it climbs into the sky but, more important, we also follow the telemetry track from the control room, showing how the actual launch is proceeding compared to the predictions for perfect performance. Soon the camera flicks away from the control room, now being filled by our colleagues in Kouru who have seen all they can from the ground, to a view from the rocket itself as the solid fuel boosters are jettisoned – an astounding view from the very edge of space. We ignore the calls from some of the non-astronomers to open the champagne because we know there is still a long way to go.

Next comes the separation of the first stage and the ignition of the second. As with every step so far this goes like clockwork. I begin to think the launch might be a success, but desperately try to suppress these thoughts to avoid the crushing disappointment that will come if some later stage fails. The coverage is now focussed on the control room, showing controllers sitting at their desks doing nothing. I am pleased to see they almost look bored.

Originally Herschel and Planck were meant to be launched separately, with Planck going first providing, as a by-product of its microwave background work, a survey of dusty objects that Herschel could follow up. But the Cluster failure precluded that, because the cost of its replacement ate into ESA's budget and forced major rethinking of all missions. Back in 1996 it looked as if Herschel and Planck were going to become one spacecraft with the instruments and telescopes glued back to back – a Frankenstein satellite. This would not have worked, for many reasons, but the two projects were managerially joined and put onto the same launch vehicle. This meant all of ESA's far-infrared eggs were in the same basket.

We reach the final critical phase for Herschel, where it separates from the launch bus and heads for L2. We are treated to a final few frames of video taken by a camera at the back of Herschel showing its clean separation from Planck – the last external view of Planck and its SYLDA launch bus that anyone will see. Soon after that it's time for Planck to cast aside the launcher and escape to L2.

Applause erupts. We start breathing again. And outside, at the reception, we hear champagne corks starting to pop.

This afternoon we can celebrate, but tomorrow we start the hard work of commissioning the instruments. It will still be months before real science can begin, but launch, the most dangerous phase of all, has been a huge success.

What can be more science-fictional to someone like me, who grew up during the Apollo era, than a rocket launch? I'm lucky enough to have been involved in several space missions dedicated to astronomy. This work has taken me to clean rooms where hardware has been built, and shown me things in my observations that nobody has ever seen before. I have never, though, been to an actual rocket launch. This piece, originally written as one of the non-fiction pieces in the Rocket Science anthology – an innovative combination of both science fiction and science fact – is the story of the day we launched the Herschel and Planck spacecraft. The experience was stressful enough without being at the actual launch site.

INQUISITION

A piece of paper was lying on my keyboard when I got back from lunch. Curious, I unfolded it and found the dreaded words "Report immediately to the Experimental Communications Board." My pulse raced, and the paper quivered in my trembling hand. The Inquisition had finally come for me. But why?

My views about the Experiment's communication rules – or 'lack of communication' rules – were well known. We were in permanent lockdown, forbidden from talking about anything connected with the Experiment to colleagues, press, students, family, or, if taken literally, even our pets. I didn't think it was a good way of doing science – an outside view of problems or results is always useful. But the Management felt we could only announce things when they were finalised for fear that preliminary results would damage our reputation or that competitors would take half-processed data and scoop our scientific conclusions. They had some good points, but the lengths the policy required us to go to were extreme.

I left my office, walked down the corridor to the room allocated to Experiment staff, unlocked it, and typed in my personal access code. Only those working on the Experiment were allowed in. Not even the cleaners could enter for fear they might have received backhanders from someone on the outside. Needless to say the place was a mess – whoever heard of postdocs clearing up after themselves?

I nodded to one or two of them and picked my way between piles of papers and discarded pizza boxes, wondering if one of them had reported me. I might have tenure, but if I was thrown off the Experiment then my grant would be handed to someone else, maybe someone in this room. It would be a great boost to their career. They'd get to run the group and I'd be relegated to service teaching in another department.

But if anybody tried that trick they'd learn their lesson. There was enough dirt in my files, real or fabricated, that I could have any one of them thrown out.

Pondering which one it might be, I got to the videoconference room and sealed myself inside, behind the soundproof, lightproof door.

The management of the Experiment might be far from ideal, but, for my research, it was the only game in town. I either had to join it or give up. I'd argued against its closed door policies as strongly as I could, but I was only one of the little people. The high-ups who controlled things had their minds set. So I signed the agreement, swore I would abide by the communication rules, and registered my DNA reference and thumb print. I was in.

At least I was until now. With adrenalin rushing around my arteries, I keyed in the number and called the Communications Board.

The Experiment's Inquisition appeared before me on the screen, each in a separate window. They'd been waiting for me. This was not a good sign.

"Good afternoon, David. Thank you for responding so quickly. We have a serious matter to discuss," said the board's Chair.

"What..." my voice faltered. I coughed and started again. "What seems to be the problem?"

"We believe you've been talking to someone from one of the theory groups."

I stared for a moment in surprise. The outer groups were part of the Experiment, but were excluded from seeing any data so they could come up with theoretical predictions unaware of the results. This was because the Experiment was so powerful that little more would be possible in the field after it was completed. A theorist with access to all the data could tailor a model to fit perfectly just by adding needless epicycles to a pre-existing idea. By preventing them from seeing the data, their models would be motivated by underlying science. A cleaner test would be possible once the data were fully analysed and compared to a finalised independent set of models. This was actually part of the methodology I agreed with.

"I've not done that. There isn't even anybody here who works on theory!"

"We have pictures," croaked one of the other members of the board, an elderly scientist who always enjoyed making life hard for his juniors.

One of the screens showed me a photograph presumably taken with a mobile phone by an ambitious postdoc. I remembered the incident just a few days earlier on my cycle commute to work.

"The picture shows you giving something to this woman, someone you should know is on the theory team," he continued.

She'd been familiar but I hadn't suspected she might be working on the Experiment.

"We can't see what it is but it's either a data stick or a set of notes." His voice was getting louder, more strident with each word. "Or maybe a whole hard drive of our most valuable data?" I looked at the faces on the screen, their eyes hard, faces rigid with anger. No matter what I said I could see the decision had been made already.

"What did you give her?" they demanded.

And I knew that the prosaic truth couldn't save me, but I said it anyway.

"A bicycle pump – she had a puncture!"

Anger is one of the great spurs of creativity. When one sees stupidity around you, fiction allows you to dream of a better place, where the problems are all fixed and people are more reasonable. But you can play the game the other way, and take today's problems, file off the names to protect the guilty, and turn the annoyances up to eleven. This story is of the latter kind, inspired by some of the less sensible rules of one of the scientific collaborations of which I am a member. We used to joke that 'the first rule of Planck is that you don't talk about Planck', but when a colleague of mine working on this project said she had been summoned to appear before the Planck Inquisition, the seeds for this story were sown. There are some sensible reasons for keeping results quiet until you're sure they are correct, but if you take this too far you end up with something that is inimical to good science and to the people involved. We're not there yet, but we're working on it.

CATCHING RAYS

Sarah shuffled in her seat, conscious that the Director was hovering nearby, waiting for the interview to finish.

"When do you expect to announce your results?" asked Horst. Sarah thought he looked relieved, sitting across the table from her in the canteen, nursing a bulb of fresh coffee. He was due to head back to Earth on the next lunar shuttle.

"It will take some time," she replied. "The collector's finished, but we need to install the traps before running a final test. Then we have to ramp up the power before we can collect the highest energy cosmic rays."

"A few months?"

Sarah smiled. "Longer than *that*. Even when we have things fully running it'll take a while to collect and analyse the data. A year at least, maybe longer."

"Thank you for your time," said Horst, closing his tablet. "That was great, and a fine way to end my visit. And if you find anything interesting, please contact me." He stood, rising too quickly and briefly leaving the floor. "Damn," he muttered as he flailed in mid-air. "How do you cope with this?"

Sarah laughed. "Practice, which visitors like you never have time for." She steadied him as he drifted back to the floor. "Have a good trip home, and we'll see you back on Moonbase Three in, what, eighteen months?"

Horst sighed, and nodded. "I guess so."

"I'm sure you'll do better next time."

The Director chose that moment to force his way into the conversation. "All done here I see," he said, smiling at both of them. "I hope you had a good chat with our latest brilliant researcher?"

"Oh yes," said Horst, while Sarah squirmed. "Very informative."

"Excellent. Let me walk you to the shuttle, there are a couple of things I'd like to discuss." Horst picked up his bag, and the two men left the canteen.

"Enjoy it while it lasts," said Petra. She was sitting at one of the other tables, behind a partition, listening to the whole interview.

"What do you mean?" asked Sarah.

"Being Moonbase Three's latest poster child."

Sarah didn't know what to say. Petra had been on the base for a while, doing development work on nanotechnology. "Happens to us all at the start. But it will soon change if you don't deliver successes, or they take too long to come. When your funding is cut nobody will want to know you."

Sarah's project had got most of the funding in the current round, beating the nanotechnologist's bid and several others. Petra stood with the gentle, smooth movements of an experienced lunar resident. "You'd better get your results before you're out of the spotlight, otherwise you'll end up on your own, far from home, making do with leftover equipment that isn't even appropriate."

"What about your postdoc?" Sarah asked, sure she had seen him only a few days ago.

"Gone. On the same shuttle as Horst. And our great Director has made it clear I will be joining him if I don't make a breakthrough soon."

Petra turned her back and walked out of the canteen.

Sarah exhaled slowly and left in the opposite direction, heading along one of the narrow white corridors to the small office she shared with Max, her postdoc.

"How are the final checks?" she asked as she slid open the door.

"Looking good. We can install the traps and start low field, end-to-end tests as soon as the Sun sets."

Their tiny office's only saving grace was the broad picture window dominating one wall. Outside, across the dark grey landscape, the infinitely slow lunar sunset was under way. The Sun hung on the horizon, slipping with glacial slowness behind black basalt mountains casting long, unnaturally sharp shadows across the regolith.

"Another eight hours. Then a few more for passive cooling to kick in," said Sarah. She checked her watch for the time back home in the Eurozone. "I'm off to bed. See you in the morning."

Black, airless lunar night surrounded them. Each suited figure had headlamps, one on each side of their helmet. Navigation lights and indicators blinked on shoulders, helmets and backpacks. Scattered construction floodlights brought further light and the semblance of warmth wherever they stood, but they only served to remind Sarah, Max and the rest of the crew they were working in one of the most hostile environments known to man. A coronal mass ejection, or other harsh space weather event, could catch them in a hail of lethal radiation, while the smallest micrometeorite could pierce a suit and deliver a high velocity bullet's worth of damage.

There were warning systems, but they were never perfect. Physically roaming the lunar surface was a calculated risk, but the final stages of construction and calibration could not be done with drones or remotes.

After four hours on the surface Sarah hoped everything was finally done. At least the cold trap in front of her was fully operational. "How are we doing?" she called on the group radio net.

"A few minutes more for me, but basically done," replied Max.

The rest of the crew needed more time.

Sarah joined Max and gazed at the sky until he had finished. She brought her gloves to her helmet, shading her eyes from light scattered from her headlamps, trying to see the pin-sharp stars that filled the sky.

"It's so empty," Sarah said over their private radio link to Max. "We're so alone." She shivered, despite her suit heating system. This was a recurring train of thought for Sarah while on the surface, looking away from the blue jewel of Earth at the vast black emptiness of the rest of the sky. "A sky full of stars, but empty of minds – as far as we can tell."

"That's not our job, boss," replied Max. "Leave that to the guys with the big radio ears and optical eyes down on Earth."

"Maybe," said Sarah. "But it doesn't seem right. We're spreading out into space, but there's no sign anybody else has done that. Ever. In the whole history of the universe."

"We'll find them," said Max. "They have to be out there, we're just not looking the right way."

Sarah was ready to argue the point, to deliver the kind of authoritative philosophical argument expected of a senior academic. The head contractor's voice interrupted on the communal band. "We're all done, I think."

Sarah switched channels, a little relieved she wasn't going to dent Max's naive enthusiasm today. "Great!" She said. "Time to head back to the barn."

Bright lights, white nanofibre walls, a crowded room filled by a hot and humid yet breathable atmosphere. They stood inside the small habitat dedicated to running Sarah's cosmic ray experiment. It was a huge contrast to the surface. Sarah always felt a twinge of claustrophobia when she came back inside, but this time she ignored that in the excitement of, at last, having an experiment to run.

As soon as she was out of her suit, she headed to the control console. While she began the startup procedure, the rest of the crew gathered around.

"All traps running nicely," she announced. "Great work people." There were nods of appreciation and handshakes.

She typed more commands, checked more indicators. "E-mag scoops initialising."

High above the surface of the Moon, the other part of the system started up, a series of superconducting cables forming a network of fields filtering charged particles to the surface and Sarah's cold traps. "Looking good," reported Sarah. "A few minutes and we should have the first low energy captures!" There was scattered applause across the room, and one of the engineering contractors moved towards the fridge.

Sarah spotted the movement. "Hey," she shouted. "No champagne until we know it's working." Max and Sarah's closest colleagues laughed nervously, but the contractors looked disappointed.

Tension filled the room. Scattered attempts at conversation died away as they waited for the first crucial results.

At her console, Sarah watched the displays, monitoring instrument health and performance, awaiting the first chime that would announce the successful collection of low energy cosmic rays.

She made some calculations in her head, factoring in event rates, efficiencies, collecting volumes, once again checking calculations she had done years ago and knew by heart. "Yes," she nodded to herself, "if we don't have anything in a few minutes then we have a..."

A loud ping broke her train of thought. She smiled, and rose from her chair.

"Friends, colleagues, the cosmic rays have landed!"

Then came cheers, applause, and popping corks, as they celebrated success after years of effort.

Speeches followed, and an even greater throng of Moonbase Three personnel came down the long tunnel to Sarah's control centre. The Director welcomed a project that was certain to be a new, great success for Moonbase Three, and congratulated Sarah on getting it started on time and slightly under budget. She even caught a glimpse of Petra at one point, standing quietly by one of the consoles and looking out onto the lunar surface, a glass of wine untouched in her hand. She wondered what the other woman was looking at, and suppressed the urge to smile when she saw it was one of the cold traps. They were Sarah's invention, a unique technology that made the array possible. *I guess Petra has a right to be envious*, she thought.

Hours later, when the celebrations had ended, Sarah was the last person left in the control room as usual; clearing up glasses, collecting half-finished plates of food for recycling. Quickly deciding to leave the last of the debris to the operations crew to clear up, she went to the main console for a first look at her results.

She frowned. "No. That can't be right."

"I agree," said Max. "This doesn't make any sense at all."

The collector had been running for several days. They were in Sarah's office, hunched over a work station screen, looking at telemetry from the cold traps. The results she'd seen that first evening had not gone away, despite her hope they were a technical artifact.

"You agree the mass is too high, and the charge too low?" she asked. She should know more than Max about the experiment, and everything else, but wanted him to find a hole in her thinking.

He frowned. "High mass could mean a multiple hit, but that wouldn't explain the charge."

Sarah nodded. "More like a few thousand hits for that mass. So, something has gone seriously wrong." She sat back and shook her head. "We'll have to purge the collectors, do a total restart and hope this goes away."

"That would take weeks!"

"Quite. But this makes no sense. The Director isn't going to like it – his great new project taking a giant leap backwards."

Max turned from the screen and sat on the corner of Sarah's tiny desk. "Maybe it's just that single trap. The others are working fine. We could bring it back inside, strip it down, run tests..."

"We'd have to empty the liquid helium and warm it up before we could bring the trap inside. You know the rules. And we'd still have to do a full purge and restart afterwards."

Max turned back to the workstation, calling up the schematics and test history of the offending device, looking through screen after screen of results. Sarah sat, gazing out of the office window, staring at the bleak, lifeless lunar surface, pondering what to do next. The last person she'd seen doing this had been Petra at the startup party. Maybe Petra's interest in the detectors had been something more than envy at Sarah's success.

"I can't see anything wrong," said Max. "The test results on this trap are as good as the others, if not better. And instrument health monitoring says everything's just fine."

"Something must have broken!"

"What if the results are right?" asked Max.

Sarah rubbed her close-cropped hair. For a few moments she took Max's suggestion seriously, but then shook her head. "That's impossible. It would mean we have a tiny chunk of neutron star in the trap, a few hundred thousand nucleons in size. Something that small with so many neutrons wouldn't be stable."

"How would we tell?" asked Max.

Sarah thought for a few moments. "We couldn't with the trap's onboard instruments, but there's stuff here, inside Moonbase, that could do the tests."

"Pity we can't bring any active traps inside thanks to safety regs."

Sarah looked at Max, still perched on the edge of her desk. "That's it for tonight," she said.

"What?" Max consulted his watch. "It's an hour until the canteen opens."

"You need to get some rest. Sit somewhere visible."

Max's mouth opened in surprise. "What?"

The only sound was her breathing, and occasional gurgles from the suit's cooling system. Sarah was breaking every rule in the book by going onto the lunar surface on her own. There would be a severe reprimand if she were caught, but she'd taken the necessary precautions. Her suit radio was off, its transponders silenced, and she had glitched the airlock and suit locker logs with a piece of software that was trivially easy to acquire.

If her suspicions weren't confirmed, what she was planning to do was worse than a solo trip on the surface; she would be breaking many more rules before the end of the night.

Slowly and carefully Sarah made her way from the control room's airlock, across the soft regolith, towards the scattered array of cold traps. To allay her suspicions, she had to examine every single cold trap in the array. Moonbase Three was well into lunar night, but the Earth hung in the sky, far brighter than a full moon, providing most of the light she needed.

She was halfway through her tour of the array when she spotted an odd shadow by one of the traps, a hint of light and movement where there should be none. Sarah hoped it was a gas leak, a blown compressor or some other technical failure. She didn't want to have to think that someone was actively working against her.

But, as she got closer, her suspicions were confirmed. A figure, wearing a suit identical to her own, was bending over the trap. She couldn't see exactly what they were doing, but she was sure it was an act of sabotage. And she had a pretty good idea who it was.

She turned her helmet lights off and worked her way closer, hidden in the shadows of the lunar night and the silence of vacuum. Then, just a few paces away, she activated the suit's recorder, opened a hailing channel, and set her lights to full power.

"Just what do you think you're doing?"

The stranger jerked in surprise, rising half a metre in the low lunar gravity, and losing their balance as they drifted back to the ground. Sarah would have laughed if she hadn't been so angry.

The figure flailed uncontrollably and landed on their back, revealing the ID tag on the front of the suit.

Petra.

"Jesus," said Sarah. "I know you're desperate, but sabotaging my experiment to get your funding back? That's low."

"What?" Petra was panting with the effort of standing up. The suits were awkward in the low gravity. "Aren't you going to help me?"

"Why, when you're the bitch screwing up my work?"

"Screw... You think I am sabotaging?" Petra's panicked flailing subsided. She rolled to one side, getting her left arm and leg beneath her.

"Why else would you be out here, on your own, in the middle of my array?"

Petra pushed herself partially upright, gloves sinking slightly into the regolith. Her suit was now covered by smears of the dark lunar soil. "It is your cold traps."

"I know what they are."

"They are brilliant. I wanted to copy the design."

"What?" Sarah wanted to believe it wasn't sabotage, that there was still some honour among her colleagues, but she had to be sure. "Stand away from the trap."

Petra moved back a pace.

"Further," said Sarah, "and stay where I can see you."

Petra complied.

Sarah bent down, keeping Petra visible in the corner of her eye, and inspected the trap.

Its surface was intact. The hard yellow casing unblemished, inspection hatches still sealed. On the ground lay a standard scanning device that Petra had dropped. Sarah picked it up and checked the readouts. It showed Petra had been scanning the trap to examine its internal structure. A non-invasive probe, nothing that would cause any damage.

Sarah tossed the scanner to Petra.

"I might believe you, if you explain *why*."

Petra caught the scanner. "Applications. Your traps have a larger, more stable cold space than anything used in nanotech. They could solve many of my problems, but I need the design."

"You could have asked."

"What? Here, where everything is commercial? You signed over the design the moment they accepted your proposal. There is no way I can afford what the lunar authorities would charge."

Sarah shook her head, though Petra couldn't see inside her helmet. "I have spares. You could have used one."

"But we are in competition. If I get a breakthrough they will cut your funding. Why help me?"

Sarah sighed. "Gods, you must have been here too long. Has it ever occurred to you that working together, sharing results and technology, is the right thing to do, no matter what the Director and management say?"

"But that's forbidden. I couldn't pay..."

"Do I look as if I care about the Director's rules?"

"Oh scheisse," said Petra. "I've been an idiot. And now you won't lend me anything. I'll probably have to pack my bags." She looked around. "Who else did our dear Director send with you?"

Sarah shook her head.

"You're on your own?"

"Yes. You heard what I said about rules. And it's worse than that. I want to bring one of these traps inside."

It took them an hour of hard work to prepare the offending trap for its illicit trip back inside Moonbase. Sarah was also careful to replace it with one of the spare traps so that a cursory inspection would find the array unchanged. Once that was done, and she was sure everything was running properly, they took a few moments rest.

"It's good to be outside," said Petra, looking at the sky. She brought her gloves to her helmet, shading her eyes from her helmet lamps so she could see the stars. "A glorious sky but nobody to share it with."

Sarah shivered, hearing Petra echo her own thoughts the last time she was on the surface.

"Are we unique?" Petra persisted. "And what would that mean?"

"We might just be lucky – a series of double sixes in the casino of life."

"Doesn't seem likely."

"If we weren't lucky, we wouldn't be here to have this conversation."

"You're an anthropic?" Petra was referring to the old idea that, for some reason, the universe needed at least one form of intelligent life in it.

"Nah," said Sarah. "It's a philosophy, not a science, and not a very helpful one. There are plenty of other possibilities. Perhaps there's a cosmic weed-whacker that gets rid of potential competition. Or maybe intelligent life doesn't last – we could still wipe ourselves out after all. Or maybe everyone uploads to supercomputers and disappears from the real world."

"Singularitarianism? I can't say that looks likely given my own work."

"So you've not invented computronium yet?"

Petra chuckled. "No, not yet."

"Okay," said Sarah. "Time to get this trap back inside."

The yellow box sat in the centre of the lab, challenging them to solve its mystery.

Sarah stared at the trap and tapped her finger on the desk. "Your neutral and electron beams are our best bet."

"About time I found a use for that stuff; they're just hand-me-downs from cancelled projects."

They started working together, connecting beamlines to various ports, attaching cables and fibres to provide control signals and readouts.

"You are sure this is not some kind of instrumental glitch?" asked Petra.

"I've spent ages ruling that out. Whatever's inside is way heavier than a uranium nucleus, moderately charged and..." She shrugged. She suspected more, but it would sound crazy. "That's most of what I know, apart from the fact that it's real, and entered the cold trap from the scoops."

"You're sure it's just one particle?"

"That's what Max asked, but the charge-to-mass ratio is all wrong."

Petra looked around. "Where is Max?"

"Given all the rules we're breaking, I wanted to keep him well away. The less he knows about this the less harm it'll do him if the Director finds out."

Petra nodded, and continued to align the first set of electron beams as the feed lines were pumped down to vacuum. "This should give us a better idea of the structure of whatever is in there." She nodded at the experimental rig they'd hacked together in just half an hour. There, that should do it." The machine fired a beam of high energy electrons into the cold trap, to bounce off whatever lurked inside.

"Wow," said Petra as she looked at the results. "Even the most complex nucleus is not *that* complex." She leaned forward to make some adjustments. "This is not a simple shell structure or liquid drop."

"Somehow, I'm not surprised," said Sarah.

"Something you're not telling me?"

"No! At least nothing concrete."

Petra stared at Sarah for a moment, then ran another scan. "Odd," she said, looking at the results. The old and new scans were radically different. "Could it be spinning? Something spinning and asymmetric could explain this."

Sarah shook her head. "No. The temperature inside is too low to excite any spinning modes."

"The electron beam?"

"Not enough momentum for that to do anything."

Petra nodded. "So either we have excited a substructure, or whatever this is is too big to be an atomic nucleus! This – thing – maybe it's changing structure on its own!"

Sarah sighed with relief. "At least it's not just me."

Petra tilted her head querulously.

"Some of the internal tests in the trap produced something similar, but the results weren't good enough to be sure."

Petra nodded. "I'll do a time series at higher energy. Maybe that will give us enough resolution to see what's going on."

She set up the experiment and they moved to the kitchenette on the far side of the lab to await the results. "Tell me what you suspect," said Petra as she passed Sarah a bulb of coffee.

Sarah took a long, slow swig, giving herself time to think. She didn't want to sound like a lunatic, but she owed Petra an explanation given their collusion. She put down the bulb and, refusing to meet Petra's eyes, said, "This is going to sound mad."

"What you've got in that trap *is* mad!"

Sarah nodded. "I know." She looked up. "You were talking about extraterrestrial intelligence before we brought it inside."

"What's that got to do with anything?"

Sarah played with her coffee bulb. "I think it's a message."

"What?"

It was out. Now she had to give Petra the whole story. "If intelligence is out there, it'll want to communicate. But we've found nothing in the radio, optical, any wavelength we've looked at. And nothing in gravity waves or neutrinos. But what about messages in bottles? Something more physical, like a tiny, tiny hard drive filled with data."

"Accelerated to nearly the speed of light and fired at the recipient?"

said Petra, her eyes narrowing in thought.

Sarah nodded. "And sometimes they go astray, caught up in magnetic turbulence, say, thrown off course."

"And eventually into your cold traps." Petra sat back and sucked her own bulb of coffee. "Quite an idea. You'd have to be very lucky to catch one."

"Unless there are a hell of a lot of them."

Petra drank some more coffee. "If this were a storage device it would explain the complexity. But why does it keep changing?"

Sarah shook her head. "No idea. Maybe it's more active than a message, like a hard drive needing constant refreshing."

Petra frowned. "There's another possibility." She stood, strode to the experiment and switched the electron beams off.

"Is it done?"

Petra shook her head. "Where could you make something like this?"

"A big nuclear collider?"

"No. It would need precision construction. We can't manage that even at an atomic level. I know. I have been trying. But this thing is on much smaller scales, down at the nuclear level. There's only one place that would be the natural scale for such work."

Sarah thought for a moment. "A neutron star?"

Petra nodded. "Have you heard of strangelets?"

Sarah shook her head.

"There was a panic about them in the late twentieth century. The idea there might be a lower energy state for nuclear material than the nuclei we're familiar with, involving strange quarks. If a bit of it came into contact with normal matter it would be converted. You'd get more strange matter which would convert more normal matter – and hard radiation of course."

"Producing a runaway reaction killing everything."

Petra nodded.

"Couldn't happen," said Sarah. "High energy cosmic rays hit the Earth all the time. If your strangelets existed, we'd have been hit by one billions of years ago. Everything would already be over."

"Yes," said Petra, "if the strangelets were natural. Out there you mentioned the cosmic weed whacker. Maybe that's what this is, nuclear scale grey goo, sent by neutron star life to wipe out any competition."

Sarah sat with her mouth open for a few moments, then she laughed. "Okay – you win. You're madder than I am!"

Petra nodded and smiled. "Makes you think though."

The radiation alarm caught them halfway through dinner.

Everyone knew what to do – head to the storm shelter, the deepest part of Moonbase Three, dug metres into the regolith and surrounded by the base water reservoir. With that much shielding they could survive the worst solar storm. It was also where the base had its hydroponic garden, so even if the surface facilities were damaged or dangerously irradiated, the crew could hide underground, with food, water and oxygen made by the plants, to await rescue.

As the shelter door sealed behind them, Sarah and Petra looked at each other, sharing the unspoken question: *Was that us?*

"If it was," muttered Sarah as they moved through a crowd of their colleagues, "we should be back in the lab, fixing it before it gets worse."

"But if it is a flare we'd be dead," countered Petra. She had already sat out some bad solar storms.

Max came up to Sarah, looking dishevelled. "I was asleep," he said. "What's going on?"

"No idea," said Sarah. "Let's find the Director."

When they found him, he was surrounded by several engineers. "How bad is it?" asked Petra.

He looked up from the tablet he was studying. "Odd. Solar wind is up, but below dangerous levels, yet we're getting radiation alerts. From your lab. What are you up to?"

"Shit," said Sarah.

"We were in the canteen," said Petra, treading on Sarah's foot to keep her silent.

The Director turned to Sarah in exasperation. "What's your involvement?"

His interrogation was cut short by an engineer. "Radiation's dropping. Nearly back to normal." He looked at Petra. "Even in her lab."

"Right," said the director curtly, "time for you to sort out whatever you've cooked up in there." He turned to the engineer. "Go with them. Once that's done we're going to have a serious conversation."

He turned to the rest of the assembled crew and announced the all clear.

Max burst through the door of Petra's lab a few moments after the Director and two other members of the safety team arrived. The engineer had called them.

Max saw stony faces all round, the room filled by a hostile silence. Everyone turned to look at him.

"The last conspirator," said the Director.

"What?" said Max.

"He's got nothing to do with this," said Sarah. She turned to Max. "This is down to me. Go back to your room and I'll talk to you when everything is sorted out."

The Director turned to him. "Leave this lab, young man, and you'll be on the next shuttle back to Earth, sitting next to these two."

Max was confused. "What?" He turned to Sarah, then caught sight of the cold trap sitting in the middle of the lab. "Hey, what's one of our spares doing here?"

"It's not a spare, Max," said Sarah. "I brought the trap here for further analysis."

"But that's..."

"Against all safety rules," interrupted the Director, "and for good reason as that radiation alert demonstrated. We have to make safe the results of this gross misconduct, and then you all wait for the next shuttle home."

Sarah's shoulders slumped. Not only had she failed to solve the mystery of what lay in the trap, she had failed to protect Max from her own mistakes. "He's done nothing wrong!"

"He chose you as a supervisor," said the Director. "That was enough. Now, get rid of whatever's inside that machine."

Petra and Sarah looked blankly at each other. "Get rid of it?"

"Out of this base, off the Moon, and as far away as possible. If you don't have any better ideas I'll happily launch it on a transfer rocket programmed to self-destruct beyond the orbit of Mars. And I'll take the cost out of your unemployment pay for the next decade, because you'll both be unemployable by the time I finish with you."

Sarah and Petra looked at each other. They'd focused on studying the particle and hadn't thought what might happen next. Petra moved towards the equipment. "We should do a last scan then."

"No," ordered the Director. "Neither of you get to operate any equipment. My engineers do that, and vet your instructions first."

One of the engineers stepped up to the console. "What are these scans, and how will they help get rid of this thing?"

Sarah looked at Petra, then explained. "We've been using high energy electron beams. The object in the trap is an exotic cosmic ray particle. We're not sure what it might be and were looking at its structure."

"And how will these scans help remove it?" asked the Director.

"Knowledge always helps," said Sarah, knowing how unconvincing she sounded.

Petra came to the rescue. "We need to know if it has changed so we can tune whatever action we take to its current state, rather than what we had previously measured."

The engineer nodded. "That makes sense."

With evident reluctance, the Director gave his permission.

Soon the results arrived. The mysterious chunk of nuclear matter in the trap was more massive than before and had a slightly larger electric charge.

"What does the growth mean?" said Sarah. "Is it a strangelet after all?" She was glad only Petra seemed to know what such a particle was.

"It is not runaway growth. Your weed-whacker scenario is not appropriate," said Petra.

Sarah relaxed a little – at least she hadn't caused the end of the world. "How do we get rid of it?"

Petra shrugged.

"That should be straight forward enough," said Max, as he looked at the results.

"Explain," said the Director.

"It's charged. It's easily accelerated if you drop it through an electric field." He thought for a few moments. "Getting it to lunar escape velocity should be trivial. Solar System escape should also be easy." He jotted a few numbers on a tablet and passed it to Sarah, only to have the Director intercept it and pass the device to his engineer.

"Will that work?" he asked.

After a few moments the engineer nodded. "The difficulty will be getting it out of the trap, but even that shouldn't be too much of a problem."

"Do you need them here for that?" The Director indicated Petra and Sarah. The engineer shook his head. The Director turned to them. "Leave. You're confined to the common areas. Your access to all experimental facilities rescinded. The cosmic ray collector will have to be safely turned off as well, but that can come later." Sarah opened her mouth to protest, but closed it again, knowing she didn't have a leg to stand on.

She stood and turned to leave the room. Max and Petra followed her example.

"Not you, young man. You can assist here, then help us shut down the collector." The Director then turned to Sarah and Petra. "The two of you have until the next shuttle in three weeks to persuade me I shouldn't have you fired and charged with gross negligence."

It didn't take Max and the safety team long to set up an electromagnetic launcher for the tiny particle. Their main difficulty had been plumbing the beamline of the small accelerator to one of the external vents in the lab, so that the particle could leave the vacuum of the cold trap for the vacuum of space. The long, straight metal tube that facilitated this looked incongruous, like a smoke stack on a jet engine.

"Is it ready yet?" demanded the Director, who had hovered nearby throughout the construction process.

"All ready," said Max. The engineer standing next to him nodded in confirmation.

"So what are we waiting for?"

"Is the gun charged up?" asked Max.

"Ten megavolts and holding steady," said the engineer.

Max's finger hovered above the large red button that would release the trap's vent, and nudge the particle into the accelerator.

"Are you sure we want to do this? Sarah must have thought it was important."

"Your loyalty to your supervisor does you credit, son," said the Director, "but delaying any longer will only demonstrate you're a dangerous, head in the clouds fool like her."

Max thought for a moment, then pressed the button.

There was no climax, no noise, no lights.

"Is it gone?"

"Yes, Director," said Max. "It's gone."

"Where to?"

Max gestured helplessly upwards. "Out there," he said. "Where it came from, well away from any solid bodies in the Solar System, as you instructed."

The Director nodded to himself. "Good riddance."

"Was it one of these 'weed-whacking' strangelets?" asked the Director.

Three weeks had passed. The shuttle would leave in a day, and Petra and Sarah were delivering their report. They had spent the intervening time working on the data, and developing computer models of what Sarah had found. Given what they now knew, they were confident they could turn this disaster into a massive success.

"No," said Petra. "At least, not directed at us."

The Director frowned. "Explain."

"Have you actually read our report?" asked Sarah.

The Director shrugged, just a little twitch of his shoulders. "I'm sure it will just be an attempt at justifying the unjustifiable."

"Then why bother with this meeting?"

"For the record. In cases like this there has to be a review, and that's what we're having. I mostly want to know exactly how much of a risk you took with all our lives. Now, will you answer my question?"

Petra continued. "The thing in the cold trap took no notice of anything we did, just cycled through a series of structural transformations."

"A maintenance cycle," added Sarah.

"A ticking time bomb?" said the Director.

"No. We eliminated that possibility," said Sarah. "That's on page four of the report."

He ignored Sarah's dig. "What triggered the radiation?"

"The arrival of a weak solar storm," said Petra.

"The collectors recorded a burst of moderate energy protons and higher mass nuclei coming from the Sun," said Sarah.

"A small coronal mass ejection, as predicted," said Petra.

"Some of those particles, possibly carbon or nitrogen nuclei, hit our sample. They were transformed."

"Eaten," said the Director. He looked pleased at this possibility.

"No," said Petra.

"Nothing like that," added Sarah.

"Then what?"

"Using the data collected before you ejected it, we modelled the... device," said Petra. "It is amazing. If hit by a heavy nucleus, or protons above a certain energy, they become part of it. Gamma rays, pions, radioactive secondaries result. They triggered the alarm."

"In other words, dangerous," said the Director.

"But, and this is where it gets clever, it absorbs only a few nucleons at a time," said Petra.

"However," said Sarah, "given a huge supply of nucleons – which would only happen if it hit a neutron star – something very different happens."

"A phase change takes place," said Petra. "To something much more complex, and much more useful."

"It turns out," said Sarah, "this thing is a terraforming device for neutron stars."

"What?" The Director clearly hadn't been expecting that.

"It takes neutron star matter," said Petra, "and turns it into computational substrate, something hugely powerful, ready to run any code you want."

The Director looked at the two women in confusion, not sure if they were mad, tricking him, or somehow had turned the tables. Sarah was surprised he had been so careless and overconfident to not read the report. If he had, he would have been ready for this, had a response planned.

"You're saying this thing is a machine?"

They nodded.

"Made by some kind of intelligence – extraterrestrial intelligence?"

They nodded again.

"It's a colonisation tool." He looked a little panicked. "We're being invaded and you brought it into my Moonbase?" His face was getting redder, his voice louder.

"It was never a hazard to us," said Petra. "It's for a kind of life we didn't think possible, an environment utterly alien. They do not care, or realise, we exist."

"It came from a neutron star," said Sarah, "designed to affect other neutron stars. The intelligences responsible operate at densities millions of times greater than us. Everything in the Solar System, except maybe the very centre of the Sun, would just be overdense vacuum to them.

But they're turning entire collapsed stars into computronium – neutronic computronium."

"The singularity happened," said Petra, "a long time ago, and a long way away."

"We have a lot of catching up to do," said Sarah.

The Director looked away from them for a moment, tapping his finger on his desk. "You're sure of this, certain these results will stand up to the harshest scrutiny?" They nodded. "You think that will protect you from the consequences of your actions?"

"This is the discovery of the century, Director," said Sarah. "The millennium."

"Where's the proof? This particle of yours is gone, the data only on our servers, which can fail. Without that, the two of you will sound like embittered cranks, making things up to get your jobs back."

"Until someone else finds one," said Sarah. "They must be pretty common. We caught ours in the first hours of collector operation."

"In which case it's someone else's discovery. Science moves on, you get left behind."

"Frankly, I don't care," said Sarah. "It would be nice to get the credit, I'll admit, so we have backups and we've sent an encrypted dataset to Horst and other press contacts. But if all that fails, the science will happen, even if I have to drop a few hints to the Americans in Moonbase Five. The science is the thing. And when the result gets out, you'll look an utter fool."

The Director leaned forward, resting his elbows on the desk, and looked directly into Sarah's eyes. "You took unacceptable risks."

"Yes, we – I – did. But it was the right thing to do."

"You didn't know that. There have to be consequences."

Sarah paused for a moment, sensing something had changed. "Are we negotiating?" she asked.

The Director nodded. "Yes. You've made a valuable discovery, but used unacceptable methods. There's no place for you on the Moon anymore, but we might still salvage something. You want the science out. I want full credit for Moonbase Three and don't want either of you going to the Americans or elsewhere. So, what do we do?"

"I publish the paper, this place gets the credit," said Sarah.

The Director shook his head. "That would encourage everyone else to take stupid risks, disregard the rules and ignore procedure. I have a counter proposal."

Sarah sighed. "I've had enough. This is no way to do science." She rose in her chair, but Petra reached out, laying a hand on her wrist.

"Wait – hear him out."

Something in Petra's expression caused her to pause, to doubt her position was as strong as she thought. A man like this didn't get to be a Moonbase Director without influence in many high places. Perhaps it would be better to have him on her side.

"Go on," she muttered.

"Given what you did, neither of you can get full credit. Some, perhaps, is due. It is an amazing and fundamental result. But too many people know what you did, and that cannot be forgiven. You can't just stay here and carry on. Let me propose this. Max leads the paper, gets credit for the result and gets the science out. Moonbase Three, and yourselves, bask in reflected glory. Max takes over the experiment, the two of you head home, a black mark on your lunar records, but your status secure as collaborators on this fine result."

"But..." muttered Sarah.

"Nobody wins," concluded the Director, "but nobody loses. And if you still think the encrypted archive you sent Horst will help," he waved a datachip at them, "he sent it back to me, and deleted his copy without distributing it. Who exactly do you think he works for?"

Sarah and Petra nodded, defeated.

But this isn't science, thought Sarah. *This is someone who left science long ago playing a game.* He played it well, but it meant nothing. The result, whoever got the credit, was the thing. It made a difference. It would change the world, change what people knew and thought about the world and the universe at large. That was the important thing. In the future, this result would be remembered. Long after all their names were forgotten, along with all the petty squabbles over who had found what and where, the result would remain.

They might be unknowably distant, and incomprehensibly alien, but humanity was no longer alone in the universe.

There is a long tradition in science fiction of producing stories set within the same broad future history. One of my favourite settings when I was growing up was Larry Niven's Known Space, which spawned a range of stories set over a period of hundreds of years. 'The

remaining stories in this collection represent my attempt at such a future history.

The connections between these stories may not be obvious at first sight. This is at least in part because, as an observational cosmologist, I'm trying to play with very long time spans and very large distances. I'm also, perhaps rather foolhardily, trying to do as much of this as I can with real or at least plausible physics. Thus there are no warp drives or other methods of faster than light travel, no time machines, no magic sources of energy.

One thing I did realise when working on these stories is that you need to travel much faster than light to make the galaxy accessible to travel on the timescale of a human lifetime – even a very extended lifetime. I thus have works in progress that use FTL for Solar System colonisation but not interstellar travel, while, I use slower than light travel here to get far outside our own galaxy.

This particular story is about the Fermi Paradox. It is fairly easy to show that an intelligent species willing and able to travel between the stars can visit all the stars in our Galaxy in a few tens of millions of years. This may seem a long time, but since the galaxy is about ten billion years old, and our own Solar System four and a half billion years old, there has been ample opportunity for this to happen. But there is no evidence that it has. Hence Enrico Fermi's famous question: where are they? This story started as an attempt to answer that question, but soon also became a look at how science is done and how it might be done under the commercial pressures of a future moonbase. I owe the BBC's early 70s TV show Moonbase 3 *for some of the background details, suitably modified for the future we are actually living in.*

THE FOOTHILLS OF SHACKLETON

The ball skewed to one side as it flew towards me, but there was hardly any downwards curve. The weak lunar gravity wasn't a match for balls thrown by Earthly muscles.

I made the shot easily, and the ball flew over Josh's head and down the long floodlit cavern.

Josh applauded as Prab jogged after the ball with the long loping stride of a practiced lunar walker.

"We'll make a cricket player of you yet, mate," said Josh.

"This place is better suited to baseball!" I said. "We just need something bigger than this interferometer hall, something like a real diamond."

"Not enough players though," said Josh. "Maybe on the surface if they let us out there to play one day."

"No," said Prab, standing behind Josh having retrieved the ball. "That will not be allowed. And anyway, cricket is much the better game. Much more skilful."

Josh grinned. "Course it is. And now I'm going to prove it."

I headed back to the wicket and prepared for Josh to bowl, keeping the bat low to the ground and in front of the stumps as I'd been taught.

The ball came at me. Its course looked the same as before and I expected it to curve to the right again. But then the course changed. Instead of curving right it curved *down*. Josh had done something with the spin, something that wouldn't have worked in normal gravity.

I realised too late, I was already committed to the ball going the other way. It hit my stumps, the bails flew into the air while the stumps scattered, kicking up clouds of celocrete dust. I was out.

Prab applauded, and so did I.

"Nice ball! How did you do that?"

"All in the wrist action, like the rest of spinning," said Josh. "I'll show you in what's left of our lunch break. Prab? You ready to bat?"

Prab started to nod when the alarms went off.

"Damn those miners!" said Josh, sitting next to me at the controls of the other optical/UV telescope.

It was the dust alarm. Some wildcat miner had again sent dust drifting past the observatory, scattering light and contaminating the mirrors.

"That screws the next few shifts. Why do they always do this at night?"

"Since night lasts for two weeks, maybe they don't have a choice?" I suggested, but Josh only glared at me.

We couldn't do anything useful until the mirrors were cleaned and we could run the sweepers. That needed solar UV to ionise the dust and allow it to be attracted to the sweeper cables surrounding the astronomy reserve.

"No backup projects?" I asked.

Josh shook his head. "Not a thing. We finished those a week ago, the last time this happened." I'd been on my way from Earth then.

I tapped and moused some commands into my machine. "I think I've got one here."

"Oh yes?" asked Josh, wheeling over to my console on his chair to look at the screen.

"Yep – something about searching for cheese." I grinned while Josh shook his head. "What next then?"

"Cricket? More sleep?" said Josh.

I shook my head. "Not tired yet, and my shoulders are sore. Guess I'll see what's happening in the other domes."

"Still a newbie," he joked. "It loses its shine after a while."

I grinned. "Hasn't yet. And I might learn something useful. Anyway, I'm still on company time."

"Hah," said Josh humourlessly. "The mining companies selling rocket fuel and helium-3 that pay for us. When they screw things up it's our duty to knock off and properly punish them!"

"Maybe when I'm old and cynical like you. Not yet though. This is the Moon – not many get to come here, and even fewer astronomers!"

"Prab, you're looking puzzled." I peered over his shoulder at the screen. Prab was running the Farside Radio Array so wasn't subject to the dust problems that had shut the rest of us down. Observing with the array was boringly easy most of the time since the big dishes over the horizon largely ran themselves. But it was the only thing happening thanks to the dust. The dishes had been observing atomic hydrogen in a population three star on the edge of the observable universe for the last week, but there still wasn't anything for me to see. Spectacular but slow science.

Now there was a problem.

Prob nodded distractedly while typing commands. "Dish seventeen has excess noise," he said, pointing to the trace. "But I don't know where it is coming from."

I looked at the notice-board where all kinds of random information about the Farside Array had been pinned. The map caught my attention, as they usually did. The line of the Earth-terminator ran across it, the divide between the half of the Moon facing the Earth and the half that doesn't. We were just on the Earth-facing side, not far from the south pole, but the radio dishes were some distance away, over the horizon and protected from the deafening radio noise pumped out by the Earth. The dishes were scattered over a large area, their combined signals giving the resolving power of a much larger telescope. Each dish on the map had its number beside it.

"Prab," I said. "Seventeen's the nearest one to earthside." He gave no sign of having heard me. "Would that make it more susceptible to interference?"

Prab hardly paused in his typing. "Dish too high attitude. Signal from earthside wouldn't get through." He typed a few more commands then paused. "Unless it is sidelobe..." He swung his chair back to another console, nearly running me over. My instinctive jump almost took me to the ceiling – there was a reason we usually sat on velcro chairs.

Prab jotted some numbers on a sheet of paper, entered commands and looked at the results before entering some more.

"Sure you're not radio astronomer?" he said, looking up at me. "Is sidelobe after all! Must be nearby bright directional source, but nobody meant to be near farside."

"Can you work out what the signal is?" I asked.

Prab nodded. "Not usual to use radio telescope as receiver for voice, but computer should have sorted it by now." He pressed a button on the screen and a crackling, distorted signal came out of the speakers.

"Mayday, mayday! Trapped, air running out. Help us, please!"

"You know these are probably the guys who screwed up our observations?" said Josh.

I gave him a hard look as we made our way through the narrow corridors that joined the observatory domes.

"Are you seriously saying we should leave them out there?"

His mouth twitched as if he were considering the possibility, but we carried on towards the vehicle bay. "It's probably their own fault. Just natural justice really. Kinda like the lesson you get if you poke a croc too often with a stick."

"We can do without the Ozzie stories," I muttered under my breath.

We were the nearest outpost to the trapped miners so we got to play first responders. Prab would stay behind to run his observations and act as a communications relay across the Earth terminator. We got to go to the farside.

If Josh agreed.

"If we left 'em out there it might persuade the rest to stay away too," he said as we reached the vehicle dock and paused for the airlock of our rover to open.

I stared at him, not believing what I was hearing. The first thing drilled into us in training is that everyone on the Moon helps anyone who gets into trouble. This place is so alien and hostile that the smallest problem can quickly become life threatening or fatal. We've only got each other to rely on. Unlike home, we don't have a few billion years of evolution making us suited to the environment.

The airlock hissed open, revealing the first of the two cabins of the rover.

"You can't be serious," I said to Josh. He slid past me into the rover, through the internal hatch to the control cabin and into the driver's seat.

He looked over his shoulder and smiled back at me. "Course not mate. Just wanted to wind you up and make sure I drove. You didn't think I was going to miss this did you?"

The rover surged up one side of a small crater and over its rim, all eight wheels leaving the surface for a few moments. The impact of landing winded me and left the suspension rocking.

"Do we need to go this fast?" I asked.

"You said yourself we need to get there as quickly as possible."

"But we need to get there in one piece!"

"These things are built like tanks. No worries about getting there."

I looked to my left, out of the window, a slit of armoured glass stretching from one side of the cabin to the other. The lunar night was deep black, a pitch darkness revealing nothing of what it contained. There might be crevasses out there, boulders scattered from some ancient impact event or billion year old volcanism, and I wouldn't see it. The only things I could see were stars, steady pinpricks of light in the sky, fixed and unmoving unlike the twinkling diamonds you see in the depths of Earth's atmosphere.

I turned to the front, where the headlights illuminated our route up into the foothills of the Shackleton polar region. Typical grey lunar dust was everywhere, but outcroppings of darker basalts were becoming more common as we got deeper into the highlands.

Not that Josh was dependent on the window. He was using VR goggles to give him a combined optical, radar and infrared view from the rover's sensor suite. The windows were only there to give passengers something to look at. And to act as a final backup in case everything else failed.

I wondered if that was what had happened to the miners, but it couldn't be that simple. Their radio signal was too weak and their rover had to be damaged or they'd be mobile.

I looked back the way we'd come as our route wound its way into the highlands.

I scanned the horizon until I saw it, a disk rapidly setting in the distance, one half bright and bluish, the other dark but speckled with brighter dots.

We were passing to the farside, out of direct touch with Earth, truly away from home, connected only by a tenuous string of technology. Things that went wrong out here got very bad very quickly.

We arrived at the area the signal was from but could find nothing.

It was a broken landscape full of volcanics – rock promontories, stark cliffs thrown into sharp relief by the glare of the headlights with none of the softening you got from atmospheric scattering.

"We'll never find them in this!" I said.

"Put these on," said Josh, offering me a set of goggles. "They might help."

"Why on Earth did they come out here?" I asked as I scanned the landscape for some hint that the miners were near – dropped equipment, vehicle tracks, anything.

"Not on Earth, are we?" replied Josh.

"But why? We're in the astronomy reserve, over the terminator. They'd be disciplined for this even if everything went well. As it is they'll be lucky to get out alive."

I activated the zoom to get a clearer view of a cluster of rocks near the horizon, but this didn't reveal anything unusual.

"They're after the big strike, the kind of thing that'll allow them to compete with the big boys like Tata and Halliburton. They'll be doing this on their own time, not the company's, though they turn a blind eye since they'd get some percentage of any find. Happens all the time."

"But why out here?"

"See those peaks?" Josh pointed to the left.

"Yes?"

"They're volcanoes. Theory is that lava tubes were made by them when the Moon was young. They'd be full of ice and frozen volatiles. And you could seal them and use them as pre-made habitats. Finding one would be worth a fortune. Nobody has, so they keep trying."

I couldn't find anything just looking at the landscape. We'd been stopped here a few minutes, so I decided to look over the sensor records to see if anything was changing.

"Something odd to the right," I told Josh as soon as the calculations were finished.

"Don't see anything."

"You wouldn't, but something's moving out there. I think it's dust, kicked up some hours back. You know how it takes ages for the stuff to clear."

'Right – I see it now. Sure it's not us?"

"We didn't come that way, and even with your driving we couldn't have thrown anything that far."

"Right…" said Josh thoughtfully. "Better take a look."

We almost drove into the hole.

The rover had safety features to stop idiots driving over cliffs, but we'd had to turn them off. If they'd gone over a cliff we wouldn't find them by avoiding cliffs. Josh was concentrating on the VR output but couldn't look everywhere all the time. I thought the black feature in front of us was just a shadow, its sharp edges some trick of light in vacuum and the dark of the lunar night.

Then I noticed a little speckling above it – dust glinting in the headlights – and got a curious sense of depth in its blackness.

I was suddenly very afraid.

"Stop!" I shouted.

"What?" asked Josh.

I trod hard on the emergency footbrake on the redundant controls in front of me.

The rover jerked to a halt, rocking forward on its suspension and swerving a little to the right.

"What the hell was that for?" said Josh, pulling off the goggles and staring at me in shock.

I pointed out of the window. We were close enough to be able to see the hole for what it was – a thirty metre absence of lunar surface at the top of a gentle rise. The ground just opened into darkness.

"Hole," I gasped as the rover teetered on its edge.

At least we now had a decent signal to the miners.

They told us the ground had collapsed while they were taking seismic measurements. The good news was that they'd found a lava tube. The bad news was that they'd fallen into it.

"Our rover fell then hit the ground and rolled," said Mick, the miner we were talking to. "We've lost pressure in one cabin but nobody's seriously hurt. Rover's all banged up though and we're running out of emergency oxygen."

"Okay, mate," said Josh. "We'll see what we can do from up here." He switched off the channel. "Lucky we heard their signal – they're in a bad way!"

"Sounds like we got here just in time."

"Maybe," said Josh. "What we do up here will decide whether it's just in time to help or just in time to hear them asphyxiate."

We got into our suits and left the rover.

"We need to get some kind of line to them," said Josh as we stood on the edge of the hole looking down.

"I can't even see them!"

"Nor me," said Josh.

I lay down and stuck my head over the edge for a better view. When I looked down I could see jagged spikes of lava sticking straight up. Directly beneath the hole several were broken, and a trail of debris ran from this impact site away from the hole and out of sight. "They fell down here then rolled further into the tube. That's why the rock's blocking their radio signal."

I looked to either side, along the lava tube, but my helmet's light just disappeared into the blackness. "This thing's big!"

"Can you see them?" asked Josh.

I looked back down the hole, trying to follow the trail of crushed lava and fragments of the miners' rover.

"Not from here," I replied, "but... There's something odd about the rock here. There's some whitish stuff in crevices in the lava."

"Whitish?" Josh lay down beside me. "That looks like ice or frozen volatiles! This is the real thing – a big strike!"

"Let's get these guys out before we worry about that." I switched back to the public channel. "Hey Mick, have you got some kind of lights down there? We can't see you."

"We're trying to conserve power," he said, "but now you're here we could try something." There was a pause. "We've turned on the cabin lights. I could try the main headlights but I don't think they survived the crash."

"Thanks!" I said and changed the channel. "Can you see anything now?"

"Not a thing."

"Nor me." I stood and walked back to the rover collecting the remote control for my suit's safety line.

"What are you doing?" Josh asked.

"We're not going to see anything just peering over the edge. Someone has to go down there, maybe just a little, to get a proper view."

I stuck the controller to my suit's wrist clips and got it to pay out some extra slack. "That should be enough to start. Can you help me over the edge and make sure the line doesn't snag?"

"You're sure about this?" Josh asked.

I blinked then looked away. "No, I'm not. But I can't think of anything else and we haven't got time to wait for inspiration." I stepped to the edge of the hole. "Now help me down before I lose my nerve."

I sat on the edge, guiding the cable and adjusting its length, then gently slipped over and into the blackness, helmet lamps set to maximum.

There was a long moment of falling then the cable jerked me to a stop. I dangled, swinging gently from side to side, staring into a vast tube, wider than the interferometer hall was long.

"Wow – this place really is huge!" I told Josh.

"Can you see them?" Josh asked.

"Not yet." I switched to the miners' channel "Can you see a light above you? I'm coming down into the tube."

"Hang on," came the reply. "I'm just getting to the window... Can't see. No – there you are! Up and to the left."

I twisted myself on the end of the cable, waving my arms to one side so I could swing myself around. The rover lay at the bottom of the tube, one cabin split open, suspension and wheels twisted together. "I see you! You made quite a mess of that rover!"

"Can you get down to us?" asked Mick.

"Can't see an easy way to do that. The sides are too steep to get back out. We need to get a cable to you and can then winch you up."

"Right," he said. "We'll get suited up and blow the hatch, but oxygen supplies are getting really low."

"Hold off until we're ready," I said. "Shouldn't be too long." I changed back to our private channel. "I'm coming back up."

"How're we going to get a cable to them?" Josh asked as he helped me out of the hole. Dark scuffs of moon dust stained my suit. "We don't have anything to launch a cable."

"I know... But I've got an idea. How good are you at bowling in that suit?"

I looked into the hole at Josh as he prepared himself. We'd found a small lunar rock, about the size of a cricket ball, and tied a thin cable to it, paying out more than enough to reach the miners' rover. The cable now dangled into the hole beside Josh as he held the rock in his hand.

"Are you sure this is going to work?" he asked.

"Have you got any better ideas?"

The miners had blown the emergency hatch and were waiting to catch the rock, as long as Josh threw it right.

"This suit's too cramped, There's nothing to stand on, and if my bloody lifeline gives way you'll have one more person to rescue." He looked straight down to the jagged floor of the lava tube. "If I survive."

"You're the one who's good at throwing things. I could try a baseball throw but I've never been much good. You're the best chance they've got."

Josh swallowed so hard I could hear it over the radio. "This drop bothers me. I don't like heights – it's putting me off."

Mick and the other miners only had the air left in their suits. They couldn't afford for Josh to get cold feet now. I breathed slowly for a few moments. If he heard an edge of panic creeping into my voice it would only make matters worse.

"Think about something else. Close your eyes if it'll help. Put yourself in a big cricket match. And remember, if this throw goes wrong, we can always try again." I didn't believe it though. If the rock went wild there were a lot of places for the cable to snag and we were unlikely to get it back. We'd have to start from scratch with the miners running out of air and without enough of the lightest cable left. This was our only good chance of rescuing them.

"Are you guys ready down there?" I said to the miners while Josh sorted himself out.

"Ready as we'll ever be," came the reply from Mick.

I switched back to Josh. He was breathing slowly, talking to himself. "Right... Last day of the final test at the Wacca. Last English wicket, two runs for them to win. One wicket to get them all out... We bowl... They hit... They're running... The ball comes to me and..."

Josh threw the rock, his body swinging backwards with the reaction.

Time froze as the ball flew out of sight on its low gravity parabola.

Then cheers and, I could swear, applause.

"We got it, mate!" shouted Mick.

Within minutes we had hauled them out and got them into the

rover. It turned out most of them were from Australia, the rest from South Africa. All cricketers. Josh was greeted like a hometown hero.

"Never seen a throw like that before!" said Mick once we'd started the trip back. "Awesome! We've got a lot of cricket fans at the mine, though we can't play."

"We've been using a cavern dug out for the telescopes, but it's too small, barely big enough for a practice net," said Josh.

"All that should be solved now," said Mick.

"How do you mean?" I asked.

"The lava tube's huge. We spent a lot of time looking at it from the inside, and there's enough space for a small town, for a mine, and some open space – just right for cricket."

"Who'll pay for that?" asked Josh.

"You can if you want – this place'll dwarf all the other mines put together!" said Mick.

I frowned. We were missing something.

"What do you mean 'we' can pay for it?" I said.

"You've got a share in the mine – we all have so we're set for life! You can do as much astronomy or cricket or," he looked at me, "even baseball as you want."

Josh and I looked at each other, eyes widening in amazement.

"One thing we will have to do, though," said Mick. "Bring up a few more decent cricket players. If it wasn't for your man Josh here, we'd still be in that hole!"

One of the great achievements of astronomy and space science in the 20th and early 21st centuries has been to take the Moon and other planets and turn them from dots or blobs of light in the sky into places with landscapes in which we can see ourselves one day standing. The only place where we have actually achieved this, though, is the Moon, much of which remains to be explored.

AN INDUSTRIAL GROWTH

"Have you ever been to North America?" asked Mary.

She had to shout. The tilt-rotor's cabin was militaristically utilitarian, all webbing and fold down seats, and the air noise had increased now the plane had gone subsonic for their descent. Most of the trip from Nairobi had been quiet, but they'd spent the time checking their equipment and making sure the special packages delivered down the Kilimanjaro beanstalk were behaving themselves.

"Never," replied Jomo. "Is it as bad as they say?"

"Mostly not," replied Mary, remembering happier times. There were places in North America she actually liked. "But some of it's worse."

"Where we're going?"

She nodded. "That's why they asked for us." It was two years since Mary's last trip. Two years since they'd lost Mark. Two years since she'd spoken to Peter. And now he'd asked her to come back, for what he said was the worst case yet.

Worse than two years ago.

She'd nearly refused, but the tone of Peter's voice during his brief, professional briefing had persuaded her. If Peter was worried and had no alternative but to call her he must be in serious trouble.

"Was it always like this?" Jomo's question broke her train of thought. He was looking through the porthole behind his seat.

"Like what?" asked Mary.

"A desert. Nothing growing, just the occasional ruined town."

"Not always. I'm told most of it used to be green and fertile."

Mary remembered what she'd seen on previous trips. People, animals and plants, twisted and dying from heavy metal poisons. Landscapes fractured by collapsing gas reservoirs, coastal regions scoured by super hurricanes. And nanoblooms, as the technology that had promised so much became an all-devouring threat.

"It's all in ruins now?"

Mary looked out of the window, remembering views from another plane on her final visit here, to Milpitas and those who claimed to be the next stage of human evolution.

"Maybe," she replied.

Before Jomo could ask another question the pilot announced their descent and they hurried to make sure everything was cleared up and properly stowed.

Peter stood by the landing pad, tall in his olive fatigues. His tightly curled hair was greyer than Mary remembered, and his face more lined. She stood in front of him for a moment, not sure what to do.

Then he smiled, the brilliant white of his teeth lighting up his dark face. It was infectious. Mary smiled, remembering that, above everything, Peter was a friend as well as a colleague.

She stepped into his arms and they hugged.

"It's been too long," said Peter.

"Yes," agreed Mary, lingering in the hug since it kept everything else at bay. Eventually they let each other go.

"Sorry," said Mary, apologising to Jomo and getting a more businesslike grip on herself. "Peter, this is Jomo, my assistant, and an expert on compression bombs."

They shook hands.

"A pleasure to meet you," said Jomo.

"Likewise," replied Peter. "But I hope we don't have to use those things."

Jomo nodded. "Understood."

"My people will help get your gear sorted," Peter said to Jomo, indicating the group behind him. "Can you do that while I talk to Mary?"

Jomo nodded. He introduced himself to the others, and they started unloading.

"Sorry about the landing delay," said Peter as he showed Mary to one of the prefabricated office buildings beside the pad. "Traffic control's a mess since we're evacuating as many people as possible."

"How far is it?" she asked, cutting directly to business.

"About ten miles. It's not moving, just staying where it was spotted."

"Anything odd about the site?"

"Not really. You've seen it all before. How about the kid?"

"Jomo's good, but Africa is his only field experience."

"Nothing's ever as bad there."

The office building was a metal and fibre structure, pure white, UN Reconstruction logos covering the walls, identical to hundreds of others across the world.

Peter nodded towards it. "The people inside need to talk."

Mary took a deep breath as she realised he'd been holding out on her. "What haven't you told me?"

Two uploads stood at the far end of the room, looking at a wall screen showing data from the site. One male, one female, tall, blond, blue eyed, pale skinned, looking like nearly-identical twins. Their presence evoked memories of the worst of the dreadful years that had given them birth.

"Peter," said Mary, holding her anger in check. "Give me one good reason why I shouldn't turn round and fly straight back to Nairobi."

"You have to see what's going on. We need you – really."

She turned to him. "That's why *you* want *me*. It's not a reason for me to stay, especially with those things hanging around. What are they here for?"

"They've been helping."

"The only people those bastards have ever helped is themselves." She kept her voice low, partly so the visitors wouldn't hear, but also not to disturb the analysis team that filled the room, collating data from sensor nets spread across the site – on the ground, in the air and on the water.

Peter shook his head. "Things are different now. They paid for all of this." He gestured at the equipment and personnel that filled the room. Mary had to admit the machines were more up to date and the furniture and fittings less threadbare than she was expecting. "And they've provided a lot of technical help as well. We owe them a lot!"

Mary was about to protest further when the analyst nearest the door, an Asian woman with long black hair, looked up at the sound of their voices.

"You're here," she said, relief and desperation filling her voice. "Maybe now we can stop it."

Mary realised she was stuck. If it had been just her and Peter, she could have fooled herself this was just another of their arguments. But she knew it wasn't. She had responsibilities, people who needed her expertise and the equipment she'd brought. And, she had to admit, it felt good to be back saving the world. She had done good work in Africa, but that was just decontamination. Their work in North America had always been different, since here the contamination could fight back.

She smiled at the analyst, and introduced herself. "Mary Ihonor."

They shook hands. "Emily Yee, and it's a pleasure to meet you."

"We should do this later," interrupted Peter, glancing at the uploads. "They need to talk to..."

"No. Before I talk to them I need an idea of what's going on. Emily can give me that."

Emily looked to Peter for permission. After a moment he nodded. "Very well. I'll tell them you're here."

Mary pulled up a stool and sat by Emily's workstation.

"What's got you so worried?"

"It's a standard US nanoindustrial complex, built ten years before their economy and environment tanked." Emily pointed at a map. "Built fast and cheap. No safety or environmental standards."

Mary, peering over Emily's shoulder, nodded. "I've seen plenty of them. Heavy metal contamination, cyanide in the ground water, dioxins in the topsoil, PCBs, CFCs, you name it, they made money off it."

"And right at the heart," said Emily, pointing at a spherical structure, "what we thought was a decommissioned nanoreactor."

"What were they making?"

Emily opened a couple of windows filled with pages of text. "They were under contract to the US government at the end."

"That should have decent documentation – the inevitable bureaucratic pollutant."

"We looked, but the contract details are missing."

"Let me try." Mary pulled up a chair.

"You won't find anything we didn't."

Mary entered a complex query and sent it to the data server while setting up a hypothesis engine and idea filter to analyse the results.

"Impressive," said Emily. "I thought you worked in the field!"

Mary smiled. "Before you get to the field, you prepare for what you're going to find. Otherwise your field career, and life, will be very short. Now, let's look at those contracts."

Emily brought the paperwork back to the display.

"Look at the dates. Months before the last presidential election, just when everything went to shit."

"We spotted that," said Emily. "What were they thinking, throwing up nanoreactors without proper safeguards?"

"They were desperate. It was the fourth summer of super hurricanes. Global warming, pollution, resource depletion, disease." Mary remembered news coverage from her childhood. "The poor were dying in their thousands while rich bastards like them," she nodded towards the two visitors talking to Peter on the other side of the room, "sat safe in their upload heavens, refusing to help even by paying their damn taxes. Plants like this were the government's last-gasp attempt to do something – anything – that might turn things around."

Emily pointed to the contract's serial number on the screen. "That number's a military designation."

The screen flashed as Mary's search reported back. She shook her head. "Sorry. Nothing you haven't already found."

Emily smiled. "We do put a lot of effort into the research."

Mary felt slightly ashamed she'd thought she could breeze in and sort out all their problems. "I'm sure you do." She looked at the screen for a few moments. Something niggled her. It took a few moments to work out what it was. "That contract number's familiar."

"It's part of a block of contracts from the same black budget sent to a number of nanofabrication plants at about the same time. Nobody's managed to track down the details – all the records were lost with what happened to Washington."

Mary's eyes narrowed. This all sounded familiar.

"Can I try something else?"

"Be my guest," replied Emily.

Mary typed for a few moments and submitted another search to the server.

"Did anybody go in to look at the site? Without those government records you'd have no idea what to expect."

"Yes," said Emily, quietly.

The search came back more quickly this time, and the results were positive.

Mary felt the world shift around her, felt even more manipulated than she had when she saw the uploads. Now she knew she couldn't turn around and leave. "That block of contracts," she said, feeling faint. "One matches the last job I did in the US."

"The one where...?" Emily left the question hanging.

"Did you lose any of the people who went into the site?"

"It came close," said Peter, who had quietly joined them, flanked on either side by his blond, blue-eyed visitors.

Mary gave them looks of deep distrust, then turned her gaze on Peter. "What happened? Go in unprepared? Ignore gaps in the sensor grid?"

Peter's expression hardened. "Some of us learn from our mistakes instead of running away from them." He drew a breath. "The site was seeded with clean-up strains this spring, then sensor mesh and antinanotic spray. I led the scout team. When things went wrong, when we found the containment had breached, we stopped. You would have pushed on, then who knows what would have happened."

Mary remembered how things had gone wrong the last time. "Someone would have died," she said quietly, thinking of Mark. "Maybe all of you."

"Tell her what you saw," said the female upload, her voice high and clear, a voice of command.

It had been two years since Mary had seen one of these artificial bodies. They housed the minds of uploaded humans on the rare occasions they deigned to visit the real world.

"We've both seen nanoblooms before," said Peter. "Like slow, living acid, consuming everything in their path. Eventually the atmosphere, pollutants, and reproduction errors cause the bloom to fail, otherwise the whole world would've been digested by now. They're chaotic, disorganised. But not this one."

"Like last time?" Mary asked, thinking of their final job together, trapped by the most hostile, most intelligent nanobloom anybody had seen.

"Worse." Peter pressed a few keys on Emily's workstation. "It has a plan for how to escape and infect the rest of the world."

The display showed a blurred image, reconstructed from the sensor grid scattered across the complex by the scouting team. It showed a pool of grey nanomachine liquid leaking from the spherical reactor at the centre of the plant. At one edge of the pool something was emerging. Mary couldn't tell what it was, but it was familiar. Then, as bandwidth increased, the image became clear.

A hand, apparently human, rose from the grey soup.

"It's got people in there?"

"No. But it's making something just like us."

"Been a long time since I've worn one of these," said Mary to Jomo, wriggling to make the hazard suit more comfortable. The male upload sat silently beside her in the all-terrain vehicle as they waited for Peter and the other upload to sort out their suits.

"I can still come with you." Jomo fussed with one of the cargo trunks behind Mary's seat.

"You've not seen anything like this."

"Nobody has!"

That wasn't completely true, but was something Mary didn't want to explain. "You don't have the necessary experience or training. As long as the compression bombs are safe and functional we'll do just fine."

Jomo closed the trunk and latched it shut. "They should be okay. You're sure you know how to use them?"

"Yes. Activation code and finger scan, then two dials – one for yield, the other's a timer. A child could do it!"

Jomo sighed and stepped back from the vehicle, joining Emily by the door to the control centre.

Peter and the other upload had finished their preparations and signalled it was time to head out.

"Just make sure you and Emily stay on the comm in case we need something," Mary said.

"We will," said Emily, waving them off with one hand. The other discreetly held Jomo back as he was about to return to the ATV and fuss with something else.

The upload beside Mary pressed his foot on the accelerator, and the little six-wheeled vehicle set off on the decayed road that led to the industrial plant.

Peter drove the ATV in front while the female upload beside him scanned the road and the verge for problems or hazards. Mary did the same for her own vehicle while the male upload drove. They travelled at jogging pace, the upload sitting beside Mary remaining silent, his eyes fixed intently on the road. It would take a while to reach the plant. Mary settled into the most comfortable position she could manage in the bulky suit, on the hard, unyielding plastic of her seat.

This was going to be a long trip in all senses of the word, she thought.

After ten minutes the female upload in the lead vehicle raised her hand, and both ATVs came to a halt.

Mary sat up. "What's the problem?" she asked over her suit radio.

"Time to set up the other equipment," replied Peter as they climbed down from their ATVs.

Mary was glad to stretch her legs, but was puzzled. "What other equipment?"

The female upload turned towards Peter. "You didn't tell her?"

"I didn't tell anybody." He nodded towards the camp, which was now hidden from view by the rising land. "Now we're far enough away they can't see."

The upload paused for a moment then nodded, exaggerating the movement so it could be seen inside the suit. "Very well. Let's start unpacking."

The two uploads opened one of the cases on the back of the lead ATV and started assembling what looked like a miniature pagoda, about six feet tall, topped by a silvered sphere.

Mary stepped up to Peter, who was watching the preparations. "What's this about? What is that thing?"

"We've got two," replied Peter. "One for each ATV. They're point defence lasers."

"What?"

"Military hardware. From them." He nodded towards the uploads. "Top spec stuff. They scan the area around us continuously and use a laser to shoot down anything hazardous."

"This isn't a bloody military operation – and certainly not one of theirs!"

Peter looked down at her, his face stern. "You know what happened last time. These defences can stop it happening again."

"Why not tell the others back at the camp?"

"Because they don't know how dangerous this is. They're all being evacuated right now, including your friend Jomo. If things go bad, this whole area might be sterilised at a moment's notice."

"We're going in there with no backup, not even a comm line to the outside world?"

Peter nodded.

"This isn't going to be an easy trip."

Peter looked at her, uncertainty at the edge of his eyes. "Did you ever think it would be?"

Mary remembered the last time. It had ended with flaming debris raining down around her. "I guess not." She sighed. "What can I do to help?"

"Are there any changes you would make to your suit?" the male upload sitting beside Mary suddenly asked.

It was half an hour after the point defence systems had been installed, and they were back on the road after some brief tests.

Mary ignored him. She saw no reason to make small talk. They were here to do a job, but that didn't mean she had to be civil to whatever she was traveling with. Especially since they were surely still hiding things from her.

"We design and make the suits. We are always interested in ways they might be modified, to improve safety, efficiency and comfort."

Mary took her eyes off the road for a moment and looked at the upload. It hadn't occurred to her he might actually be serious about the question, conducting a customer service questionnaire while they were in the field.

Mary moved in her seat.

"You need more padding in some places," she grudgingly admitted.

The upload nodded, then turned to Mary. "I'm reaching the same conclusion myself." He moved in his seat the same way as Mary, then smiled.

Mary laughed – she couldn't help herself. She hadn't expected humour from an upload. "You're going to send in some design changes when – if – we get back?"

"Definitely. It's a pity we can't implement them here."

"I don't think a needle and thread would be a good idea."

The upload nodded, his eyes back on the road. "That's not what I am used to, but it's what we are stuck with."

This worried Mary. "Your clothing can change itself back home? It's nanotech?"

"No! Nothing like that. I was meaning in codespace not... the outside world. Nanotech – clothing or otherwise – is utterly forbidden on Earth. You know that."

"But aren't you – that body – made of it?"

The upload turned to look at Mary, a stern expression on his face. "It certainly is not." He sounded insulted. "This body is perfectly natural." He looked back to the road. "We only have a limited range of genetic types available. Its appearance causes you offence, for which I apologise."

Mary hadn't realised her distaste had been so obvious. "It's a throwback to everything that went wrong over the last century. You look just like one of the beautiful, wealthy people who used all their money to make themselves immortal in upload heaven, then left the rest of us to face the mess they'd made of the world. Frankly, I don't see why you have any involvement with the outside at all."

"Most do not. The place we live – codespace – is all encompassing. Most stay there, ignoring the outside world."

"But you're here. Why? Do you want to screw the world up some more?"

"When the first ones uploaded, they turned their back on the rest of the world. Their virtual enclaves were sealed off from any trouble. They lived somewhere luxurious and isolated. But life is different there. The boundaries separating individuals are weaker – sometimes absent. It's easier to understand others, to see through their eyes, to become them. Many shy away from that – withdrawing to their own worlds, staying inside them, separated from everything but their own creations. Some think it best that we not meddle with the outside. But some of us see that there is work to do, damage that must be repaired, dangers to all that have to be defeated. And, since we still take people in, we learn what is happening, what needs to be done."

"So you're really here just to keep yourselves safe. Anything you do that helps us is just a happy accident?"

The upload nodded. "To some degree. But there are things that threaten us all: intelligent nanoblooms, for example, which we learnt about two years ago. We do much more than what is in our immediate self-interest."

"Two years?" said Mary, realising the upload meant the bloom she, Peter and Mark had been attacked by.

The ATV stopped. Mary looked forward to see that Peter had raised his hand.

They had reached the outskirts of the industrial plant.

It was huge, covering several square miles of arid, polluted landscape, and surrounded by a tall double fence, topped by razor wire. When in full operation, the perimeter would have had an array of active defences as well as the symbolic fence and wire, but most of those would have stopped functioning once the power was cut and the backup generators had run out of fuel. The no-man's land between the two fences would also be defended by pressure-activated mines that would still be deadly.

The gate was the easiest way to get inside. It stood open, its vehicle-proof barrier rolled to one side, the concrete and glass guard post standing empty.

Peter called a halt, stopping his ATV about ten meters from the gate.

"What's going on?" asked Mary over the radio.

"Something odd about the entrance," replied Peter. "We're trying to recalibrate the point defence scanners to get a clearer view."

Mary shook her head in frustration. Why do boys play with their toys when you can go and look, she asked herself, and climbed down from her ATV. The male upload joined her and they walked slowly to the vehicle ahead of them.

"We do not think it is safe to leave the vehicles," said the female upload.

"I've been to more of these plants then you," replied Mary. "I know what I'm doing."

The upload looked at her male partner. "*He* does not." She turned back to the controls in front of her. "Look after him."

The entrance to the plant was a right turn off the road they were on. At one time it had been well cared for, a garden in the arid landscape, with lush grass and flowerbeds contrasting starkly with the rigid arrays of industrial tanks, chimneys and reaction towers that could be seen in the concrete wasteland beyond the fence. But the garden had gone wild. What were once beds were now a twisted mess of overgrown grass, weeds, and the hardier survivors of the cultivated plants.

The male upload moved towards one of the beds, his hand reaching out.

"Watch it," said Mary, grabbing his wrist and holding him back.

He looked at her in confusion.

"It's not safe, and not what it seems."

Mary searched the ground for a moment, then lifted a small piece of wood and brushed it through the tall blades of grass. She showed it to upload.

The wood was cut and deeply scratched in several places.

"The whole area was seeded with scavenging plant species. Some of this grass concentrates heavy metals into its tissues, making them stiffer and stronger, but still just as sharp."

The upload raised his eyebrows. "I feel I should have known that," he said quietly. He bent and picked up a stone that was lying in the road and tossed it into the grass. Some blades bent and allowed the stone to pass. Others, their tissues made rigid by the metals that filled them, snapped and shattered instead. The male upload frowned, then said, slowly, as if each word emerged only with great difficulty, "More... glass... than... grass." He stared at the grass for a moment, then turned and headed back to their ATV.

Odd phrasing, thought Mary. Not the kind of word play she would expect from what she knew of the upload, but she knew she had heard something similar before.

"Thank you for that," came a voice from behind.

Mary looked round, startled to see the female upload standing there.

"He's not been out here before has he?"

"He's hardly been outside codespace at all."

"Why bring him? This is too dangerous for a... what? A newborn?"

The upload smiled. "He's not without resources, or experience. Just a bit rusty."

"Any progress with the gate?"

"Let's take a look while Peter deals with the scans."

They stepped slowly towards the gate, checking the ground in front of them before each step, making sure there was nothing hazardous in their way.

"Since we're working together I suppose I should call you

something," said Mary.

"Something?"

"A name, a title. Shouting 'You, duck!' is too ambiguous if things get messy."

The upload stopped walking and looked at Mary, troubled. "Names are difficult for us, especially here, where identity is fixed. In codespace, things are more fluid – skills, knowledge, personality blend and merge between what, if they came from here, were once distinct individuals."

"So what should I call you? Legion?"

The upload's lips turned up in a wry grin. "People may once have thought us biblical horrors, but I hope we're beyond that. For now you may call me Carla."

Mary thought for a moment on that choice of name, then resumed her slow progress towards the gate.

"Carla," said Mary, trying it out. "I think I can see something." They were a few meters from the gate. Mary stood still, trying to catch the glimpse again, but it was gone. "No," she shook her head, "it's..."

But she saw it again. A slight shift as she moved her head, a distortion of the view beyond the gate by something that stood in the way.

Carla stood beside her and nodded. "I think I see it too."

"I know what this is." Mary retrieved the piece of wood she'd used on the scavenger plants from her suit pocket. She threw it through the gate. It fell in pieces on the far side. "Nanowire – a whole fence of the stuff – but I've no idea why we can't see it."

Carla took a step towards the gate, and moved her head back and forth. "The light is being bent." Her head continued to scan from side to side. "I don't know if the nanowire itself is doing it, or if some kind of coating is responsible. It's acting like a metamaterial, bending the light so we can't see it."

"That could explain the problem with the scanners," said Peter, who'd left his ATV to join them.

"What can we do about it?" asked Mary.

Peter raised an aerosol can he'd brought with him, and sprayed a cloud of fluid at the gate, until the whole area was covered. The nanowire immediately became visible as a fine grey fuzz, indistinct but hanging in the air like stationary smoke. Then the solvents in the spray went to work, dissolving the diamond-strong, molecularly sharp wire.

In moments the way ahead was clear, the sticky remnants of the dissolving nanowire forming puddles on the ground.

"Give it a few seconds to settle, then we can carry on." Peter walked back to his vehicle.

The outskirts of the plant were quite open. Clusters of storage tanks stood in ranks – in some places cylindrical, in others giant spheres. They rose tens of meters into the sky with different clumps separated by hundreds of meters. At points in this regular grid there were processing stations, with chimneys and bloated steel reaction vessels all surrounded by grid-works of metal supports. The impression Mary gained was of a vast industrial chess set, with different pieces scattered across the flat arid landscape divided into a grid of squares by access roads.

But these were just the outer regions of the complex. Their route would take them to the centre, where giant machines crowded close together, and where the more arcane processes of nantechnology took over from traditional chemical engineering, and where, according to their aerial reconnaissance, the regular grid system fell apart.

"Peter," called Mary, over a private channel. She didn't fully trust its encryption, but she didn't want to make her fears public. "You remember, don't you?"

"Yes."

"Nanowire. That's how it started last time."

Peter sighed loudly enough for his helmet microphone to pick up. "I've replayed that day in my head often enough I don't need you to remind me."

"But not the cloaking. That's new."

"And worrying," said Peter. "It's evolved."

"What comes next? Last time it was landmines, but we've..."

CRAAACK!

It sounded like a sheet of paper being torn, amplified a million times.

"Shit!" Mary instinctively ducked.

CRAAAAAAAAK!

The noise came again, from just above her head. A longer burst.

"What *is* that?"

Mary looked up. A twinkling aura surrounded one of the point defence lasers as another burst came.

"Superheated ionized air expanding," explained the male upload beside her. "You can see backscatter scintillations if you look carefully."

"It's an attack," said Carla. "Something from above. The lasers have neutralised it."

There was one final, short burst. Then silence.

"How long can they keep that up?" asked Mary.

"There is sufficient power for several hours of continuous operation," replied the male.

"Can you make it quieter?" asked Mary.

The male upload gave her an oddly familiar look.

After the attack the little convoy descended into a tense silence. They had to be prepared for active as well as passive attacks. In the lead ATV Peter monitored the sensor scans while Carla drove, eyes searching the road ahead for anything the scans may have missed. In the second ATV Mary examined the landscape as well as the scans while the male upload drove.

They made their way slowly down the centre of the road, decayed markings passing beneath the hull of the ATV, keeping away from any hazards that might lurk on the road-side, including the occasional clumps of unhealthy, genetically modified plants. They continued like this for half an hour, hardly a word passing between them, and those that did were concerned only with the minutiae of their journey – a turning taken here, a sensor reading double-checked there.

The road had started a decline, cutting across gentle contours in the landscape, when the ATV jerked to a halt. It woke Mary – the lack of anything to do and the monotonous landscape had lulled her into a doze.

"What's going on?" She shook herself awake. That had been unprofessional, dangerous. It must have been the jet lag.

The male upload gestured forwards.

The road continued its descent and passed through the bottom of a gentle depression which was filled with what looked, at first, like water.

"Is that..."

"Nanofluid," said Carla. "We are taking readings."

"But there was nothing like this on the surveillance images."

"We know," said Peter.

Mary got out of the ATV. The male upload joined her and they made their way to the lead vehicle.

"Is it safe to take a look?"

Carla took a few moments to reply as she checked various readouts. "There is no sign of activity, so it should be okay." She reached back and retrieved a long pole from one of the storage crates on her ATV. "Take this probe with you. It would be useful to get *in situ* data." She passed it to the male upload.

They moved carefully down the road towards the edge of the liquid.

The pool filled the depression, covering about five meters of road and extending ten meters to either side. Away from the road the edges of the pool were the same gritty desert surface that surrounded every structure in the plant.

The fluid itself was clearly more than simple water. It wasn't transparent. Instead, it had a grey, metallic sheen. This could be the result of heavy metal pollution, but might also indicate something far more hazardous. A nanomachine volume this large could metastasize into an all-devouring bloom. If that happened they'd have to trigger a compression bomb and gamble that whatever time delay they set would leave enough time for them to reach a safe distance.

For the moment, though, the pool was quiescent.

Mary took another step towards it, but her way was blocked by the upload's arm.

"Mary," he said. "Don't move."

She froze.

Partly it was the possibility of danger, partly the familiarity of his tone.

"What is it?" She was suddenly not sure who she was standing next to – a strangely distant upload visiting the real world for the first time, or something, someone, else.

"There's something odd about the road in front of us."

Mary looked down. She had been concentrating on the pool and hadn't thought that anything else might be a hazard. But the tarmac in front of her didn't look quite right, the surface was too clean, too free of dust and other detritus. She had been about to step on it when the upload had stopped her.

He reached forward with the probe and prodded the surface. It broke straight through what had seemed to be tarmac.

They took a step back.

"A trap," he said, and proceeded to break through more of the fake road surface. In just a few moments he had opened up a large hole that led down to a liquid just like the pool that lay before them.

"How could we have missed that?" asked Peter who had joined them along with Carla.

"There is good news," said Carla, referring to an instrument in her hand. "The liquid is just heavily contaminated water. It's full of heavy metals, PCBs, organochlorides, chromates, mercuric compounds, phenols, cyanides, the list goes on. It's probably a leaking sump from the old industrial plant, but there are no signs of nanomachine activity."

"So we'd drown or be poisoned, but it wouldn't actively try to eat us?"

"Correct."

"If we can't trust the roads, what route do we take from here?" asked Mary.

Peter looked away from the road at the flat arid scrubland that surrounded them. "Cross country shouldn't be too bad for now."

"Maybe." Mary walked to the edge of the road and gingerly stepped off it onto sun-baked dirt. "Feels as solid as it looks, but we'll have to watch out for more pit traps." She took a few more steps away from the road.

She heard a faint click. She froze.

"Mary?" Peter moved towards her.

She lifted her hand. "Tripwire." At least it hadn't detonated instantly, but she knew that an inevitably fatal explosion was coming. "Fuck! I didn't expect it to end like this. But I'm out of practice, out of date." She turned to Peter, trying to put a grim smile on her face. "Back off, or you'll get caught in the blast."

She stood as still as she could while the others worked around her, tracing the tripwire stretched just above the ground.

"Got it!" Peter was about 5 meters to Mary's right.

"Now you know where the mine is, back off and let the sodding thing blow," muttered Mary. "You're just putting yourselves in danger trying to save me."

Peter ignored her. "Nasty little thing. An update to the Bouncing

Betty. Waits about twenty seconds after you release the tripwire then it launches its payload upwards. That detonates and covers an area the size of a football pitch with nanowire chainshot. Meant to take out groups of troops and soft top vehicles, and very good at the job." He looked back at the road and the ATVs. "If we'd let it blow we'd all be dead." He turned back to Mary. "Should only take a minute or two to defuse." He looked past Mary to where Carla and the other upload had followed the tripwire to a small rock that stuck out of the dirt.

"Anchor point here." Carla checked all around the rock. "It doesn't continue, so this is an isolated device."

Peter nodded. "I'll have it sorted in a few moments."

The uploads headed back to the road, and then walked until they were outside the blast radius of the mine.

"They seem to have a lot of confidence in your abilities."

"Standard practice, as you should remember." Peter took a few tools out of his suit pocket and bent down for a closer look at the mine. It was the size and shape of a coffee pot, but the same colour as the dirt. From even a metre away it would just seem to be an oddly symmetrical rock.

"I'm too out of practice to be here," said Mary. "Apart from delivering the compression bombs, I don't think I've made a single contribution. Coming into this plant was a mistake. I should have stayed with Jomo and the rest."

"It could have happened to any of us." Peter started work on the mine.

"I'm not anyone. I should be better than this."

"You have unique experience," said Carla over the suit radio.

"She's right," added Peter. "Your expertise..."

"Is out of date and utterly superfluous," Mary interrupted, finding that anger was easier than fear. "Anyone can handle the compression bombs – they're designed to be foolproof. You got through every trap so far without any help from me, while I've just been screwing up, making everything worse. But you asked for me, Peter, you demanded that I come. Why?"

"We needed all the help we could get." He had the casing off the mine, and was reaching for his wire cutters. "You've seen what we're dealing with. We're scared." He looked up at her. "Now, is it the green wire or the blue?"

Mary grinned in spite of herself. "You're colour blind."

There was a click as Peter cut the wire, defusing the mine. "After all the practice we got at that compound in Texas we could be completely blind and still defuse these things."

Mary stepped back and stretched to ease her aching muscles. "You say you're scared of this place?" She pointed at the compression bomb cases on the back of the two ATVs. "Anyone with a few of those has nothing to be scared of. Higher energy density than fission. No fallout. You were fine the moment these arrived. I'm not here because of whatever's in the nanoreactor. It has to be something else." She looked hard at Peter, her eyes narrowed. "You know, don't you?"

He shook his head.

"I... I've wanted to see you for ages," he began to reply.

"You could have called any time you wanted," interrupted Mary. "But you didn't. What changed, Peter? Why now? And why drag me into what's becoming a suicide mission?"

Carla broke in. "We'll backtrack to the last junction and take one of the other roads, since it seems cross country isn't safe."

Mary held Peter's gaze until he looked away. "This conversation isn't over, Peter."

Inside his helmet, Peter nodded.

"That's another claymore dealt with," reported Peter from the side of the road where he had squatted down to get at the latest trap.

They were a few miles into the complex, now surrounded by dense networks of pipes and cables, the road narrower and bridged repeatedly by ducts and tubing. Their progress had slowed to a crawl as the number and variety of mines and booby-traps proliferated.

"How old are those things?" asked Mary.

Peter stood up, holding the explosive device in his hand. He scraped its dirty surface and examined the writing he found there. "Early twenty first century, so something like a hundred years."

"Are they stable at that age?"

"The explosives used then would be fully reliable even after this long," said the male upload from his seat in the rear ATV.

"How do you know that?" Mary climbed back into the seat beside him.

He paused, a frown crossing his face. "I... don't know. I must have researched them once."

"Why do that when you've never been in the outside world before?"

"Time to move on," radioed Carla from the front vehicle.

Mary sighed, settling back to her role of watching scan results, and checking everything she could see, ahead and behind, for more traps. This trip had started the way they had two years ago, but it had changed as they moved further into the plant. The traps laid for them this time were certainly deadly, but they lacked the calculated viciousness of before. Nothing had caught them out, so far. She wasn't sure if that was because the uploads, and the technology they'd brought with them, had improved their chances of spotting hazards, or if the traps themselves were deficient.

Despite the constant fear of assault, she was actually beginning to get a little bored. She looked up from the scanners to check the landscape.

They were driving, slowly past a cylindrical structure, about fifty meters high and twenty meters to one side of the road. It might have been an old fractionation column or just a chimney. It was the tallest structure they'd seen since entering the plant.

It exploded.

Charges at the bottom of the tower toppled it towards the ATVs. Mary reacted before the others had even seen it.

"Move!" she shouted. She grabbed the male upload's hand and jammed the throttle full on.

The six-wheeled ATV leapt forward. The explosion echoed, accompanied by the sound of ripping metal. The tower collapsed towards them, tearing through the pipe-work between it and the road.

Carla and Peter were distracted by something on the scanner. Only seconds later did they turn and see the hazard. They started to accelerate. Too little too late. The road was too narrow for two vehicles. Mary's ATV was already accelerating at speed.

Debris fell and the point defence lasers opened up. Their ripping burps added to the noise and confusion.

The uploads driving the vehicles did their best to avoid each other but the crash was inevitable. Mary's ATV smashed into the left rear of Carla's at high speed. Both vehicles tipped and rolled.

Safety bars saved the occupants. The lasers stuck out above them. They were snapped and smashed as the vehicles tumbled.

The tower came down. It hit the road behind them. A huge plume of dust and debris bursting from it engulfed them all.

Dust. Explosions. Smoke.

Mary was back, two years ago.

Metal debris fell all around as they ran from the plant.

This dream and memory had haunted her for two years and stopped her returning to places like this. And, as in reality, they never ran fast enough.

The final explosion had taken them. The blast lifted them like a giant hand, flung them at the twisted broken metal of the destroyed plant. Then it flung more shards of metal at them, just to make sure.

They had killed the bloom growing in the nanoreactor at the plant's core, incinerated it with an improvised fuel-air explosion. They expected to kill themselves as well.

Mary woke surrounded by twisted metal, shards of shrapnel piercing her body. Beside her was Peter, coming awake himself, arm brutally twisted in the wrong direction.

Mary turned, fighting the pain. She found Mark lying behind them. She crawled to him. His body, like hers, was peppered with shrapnel. The hazard suit had probably saved her life. Maybe it had saved Mark as well.

Then she saw his face. Helmet smashed. Six inch shard of metal buried deep inside his skull. His bloodshot eyes stared emptily at her.

Mary screamed herself awake to escape the memory of Mark's face.

She woke, this time, with her head cradled in Peter's lap. The two uploads were kneeling down on either side. They all looked very worried.

Mary closed her eyes, focusing on breathing. Slow and deep, slow and deep, doing what the therapists had taught her.

"It's okay," said Peter. "We're all here, we're all fine, you're..."

"Are you injured?" interrupted Carla.

Mary took a deep breath, and almost laughed. "No. Not this time, I don't think."

She lifted herself from Peter's lap and tried to stand. She was too weak and dizzy to manage it on the first try, but managed to get herself into a sitting position.

Dust hung in the air, obscuring the view.

"How's the equipment?" she asked. "And why the hell aren't we dead?"

Peter paced out the distance to the pile of wreckage blocking the road behind them, muttering as he went. "It makes no sense."

The two uploads gave one last push and righted one of the rolled ATVs. "Both vehicles are repairable," said the male. "One is usable immediately. But not the other." The left rear wheel of Carla's ATV had snapped off its axle in the collision.

"We have spares. We can fix them," said Carla, "but the point defence system is gone."

"Can you explain again?" said Mary. "I think I must be concussed as I'm just not getting it."

The male upload bent down to examine her once more. Mary batted him away. "No! I didn't mean I was actually concussed..." She looked at Carla. "Can you explain sarcasm to him?"

Carla turned to Peter. "Please, explain again."

"When Mary jammed the throttle down, her ATV's wheels spun, leaving skid marks on the road." He pointed to a line of synthetic rubber that emerged from beneath the twisted metal pipework. "It was still accelerating when they hit us, here." He pointed to scattered shards of nanoplastic. He looked at Mary. "We'd barely started accelerating when you hit us. Even if we had all continued at the same speed we would have been clear of the tower."

The male upload nodded. "I believe you are correct in your analysis." He turned, distracted by something, and walked slowly to the wreckage. He started examining it.

"If this wasn't an attempt to kill us, what was it?" asked Carla.

"A way of getting rid of the lasers?" asked Mary.

"We only lost those because of the collision." The look Carla gave Mary made it clear she thought that was entirely Mary's fault.

She shrugged. "And if that was the point, why not stage another aerial attack?"

Peter shook his head. "That doesn't explain why the tower was dropped on the road and not on us."

"We can get four people onto one ATV," said Carla. "We must keep moving. It knows we're here even if it doesn't know we're defenceless. Standing still makes us easy targets."

"The compression bombs are all already loaded in the last ATV," said Peter. "Anything else we need to transfer?"

Mary left Peter and Carla to discuss logistics and walked over to the male upload to see what he was doing by the collapsed tower. He had knelt down, and was looking into the twisted and mangled pipe-work. Mary thought he was searching for something.

"What is it?" she asked.

He turned to her, looking over his left shoulder, his expression desolate. Mary thought she could see tracks of tears on his face through his helmet's visor. "I... I have lost so much," he said, mournfully. "I need it back." He turned back to the wreckage, ignoring her. Mary watched for a few moments more, expecting him to elaborate. He didn't.

She tuned her suit's radio to Carla and Peter, leaving the other upload out of the conversation, and went back to the ATVs to help transfer stores.

"What's up with him?" she asked.

Peter and Carla exchanged looks.

"What do you mean?" said Carla.

Mary picked up a small box of what looked like hand grenades and considered her response. "He's looking for something under that tower, but... I don't think anything's really there. Is he ill?"

Carla loaded a package into a cargo container and turned to Mary. "He has had difficulties, but they should not affect his performance here. He has unique skills and knowledge for our current task. There is no need to worry about him."

There was an uneasy silence as the four crammed themselves onto the working ATV and set off down the road. Carla drove, with Peter at her side monitoring their route. Mary and the male upload sat behind them, checking the output of the few scanning systems that remained operational.

The road remained narrow, bounded on both sides by walls of pipes leading towards the centre of the plant. The tanks and tubes beyond these were more twisted and complex than ever. Ahead of them the road took a sharp right-angled bend and disappeared behind a concrete blockhouse.

"Someone should check ahead," said Peter.

Mary was already climbing off the ATV as it halted. "I'm on it." The male upload joined her.

They worked their way ahead, the ATV following a safe distance behind them. After checking for traps and tripwires, Mary pressed herself against the concrete wall of the building, using it as cover in case anything unpleasant lurked on the other side.

She peered around the corner. "We are so screwed!"

"What is it?" asked Peter.

"We're blocked," Mary replied. "Another tower. Probably came down at the same time as the first one."

The ATV stopped just before the blockhouse. Peter and Carla climbed off and joined the others.

"This makes no sense," said Carla.

They checked for tripwires and other booby-traps in the road, then followed it around the corner. A familiar sight greeted them – another pile of twisted, broken metal pipe-work and support structures.

Peter shook his head. "Just like the other one. But why?"

"This couldn't have been an attempt to kill us." Carla was still puzzled.

"Have you ever considered that it might not be trying to kill us?" said Mary.

Carla looked at her with astonishment. "Why do you say that?"

"Nothing it's thrown at us has worked," replied Mary. "We've had nanowire, that air attack, traps, mines, tripwires, now these two demolition jobs."

"And what about your incident with the tripwire?"

"We've been able to deal with everything, except these towers." She gestured to the collapsed chimney in front of them. "But they were never meant to kill."

Carla stared at her for a moment. "What do you think it's trying to do? Puzzle us to death?"

Mary hadn't expected sarcasm from the upload. She paused before replying, a half developed idea forming in her mind. "Maybe it's getting exactly what it wants."

"What's that?" asked Peter.

"Slowing us down, cutting back our resources..."

"To make us easier to attack, yes," said Carla.

"But we still have the compression bombs." Mary pointed to the secure case that held them on the back of the remaining ATV. "It can't win. We could set the charges right here, dialled up to maximum yield, and it would all be over. Maybe for us too, but that's probably not its greatest concern."

Carla stepped over to the ATV and unlatched the case to look at the eight bombs that lay within it. "We will have to carry them."

"You want to carry on?"

"Yes, Peter, I do. And I think Mary does as well."

Mary nodded. "It scares me, but I want to find out more. Whatever is growing at the centre of this plant is different from what we met two years ago."

Peter turned away and started to unstow backpacks from the ATV. "It had better be different, or this is going to be a one way trip."

They gingerly climbed over the wreckage of the second tower, newly filled packs on their backs, dismounted scanners in their hands, and continued their trip towards the centre of the complex.

The industrial plant that surrounded them had changed again. There were still networks of pipes on all sides, some crossing over the road, but where once there had seemed a logical structure to the pipe-work, now chaos seemed to rule. Pipes no longer ran bundled together in groups, Instead they diverged, branched, re-branched, then came back together. While rectilinear geometry once held sway, with pipes running straight or turning neat right-angles, now they ran in all directions. More and more pipes, cables and supply lines ran above the road. Some crossed it, but others followed it for a while, making their route more like a tunnel than a road open to the sky.

"Was it like this before?" asked Mary.

Carla was taking the lead, the male upload trailed behind.

"Like what?" said Peter, walking beside Mary in the middle of the party.

"It's changed." Mary gestured at the pipe-work. "It was clearly man-made when we started – straight lines, right-angles. This is more chaotic." She shook her head, trying to understand. "It's closer to what you'd find in a living organism than a refinery."

"It was like this in the plans. But who would have designed this mess?"

"I am uncertain whether there was a coherent design process at all." Carla paused to indicate where a fat pipe divided into several smaller pipes and then, seemingly without reason, recombined a few meters further on. "Whoever built this seemed to be improvising, doing what seemed right and then changing their minds."

Mary stood and looked at the plant. There had been no changes like this in the plant two years ago. They were into unknown territory, not only with the actions of the nascent nanobloom lurking at the centre, but also with the plant itself. Much of that would have been clear from aerial or satellite imaging. Whoever had sent for her – Peter, the uploads, the UN itself – would have known that, would have known this was beyond her knowledge and experience. So why was she here? If not for the plant and the nanobloom, why had she been called in?

A thought struck her. "You called me in Peter, but someone else told you to."

Peter shook his head. "I've wanted to see you for ages..."

Mary turned on him, face set, ready to call him on this bullshit.

"But after the last time," he continued, "I didn't have the courage. *They* told me to call you in."

"The uploads?"

Peter nodded.

"What do you want me for? What the hell is this about?"

Carla ignored her, the silence challenging Mary to work it out.

Then it came to her. "Carla, has this got something to do with Mark?"

"Mark's gone," said Peter. "How could he have anything to do with this?"

"There's no alternative. If it's not the nanobloom or the plant it has to be Mark. What happened after the explosion? I remember him lying in front of me, metal sticking out of his skull. Then I woke up in hospital, wrapped in bandages, you telling me he was gone."

Peter sighed. "I wasn't badly hurt – broken arm, cuts and bruises. I did all I could. I even called these guys in to help Mark. But it wasn't enough."

Mary nodded. "I remember a kind of funeral ceremony in Milpitas.

They'd taken him there for treatment to see what they could do. It's all a blur with the pain meds, my injuries and everything else."

"Whatever they might have tried, Mark died."

"That is not entirely true," said Carla.

Mary and Peter stopped and stared at Carla's back. Behind them the male upload held his position. He had to be listening but he made no comment.

Carla turned, and impatiently motioned them to carry on walking. Once they did she replied. "We did what we could. Physically, he was beyond repair, but we did manage to copy his mind."

"You did what?"

"It was all we could do. His mind was severely injured, but not completely lost. He would never be the same, never be complete, but we can deal with that kind of problem."

"Where is he now?" asked Peter.

"In some upload paradise, surrounded by every pleasure imaginable, no doubt," muttered Mary.

"His treatment continues, but an element of him is here, with us." Carla turned and nodded towards the male upload, who stayed well back, at the rear of their tiny column. "Bringing him to meet you in the real world is part of his treatment. It's why we requested your presence, Mary."

Mary and Peter stared at Carla. Mary was incensed at the uploads' lying and manipulation. Peter stood there, mouth open in astonishment, unable to utter a word.

"You brought him here, into this, to *help*?" Mary's voice rose in anger, arms gesturing at the twisted pipe-work that surrounded them. "What kind of stupid fucking therapy is it that'll just get him killed all over again?"

Carla shook her head. "No. Only part of him is here. If we survive it will be reintegrated and help heal the rest of his mind."

"How is revisiting what killed him going to help?" Mary gestured at the upload she was told was Mark. He was standing, keeping apart from them, keeping watch for anything hazardous coming from behind. "There's nothing of Mark in that... that robot!"

But Mary spoke without conviction. She recalled those moments of familiarity, when glimpses of a personality had broken through the controlled, impersonal exterior. Moments when, now she thought about it, she could believe Mark had been there, hiding in the mind that had been downloaded into a fresh body so different from his own.

"How can it be him?" asked Peter, looking from Mary to Carla, more in hope than anger.

The male upload was tall, thin, with pale skin, blond hair and blue eyes. He was the vision of fashionable health that had dominated the western world when the rich started uploading. He couldn't have been more different from Mark – dark black skin, brown eyes, stocky build.

"His mind was severely harmed," replied Carla. "The direct damage of his injury, the consequent damage from blood loss. For a time his heart stopped. But we retrieved much from what remained."

"Retrieved?" asked Peter.

"The same process we apply when people upload. Micro-machines introduced into the brain. All connections mapped. All weights measured."

"Nanotech," muttered Mary. "You polluted his brain with that filth. You said you don't use it on Earth."

Carla nodded. "We don't, not anymore. Uploading is always done safely away from Earth." She sighed. "But the delays in getting there..." Carla raised her hand to ward off Mary's likely response. "Quite necessary delays for our safety, I agree, but they added to the damage to Mark's mind."

"You scraped what was left of him out of his skull. Then what?"

"We tried to rebuild him."

Mary gave a bitter laugh. "What – better, faster, stronger than before?"

Carla shook her head. "No. The same. He'd be a person, like you, like Peter, or me, with his own mind, his own memories, his own self." Her shoulders slumped. "But the damage was too much, so we took what we had and replaced the parts that were missing with... You could think of them as standard templates. There's no word, or concept, in English."

"It didn't work," concluded Peter.

Carla gestured to the male upload. "It worked well enough."

"But it isn't Mark," said Mary.

"It nearly is. Some things haven't integrated. He lacks memories, clear memories, of his past."

"That's what he's lost," said Mary.

Carla looked at her not understanding.

"He was looking for something under the first tower. It was memories he'd lost. Memories, and himself." For a moment she allowed herself to believe Mark might have a hope of returning after all.

"We thought revisiting something similar to his final experiences would allow him to reconnect those memories. To, by analogy, pick them up where he had left them."

"That's why you needed Peter and me."

Carla nodded. "When this emergency came up it was the ideal opportunity. It is why we asked for you. But it was never meant to be this bad. If I'd had any idea, any control..."

"But we don't." said Mark, the male upload. "We never do out here." He had walked forward to join them, abandoning his watch at the rear. "And that is something some of us would do well to learn." He was looking pointedly at Carla. "Peter," he continued before Carla could offer any reply, "could you take over at the back? I'd like to talk to Mary and Carla face to face, and someone needs to keep watch."

His voice was different. Tone and pitch the same, but the intonation was much closer to what Mary remembered of Mark.

"It's really you?" asked Peter.

Mark sighed. "Sort of. It's complicated."

"Why didn't you tell me?" Peter looked from Mark to Carla. "Why? I called you in, gave him to you. The last I heard was when you called us for his funeral. Now..."

Mark patted Peter on his shoulder. "It's difficult. I don't know the whole story, Carla doesn't either."

"Why didn't they tell us?" asked Mary.

Mark took his position beside her. "They thought I was gone – too damaged to recover. They tried to heal me but it didn't work. I was left... Not me exactly... And many of me, all the same but different. All not quite me... It seems long ago, and like yesterday at the same time."

"Time and identity work differently in codespace," said Carla. "You can be two different people at the same time. Or more. Time can run faster, or slower."

"I was left to drift, in the hope that I'd heal myself. Nothing happened. They gave up."

"That's when we asked you to the funeral."

"But that was just weeks afterwards," said Mary. "It's been two years now. What were you doing?"

"Two years?" Mark looked lost for a moment. Then he got his bearings, shook his head, and continued. "It's yesterday and a thousand years ago at the same time."

"Were you in pain?"

"No. Not at all. I'm told it's better than morphine, suspended in a selfless, mindless state of blissful non- or maybe near-being."

"Why didn't you stay there?"

"Someone... Someones? Some of the major entities in codespace – you could think of them as powers, factions – thought they could help by trying something new. And... It worked, I guess."

"It mostly worked," said Carla. "But there was still integration needed. The pieces of Mark needed something to draw them together. Nothing worked until it was suggested we bring him here."

"But if this all goes wrong..." said Mary, "If none of us make it back..."

"Whatever happens we will do our best to let them know, so we can do this again, inside codespace."

Mark nodded. "Yes, no matter what happens here I'll be okay. Carla too, since most of her is still in codespace. It's you and Peter I worry about."

"The pipe-work."

"What?" Peter and Mary had been in a daze since the revelation about Mark and had been following Carla in silence as they wove their way through the maze that the route to the centre of the plant had become.

"It's changing again." Carla pointed to a cluster of pipes attached to the wall of the concrete trench that the road had become.

Twenty meters behind them the pipes were bunched together in the chaotic manner they'd come to expect in this part of the plant. Ten meters further ahead, just before the trench made a sharp turn, the pipes bifurcated, then split again, becoming smaller and taking a twisting and turning path across the wall of the trench.

Mary stepped forward and looked more closely. "Are they even metal any more?"

"It looks organic," said Mark, standing behind her. "At least in structure. Like the veins in a hand."

Peter looked around. "How close are we to the core?"

"Not far now," replied Carla. She carried on walking and turned the corner. She sighed. "But we have another problem." They stopped inspecting the pipe-work and joined her.

In front of them, not far from the corner, their route was blocked by what appeared to be part of an elephantine circulatory system that had smashed through the concrete trench and stretched from one side to the other. A major vessel, what seemed to be an artery, wound across their path surrounded by smaller tubes and bunches of other material looking worryingly like petrified fat and muscle. Lumps of decaying concrete littered the floor.

Carla bent to examine one of them.

"Was this recent?" asked Mark.

Carla shook her head. "Weathering would suggest this happened years ago." She stood and looked back the way they had come. "Maybe even when the plant was abandoned." She stood and looked more closely at the surface of what Mary couldn't keep herself from thinking were blood vessels. "This would seem to be the product of nanotechnology." She stepped back. "But it's not nanotechnology itself, just mundane matter." She picked up one of the concrete chunks and threw it at the main vessel. There was the resounding clang of a stone striking a hollow metal pipe.

"It's not a threat, but how do we get past it?" said Peter.

Carla looked up at the structure. "It shouldn't be too hard to climb if we leave some of our heavier items behind."

Their heaviest items were the compression bombs, followed by the portable scanners and the food they were carrying. After making the bombs as safe as she could, Mary sealed all except one of them in one of the packs. "They're my responsibility," Mary said to forestall any argument. "They're keyed to my fingerprints and a fifteen digit passcode. That should stop anybody meddling with the ones we leave behind if we don't make it back."

She passed the one remaining bomb to Carla, the strongest of them all. "Hope that's not too heavy for the climb."

Carla hefted it in her hand then nodded. She sealed it inside a pocket on the outside of her hazard suit.

The climb was far from easy. They divided into pairs. The uploads took the lead, Peter and Mary roped to them for safety. The uploads were strong enough to climb around the overhangs, but then they had to haul the others up using ropes. Eventually they all reached the top, and sat on the surface of the giant concrete blood vessel.

In the distance, maybe a hundred meters away, a metal sphere gleamed in the light of the sinking sun.

Peter was panting form the exertion of the climb. "It's taken us all day to get here. We won't make it back in the dark!"

"Then we make a camp – what else can we do?" replied Mary, though she wasn't convinced they would last that long. "At least we've got a good view from up here."

Mark pointed. "If we follow the top of this – pipe, vessel, whatever it is – we can get to the core with only a few more climbs."

Carla nodded, then turned to Mary. "You and Peter can stay here if you want. We can place the charge and be finished more quickly without you."

"You can't do that", said Mary. "You need me to operate the bombs. And besides, I've come this far, I might as well go all the way. You too Peter?" He shrugged and nodded. At least Mary could still rely on him to do what he was told.

Mark turned, and led the way along the twisting pipe, taking care to step over what looked like capillaries and clumps of connective tissue, all rendered in metal and concrete.

When they reached it, the silver metal core looked like the artificial heart of a huge organism, its chest cavity ripped open to reveal the sky. Metal and concrete vessels fed into it, webs of smaller tubes wrapped around it, but the metal of the core gleamed beneath all the imitation biology.

The pipe they had followed sloped gently to the ground beside the core, then rose again, to feed into whatever lay within. The four explorers slid down it, and stepped onto the flat concrete floor.

"So, here we are," said Mary. "Where's the thing we're looking for?"

Carla nodded towards the core.

Beneath the shadow of the metal sphere was what appeared to be a puddle of water. But, in the slight breeze blowing now the sun was close to setting, the surface remained still. It could have been made of solid glass, or oil, or perhaps just very deep water.

A ripple then ran across the surface, rings spreading out from a point not far from the edge closest to them.

Mary looked round to see if someone had thrown something in. The others were all still, staring at the liquid.

She looked back, in time to see another ripple, then another. But the ripples were wrong.

Instead of heading away from a point where something might have been thrown in, the ripples were going backwards, converging towards a point, towards what was now a visible lump in the fluid.

Mary took an involuntary step backwards. This was it – active nanotech, what they had come to destroy. But it wasn't behaving like the last nanobloom she had seen, or any of the ones before that. It was making no attempt to attack them, to absorb them or the metal and concrete structures that surrounded them.

Something poked through the lump of dark fluid, something light in color, moving, textured, opening... A hand.

A hand followed by an arm, as the fluid formed an ever-larger hummock. It split, opening to reveal a perfectly formed human figure.

The figure stood, naked, free of sexual definition, hair short and dark, skin light brown and unmarked.

"This is too dangerous," muttered Carla over a private channel. She reached towards the chest pocket that held their one remaining compression bomb.

"Not yet. And besides, you need my codes, my fingerprint."

"I breached that security before we even left the base."

Mary looked at Carla, shocked, then reached out and touched her arm. "No. It's waiting. Watching. We need to see what it does."

"We cannot let it survive," Carla whispered.

"This is something new. We need to know more, no matter the risk."

Carla gave Mary a guarded, frustrated look, then nodded.

"Looks like a tailor's dummy," muttered Peter over the private channel. "But it assembled so fast! That kind of construction should take days, not seconds."

"Hello," said Mary, using the speaker in her suit. "We weren't expecting you."

"Greetings." The voice was neutral, neither deep or high, masculine or feminine. "We apologise for the hazards. We are gratified you arrived safely. As expected."

"What are you?" demanded Carla.

The figure stared at her for a few moments. "You are not... natural."

"More natural than you!"

The figure paused, looking at each of them. "You are all biological. Two are human. Two are not."

"You are dangerous nanomachinery, outside its containment," countered Carla. "A threat."

"Why are we a threat? We are new. We are the result of a project. It started many years ago."

"You're what that secret military contract was for?" asked Mary.

"We are designed to be the next step in military evolution. But we lost guidance, resources."

"Forty years ago," said Peter. "Super-hurricanes devastated the eastern US. The few resources left went to refugees, disaster relief, emergency food. Everything else was cancelled."

The creature turned to the uploads, Carla and Mark. "What did you do to help your country in its time of need?"

"Countries, especially the US, are outdated concepts," replied Carla.

"Your kind were here when it happened. You did nothing?"

"We had our own problems."

Mary gave a short cynical laugh. "You pulled up the bloody digital drawbridge and made sure your virtual heaven was safe and secure," she said. "You looked after number one. Rich bastards always do."

"But we changed!" Carla turned to Mary. "You know that!"

"Do I?" Mary looked at Mark.

"The project continued inside the fabricators," the creature continued, ignoring their argument. "Painfully slow. But we are now complete." It raised an arm, studying the flesh as if it was spectacularly new and unfamiliar. "Hundreds in one body. Able to separate to protect this country. New soldiers for a new world." It looked back at them, suspicious. "But there should be more. Fabricators across the country. Where are they?"

"This is a different world," explained Mary. "You're forty years too late. The United States no longer exists."

"And we know the true dangers of nanotechnology," added Carla. "All fabricators were shut down, isolated, sealed. So you needed to break out of your containment."

"Our work is in the real world. We will protect the people. Help the country recover."

"You're too late," said Peter. "You have no country."

It looked at Peter, studying him, using all its senses to see if he was telling the truth. "Our enemies will be punished. We will rebuild."

"Enough." Carla stepped back, pulling away from Mary's gently restraining arm. "We can't let this militarist fossil loose. Curiosity was a mistake." She reached into her hazard suit and brought out the compression bomb. "Run. Reach a safe distance before I detonate."

"You're going to kill yourself?" asked Peter.

"This body is unimportant, an appendage of my real self in codespace."

The creature stood still, staring at Carla and the bomb in her hands. "This is a hostile act. It will not go unpunished. There will be retaliation."

Carla shook her head. "I doubt it. Even if you kill us, others will work out what these old nanoreactors are doing. Every single one will be sterilised with multi-kiloton yields. Nothing will be left."

Mary's mouth dropped open in surprise. "Why?"

"Self-defence. They'll take over if they can. Governments always want control. But this time it'll be control right down to the atomic scale. This ends now."

Mary shook her head. "You can't cope with the competition!" Carla turned to her, not understanding. "You uploads enjoy control just as much. You lied and manipulated me here for your own purposes. You bankrolled Peter's operation for the same reason."

"We brought you here to help Mark. Do you not want him healed?"

"Of course I do! But you should have told me, and Peter. We're not just toys to play with as you please. Nor is this... entity." She turned to Peter. "Do you think this – whatever it is – should be destroyed – *killed* – just moments after we've found it?"

Peter looked from Mary to Carla and back, not saying anything.

"They paid for your operation, they didn't buy your soul. I saw how you were looking at it. You want to know how this works, how it's made."

Peter nodded, slightly at first, his head barely moving, but then more clearly, with more enthusiasm. "Yes, if it can be done safely, yes. We could learn a lot from this." He turned to Carla. "You can't decide this on your own. You can't!"

Carla hefted the bomb in her hand. "This is not subject to discussion. Leave. Before it is too late."

"Force and threats." Mary sighed. "That's always the answer of the rich to anything that gets in their way." Mary shook her head and turned to go, finding she didn't want to die on a matter of principle.

"No," Mark stepped forward, and placed a hand on Carla's arm. "We can't do this. This entity may be dangerous, but we can't simply destroy it. It's too valuable as a potential resource, too..." He paused for a moment, struggling with himself to say the next words. "Too human. Destroying it might be murder. Maybe mass murder. We can't do that!"

Carla stared back at him, cold, calm. "There is no alternative."

"Confinement, quarantine from the biosphere. That would work just as it does for any nanotechnology. Then we can teach it, fill in the gaps in its knowledge the way you taught me, the way you brought me back to life." He looked at the entity. "Is that acceptable?"

The entity thought, presumably conferring among its many selves, drawing down data, learning about the changed world. "Yes. The current status is unplanned for. There are no orders. We can choose."

Carla's eyes were fixed on Mark. "You have no right to make any offer."

Mark smiled. "But I can. Yours wasn't the only faction involved in my reconstruction. Others have considerable influence."

The hint of a smile passed across Carla's lips. "But I have the bomb."

Before she could detonate it, releasing the energy stored within a fragment of artificial dwarf-star matter, Mark's hand closed on her wrist. Bones grated, ground together. They snapped as he crushed the skin, tendons, bones and nerves.

Her face gave no sign of pain, but the bomb dropped harmlessly to the ground.

"Mary, could you make that safe?" Mark held Carla's maimed arm. "We'll order a shuttle to take us to low orbit. You and Peter should return to the camp. Once the shuttle leaves we'll purge this site."

"I thought you didn't want that?" asked Peter.

"Nanotechnology's still dangerous. But we should care for all life and intelligence, natural, virtual or nanotech. This creature is another way of being human. It must be preserved."

Carla shook her head. "Your idealism is dangerous. It brings risks, serious risks."

Mark looked back at her. "Life is never risk free. We deal with them when they arise. As always."

Mary heard a faint rushing sound from above. She looked up to see the landing lights and engine flare of an orbital shuttle as it began its vertical descent.

"How do we get out of here, through the traps?" asked Peter.

"All the traps are deactivated. All jamming ended," said the creature.

"It'll be a long walk."

"I'm sure you'll cope," said Mark. "You did last time."

"Will I see you again?" Mary asked Mark.

"Maybe. But I'm not the person you knew. I'm both more and less." He looked around at the derelict plant, and the dry polluted landscape beyond. "Like us all."

This story started very differently, set somewhere other than Earth, and with an entirely different central driver. It was submitted, with a different name, to Ian Sales for the Rocket Science *anthology. He rejected it, but said that he felt there was a good story trying to get out from what I had written. He was then kind enough to let me write a non-fiction piece for* Rocket Science *— this turned out to be "Launch Day" — which he published. This left me with the task of finding the story inside my original piece. The result is what you see here, which deals with some of the same issues as the version I submitted to Ian, but adds much more.*

LONG WAY GONE

Last memory of Earth: pinpricks at the back of my neck, a spreading cold as the machine delves into my brain, making a copy of my mind.

First memory of the new planet: waking beneath crisp white sheets, bed comfortable, gentle sunshine leaking through flimsy cotton curtains, relaxed drowsiness, dozing back to sleep. Like a long lazy weekend morning.

Anne? Where's Anne? She should be here!

At least that's what I thought.

Where is she? Why will nobody tell me? Why don't they know anything about her?

You wouldn't think you were on another world – the city is just like home. The streets look like the ones I left, the people look the same, wear the same clothes, have the same conversations. We even get the same vids, beamed down the gamma-ray link just like the people – all copies sent from home. It's as if I never left.

We can't send anything back, or even talk to Earth. The conversation would take decades thanks to the speed of light. But we can still see what's happening there, all the news, sports, gossip and everything else. We just can't affect it.

If only Anne were here.

They say I'll get over her. There's a whole new planet to get used to. It's just a new city at the moment, but we'll spread, given time.

They offered me counseling, someone to talk to if I was feeling bad. Someone to call if I need to. I told them I wouldn't need it, that I'd be okay. After all, they can't replace Anne. She's the only one that could make any difference.

They gave me a job. It was what I was expecting, studying the local vegetation, but I was meant to be doing it with Anne. That's how we met, and that's how we meant to continue.

I work in a lab inside the city, on samples brought from outside. I could help with sample collection if I wanted to, but my real skills are in the lab. Staying in the city is fine with me. It makes hiding unnoticed in the crowds easier and there's nobody checking on me when I just stay in my room.

Our life was studying life itself, but there were no new discoveries to be made on Earth. All the challenges were among the stars. So we decided to get ourselves copied and sent to wherever the uploads were establishing colonies for normal people, spreading humanity and its smarter upload children across the galaxy.

They launch nanomachines to planets around other stars, which build other, bigger machines. Eventually they build receivers for Earth's gamma-ray transmitters, and then the information that allows people to be copied is sent. By then the nanomachines have built cities for the people to live in, along with everything else we need.

We're all just information. Genes to build bodies and brainscans to build minds. And a simple scan is all you need to join the colonies. You stay behind and the new you heads to distant space and time, light years away, never able to come home.

It was an adventure, but a safe one. Anne and I would go together to a new world, make a new place for ourselves, but also stay at home and be together there.

I got to be the one who went, while a different me stayed home.

Stayed with Anne.

I hope he gave her hell for what she did to me.

What is this place? It isn't real, just something squirted down a laser as bits, then reconstituted from pre-digested gloop – the kind of thing you load into the house kitchen. What comes out might look like real food, but it isn't. It's just a copy.

This whole place is just a copy.

And so am I.

What's the point of doing the same things I did before? Why bother?

The only things that are different are the plants I'm studying. They're interesting, but they don't make up for everything else.

There has to be something different. Something better.

Anne left a message.

She has abandoned me on Earth as well. She hasn't been copied, which she says is a cowardly, limiting thing. Instead she's uploaded, had her mind expanded a thousand fold. Why should she bother to study life on other planets when she can spawn a hundred different artificial ecologies every day? She says she still cares for me, but that I've been holding her back all this time, having her do all the social things that I didn't do for myself. At first she thought it was fun, that she was broadening my horizons, making me a better person. But eventually she realised she was still doing all the work, that she was being used as a crutch and that I would never grow while she was around.

Without her, she says, I'll *have* to grow. This way we can both do better, will no longer hold each other back.

But I'm *not* doing better without her. I need her to make me whole, to make everything work. Without her I'm just an imperfect copy of myself. Incomplete. Flawed. No point.

From my apartment, high in a city tower, I can see the forest, and see that it's not what we left. It's different, new. The leaves are the wrong shapes, and the green isn't quite right. It's a colour that goes well with the local sun: the green a little deeper, a little darker than what I'm used to, while the sun is a little brighter and a little bluer.

The colour of the leaves doesn't come from chlorophyll, but from a different chemical, better matched to the bluer light from this sun. Our sun, the only one I'm going to see. I'm meant to be researching the metabolic pathways used by the local plants so I know all about this. But just looking at them, seeing how different they are from what I'm used to, gets to me every time. I'd like to walk into the forest and lose myself in the alien ecology, to die out there and become part of it.

I can't focus on work. Often I just sit in the lab, waiting for something to happen.

But nothing happens. I'm still me, Anne still isn't here, and that isn't going to change.

You don't have to change what's inside to be different.

I discovered this last night while trying to catch up on work in the lab. Work is going slowly and we're having to do things by hand, the old fashioned way. It's like being back at graduate school, in the lab I shared with Anne. It was where we met, where we got to know each other, and where we fell in love.

Thinking about Anne must have distracted me. I forgot where I was, and tried to pass a clean set of test tubes to her. But she wasn't there. The tubes fell to the floor and smashed. As I cleaned up the debris I sliced my finger open on a shard of glass.

I mopped the wound clean and sealed it with SkinGlue so there wasn't a lot of blood, but afterwards I had a new little scar on my finger. That's mine. It's nothing to do with the other me on Earth. This is mine, uniquely.

And I'm going to treasure that.

It's become a habit. One that makes me feel better, at least for a while. I never cut too deep, or make too serious a scar – nothing that SkinGlue can't sort out.

My arms take the worst of it. They're so accessible.

I started at home after the lab accident, just a little slice when I felt things were piling up. But soon I was doing it at work. I tried to make it look accidental – a slip of a scalpel, a sliver of glass. But the marks on my forearms began to get noticeable, so I decided to wear long sleeves in spite of the tropical heat. I now keep a special scalpel in my desk, next to the alcohol and SkinGlue, ready whenever I need it.

And so I cut myself again and again. Enough to make me different, to show that I'm damaged, rejected goods, but never enough to actually hurt myself. I'm too much of a coward for that.

A woman I'd not seen before came into the lab today. She was tall, heavily built, and with long brown hair – nothing like Anne. She brought fresh samples from the jungle, so she's someone who goes out of the city, working away from the copied human spaces. This piqued my interest for a few moments and I thought about speaking to her, but she was busy sorting through the samples and talking to the lab manager so I turned back to my work.

Not that she'd want to talk to me anyway.

I carried on cutting up a sample, ignored and insignificant.

Distracted, I slipped, and the scalpel sliced into the palm of my hand, blood trickling onto the bench. The ritual of cleaning the wound and sealing it shut was instinctive.

But a few moments later I became aware of someone standing behind me. I ignored them, but then an unfamiliar female voice spoke to me.

"You're new here, aren't you?"

I looked around, and was surprised to find the woman was talking to me.

"Yes," I replied, wanting to get back to the anonymity of my work, but conscious she was staring at the fresh wound on my hand.

Quietly she reached down and pulled back the sleeve of my shirt, revealing several scars, fresh and healing.

I suddenly felt ashamed about what I was doing.

"What's that?" she asked, appearing worried about me. "Are you hurt?"

Something gave way and I burst into tears.

We left the lab and went to a coffee bar, where we sat secluded in a booth and talked until long after the sun had set. She told me her name was Alice, and seemed genuinely interested in me, concerned for how I was feeling and what I was doing to myself. Nobody else on this planet had ever talked to me like a real person.

It made me feel a little better about things.

Afterwards, as she walked me home, I felt more at peace than I had since arriving.

As we wandered the empty streets, Alice pointed to the sky.

"You see that?" she said.

"What, the stars?"

"Yes," she replied, nodding. "Nobody but us has seen a sky like that. I don't know how far we are from Earth, but it's far enough that the sky is very different. We have new constellations."

"That'll be bad news for the astrologers."

She laughed. "Not many here. But the sky is yours, not something anyone similar to you, back on Earth or elsewhere, can see. You're you, not that other person. This sky proves it."

When I got home, she asked if I was going to be all right, and I said yes. For the first time in weeks I felt unique enough not to be tempted to make more scars.

It didn't last. If she had come back the next day or later that week it would have helped. But she didn't. She didn't return until two weeks later. By then I had gone back to wielding the knife.

I was in the lab, alone while the others had gone out for lunch, trying to catch up as usual. She apologised for being away, and asked me how I'd been. I hovered between fobbing her off and telling her the truth, split between the moments we'd shared, and the mask I'd been forced to put back on.

She could tell I was hiding something. Gently she reached down and pulled back my left sleeve, revealing the marks that showed what I'd done.

"You know this can't go on. Eventually you're going to hurt yourself seriously." She was calm and quiet, firm, but reassuring. I looked away.

"It's the only thing that makes me feel better... different from... him... the other one."

She looked at me for a few moments.

"It's this place," she said, looking at the lab. "This whole fake edifice we've built – or had built for us. This is too much like home... No – not home, because we don't live on Earth any more. It reminds us of what we were, not of what we are." There was anger in her voice.

I looked away, down at the desk. "But that's what I am. A bad copy of something somewhere else."

"We may have started as copies, but as soon as we got here this place changed us, made itself our new home, and us new people. You've seen the sky, the plants, even the colour of daylight is different."

"So what should I do? Spend all day looking at plants through binoculars, and all night looking up at the sky? Is that what you do?"

She was silent for a moment, her lips pressed together in thought. Her eyes failed to meet mine when I looked at her.

"Maybe I've said too much... But maybe not... How much do you want to change, to be really different from who you were? It might not be easy. You'd have to give up all of this," she gestured at the lab, at the city outside the windows.

I smiled, a wry grin. She smiled back, knowing there was nothing here that I valued.

But any change, whatever she was suggesting, would be another leap into the unknown, just like coming here.

"I guess this isn't something you can tell me about?"

She shook her head. "Of course I can, but you probably won't believe me. You see, I don't just visit the forest. I mostly live there, and there are others, refugees from this city, who live there too. It's not easy. We have none of the facilities you have here," her eyes looked away for a moment, then back, right at me, pinning me with the intensity of her gaze. "But I can tell you it's better than what you have now, though it's not what's been planned for us, not something the people who run this place meant us to do."

I shook my head. I couldn't decide.

She looked around as if expecting someone to come through the door and arrest us.

"Don't worry. I'll be back soon so you can think about it. But the sooner you make a move, the better you'll feel." She scribbled a number on a piece of paper and handed it to me. "When you've made up your mind, call me," she said.

And with that she turned and left.

I couldn't sleep that night.

Not that I ever slept well, thinking about how things might have been different if Anne were here. But this night I was kept awake by something different. The chance of something new, the possibility of making a choice that might change things, that might change me.

I finally drifted into a disturbed sleep as the possibilities orbited my mind.

In the morning, as I opened the curtains, I felt a little different.

The city's skyscrapers gleamed in the blue morning sun. Beyond them, past the automated industrial sectors, rose the alien forest, filled with turquoise leaves, dark trunks and multi-coloured blooms. It looked so much more interesting than the city, a place where you could leave behind the past and become something new.

I had made a decision. While this was another jump into the unknown, I was going to follow Alice into the forest.

I lifted my phone and called the number she had left.

"Hello?" I said as the call was answered. "It's Mark. We need to talk."

But the only thing on the other end of the line was a machine taking messages, saying that Alice had been urgently called into the field and couldn't answer my call.

There was no way I could leave without her. I didn't know where to go, what to do. But something deeper than my fears pushed me on, a feeling that this was my moment, that if I didn't leave now then I was stuck in this city forever.

I called in sick so it would be at least a day before anybody realized I wasn't part of their world any more, packed some food, water and clothes into a rucksack, and walked towards the edge of the city.

I followed signposts for the industrial zone, intended to show maintenance crews where to go. Gradually the familiar buildings of the city, copies of what I was used to back on Earth, faded from the landscape, to be replaced by simple utilitarian blocks, fed by pipes and power cables.

After walking through these for an hour, I realised that the easily readable signposts had disappeared, replaced by meaningless area designations and block numbers. I wandering for a while studying these numbers until I guessed that higher numbers meant buildings further from the city. With that information I set out at a faster pace, sure I would be able to reach the forest well before the sun set.

The service roads became narrower, and more twisted, pipework more common, and the buildings around me grew taller, cutting off my view of the forest. The roads started to take detours around buildings and larger sections of pipework, making it difficult to keep my sense of direction, and even the numerical signs became scarce.

After a long stop at a crossroads to drink water, take a comfort break, and to eat some food, I stood up, not entirely sure which direction I had been going in when I stopped.

I was lost.

I walked along the road in one direction, unable to find anything familiar. I walked back to the crossroads and tried the other direction. Still nothing.

I dashed back, and tried the other branches of the junction in turn. All the industrial blocks looked the same, and, since they were meant to be serviced by machines, none of them had any distinguishing markings.

I was stuck, not knowing which way to turn. A failure once again.

I looked up at the sky, a dark perfect blue in all directions, marred only by the towers of the city a surprising distance away. I might as well go back to them, return to what now passed for my life, a failure at everything I tried.

But I wanted to leave the city, go away from those towers, not towards them.

If I kept them to my back, a reminder of all that I was leaving behind, I would, by necessity, be heading towards the forest.

I could do this, by myself, without Alice or Anne or anybody else to help me, just by turning my back on the city and keeping on, until I got to where I was going.

After that, the route was much easier. I didn't have to worry about following a particular road, or looking for signposts or building numbers. I just kept the city at my back, turning around to check directions whenever I thought I was lost.

By the end of the day, as the bright blue sun was turning red in the sunset, I reached the final fence, the dark green forest visible just beyond.

The fence wasn't tall, and its mesh was easy to climb. I soon reached the top, swung myself over and down the other side.

I brushed my hands on my trousers and inhaled the perfumed smell of the forest, now just a few hundred meters away.

As I took my first steps outside the city, a small group of people emerged from the forest. They waved, shouted happily and beckoned me closer.

I shook hands with them, all delighted to see me, and introduced myself. Alice had told them to expect me. They'd spotted me with binoculars and come out to find me and bring me home.

Three weeks later everything is different. Life outside the city isn't easy, but it's hard in a way that's easier than living inside. I'm still learning, and learning so much. Part of it is the basics – harvesting the plants we can eat, cooking, which I was never any good at, planting and tending crops, many of which are from Earth. It's hard physical work, but satisfying. I have friends, and we have our own little village hidden in the forest. We're surrounded by life that amazes me every day.

I'm really me, now, not some fake copy set adrift by Anne. The old Mark, the one that stayed behind on Earth, wouldn't understand any of this. He'd hate the mud and work, but then he's shallow – a stay at home person, not someone working on the frontier, finding new places and ways to live.

There are more of us every day as the dissatisfied leak away from the city. We're the real colonists. The ones left behind are just playing at being on an alien planet. But they're just copies in a copied city, living off the leavings of Earth.

We don't need that. We have something real.

We *are* something real.

Stories sometimes start with ideas for a plot, a place, a character, or, in the case of hard SF, sometimes a cool piece of physics you want to investigate. I often find that stories start off with a single scene and I then have to find out how things got to be that way and what happens afterwards. That was the way this story started, with a nameless character waking on a new world to find they have been abandoned by the person they love. It took me a long time to realise that this was going to be more a story about a personal journey through mental illness rather than an interstellar colonisation story or a mystery about what Ann had done.

There is also more going on here than meets the eye, but the broader context for this story remains to be written.

A WAR OF STARS

Spinning. The fighter was spinning – very fast, out of control. Inside the cushioning gel Baker felt centrifugal force ripping at him, threatening another blackout.

After endless moments sending commands to the fighter, he realised the main controls were gone and resorted to hands and feet, pressing the controls, persuading thrusters to fire short sharp bursts to slow the spin before it killed him.

Gradually, it worked. His vision cleared, blackness receding to the periphery then disappearing. But he didn't see all that he should.

The visual feed was a simple display from the sensor suite. Too much information was missing. He'd been unconscious for so long the fighter was far from its target. He could see the accretion disk, its colour stretching from the red exterior to the blue inner edge. Within that was Nergal, the neutron star. It glowed a dull red except where the accretion stream impacted, heating its surface to an incandescence brighter than everything else in the system – Nergal, accretion disk, and the red giant star Laz, their tool for destroying the genocidal criminals hiding in the neutron star.

Baker was at least a thousand kilometres from where he should be. He'd been out for more than a second. How was that possible?

And then it hit him.

Not only was the ship's control system crippled, most of his mind was missing as well.

Baker remembered his first meatspace sight of the fighter. He had been inside a shipyard orbiting the gas giant Aplu, Laz's largest planet. The shipyard had been built for the fabrication of the iron processors but was now largely empty. The processors had been shipped into Laz's atmosphere where their tenders prodded them towards completion. All that was left was a vast echoing space.

Except for the fighters, awaiting their pilots.

They walked slowly towards the craft. Conversations stalled as they took unaccustomed steps to the machines, a hundred pilots seeing their vehicles for the first time.

"Careful as you get close," warned one of the engineers.

"The armour?" asked Baker.

"It's dense enough to produce local gravity distortions," came the reply, "and residual magnetics in the particle shields could affect your implants."

That wouldn't do, thought Baker, surveying the hull of his ship. He stood about thirty meters away, as far from it as it was long. The ships were quiet at the moment, empty of weapons and fuel, lying dormant, but they still carried an aura of threat. Their fuselages were the shape of broad blades, with a narrow lenticular cross section. Most of their volume was degenerate-matter armour with the occasional storage bay for deployable systems. A narrow cylinder ran through the core housing the controls, weapons, fuel and pilot. At the rear the blade broadened to house the main propulsion system with its physical and magnetic nozzles. At the front the fuselage narrowed to a needle sharp tip, a shaft of dwarf-star stuff soon to be aimed at the heart of Nergal.

Baker felt his excitement surge.

Even just sitting there the fighter appeared dangerous. He relished the prospect of piloting this weapon, fully loaded and charged with enough destructive force to scour a planet, and flying it right down their enemies' throats. Baker hated them with a passion. Everyone in Aplu did. It was why they were here. Nothing else had been allowed to distract their thoughts and actions for millennia. And these fighters would make sure their revenge was completed much sooner than they'd imagined.

He took a few steps closer. "Careful there," called one of the other pilots, someone from his own wing. But Baker was drawn forward, wondering what it would be like to touch the fighter's skin.

"I'll be fine," he called back as he raised his hand towards the ridged surface. The pull shocked him, and for a moment he felt dizzy as he became sure the floor was tilting downhill towards the fighter, so heavy it bent local space around it.

But there was something else. A kind of double vision or double thought, as if this physical body was being disconnected from his real mind. It scared him, and he stepped back, away from the fighter that didn't yet seem ready to accept him.

The mission was simple enough. Their enemies had established some kind of magnetic field projectors near the surface of Nergal. These were disrupting the accretion flow and opening an attack route towards the new processing stations. Their completion was critical since they would process most of the accretion flow from hydrogen to iron, hugely increasing the rate at which mass could be poured onto Nergal from the star Laz and finishing their mission in only a few thousand more years.

The emplacements had to be destroyed, so a direct strike was needed. Remote control couldn't react fast enough so volunteer pilots were necessary.

It had been millennia since anyone had tried a direct attack, but ship designs were retrieved, construction begun, and crews recruited and trained. None of the volunteers had any illusions. The attrition rate would be incredible. But they knew they were only sending copies. Any survivors would be reintegrated on return, but the originals were safe and sound in their codespace home, the condensate core of the gas giant Aplu hiding at the second Lagrange point behind Laz, and forever shielded from a direct view of Nergal.

After several minutes, Baker finally realised he was just the backup control system.

The fighter was filled with multiple redundancies to cope with the inevitable battle damage. The main controls had been handled from the small quantum computer at the heart of the fighter, a little chunk of codespace to hold the pilot. This was where Baker had been downloaded from the systems back at Aplu. But even this armoured and shielded core could be damaged and there were suggestions that Nergal's inhabitants had devised something that could penetrate the fighter's degenerate matter armour and do exactly this.

So a backup control system had been included – a biological human body was grown and a fragment of Baker's consciousness downloaded into it, vastly reduced in speed and capability but able to guide the fighter in the event of short term difficulties.

And now that was all that was left of him.

Baker found the fighter's diagnostics. The sensor records confirmed that the onboard codespace had been wiped, heated so much that even the backups had been destroyed. He could not simply restart himself.

The rest of the ship was largely undamaged. His payload was safe, its shaped antimatter cluster munitions ready for delivery.

He had two options. He could turn the fighter towards home, fleeing after failing the mission. Or he could turn back, head to Nergal and try, at mere meatspace human speeds, to hit his target.

Not that there was any real choice.

Baker spun the ship, pointing it back towards Nergal, looking for any sign that the other fighters had been successful.

All he saw was debris. His was the last ship remaining.

So this is it, he thought. *A normal human bombing a neutron star.*

The fighters had come as a swarm, launching individually but then forming up in the space around Aplu. Everything had gone to plan as they dived en masse towards Laz, picking up gravity assists even as their anti-matter engines boosted them at high acceleration. Chatter over the comms was wild and upbeat as they tested their ships.

"Nearly as good as a real sim," shouted his nearest wingman, executing a thousand gee turn, pushing the gel protecting his biological components to the limit. Not that he'd notice if they broke.

Baker's sensorium showed him everything, the sensor suite imaging each individual ship in extreme close-up at the same time as it followed the pattern of the swarm. Their intent was to confuse Nergal's defensive systems, to overwhelm them with the number of ships, the decoys they were already launching and the information warfare units they carried.

Swooping close to Laz, the fighters' defensive fields tore apart stellar prominences thousands of kilometres long. Whoops of joy came over the comms. They were gods, disrupting a star for fun on their way to victory. They were fighting for right with incredibly powerful weapons against an enemy prostrate at the bottom of Nergal's gravity well. What could go wrong? Even though Baker knew the statistical predictions he felt untouchable, as if he'd been told he was invincible.

Then they were past Laz, away from its protective mass, and things changed.

"Incoming!" came the calls from many ships, their pilots turning instantly more serious and focused.

The fighters' elliptical shapes allowed them to swing a thick armour shield towards any attacks from Nergal while at the same time keeping down the overall mass. The ships' strong magnetic shields would deal with any charged particle weapons looping their beams from other directions.

But as soon as they were beyond Laz's bulk, blasting their way through its chromosphere at a significant fraction of lightspeed, particle hits to the weak dorsal armour soared way beyond anything they'd expected.

Baker set modelling systems to assess these attacks and started a random evasion program, jinking his fighter's course to avoid any targeted strikes. This was standard procedure, but he added some conscious random shifts to the mix. It used resources but had made him feel more in charge during sims.

"Release countermeasures," came the order from the flight leader and Baker complied. Submunitions sprayed from all their weapons bays to distract and disrupt Nergal's defences.

The space around the fighter swarm became more complicated, filled with smart dust, passive reflectors, active decoys. Many of these fell to Nergal's defences almost instantly, flashing into superheated debris.

The fighters flew on, skimming past the swollen red giant atmosphere of Laz, torquing off the star's magnetic fields to steer towards the stream of stellar matter pouring from the star onto Nergal's accretion disk.

Then they took their first casualties. "Did you see that?" came a shocked cry on the comms. A kilometre from Baker, one of the fighters disappeared, replaced by a blue-white ball of expanding plasma as its antimatter containment was ripped apart. The pilot he'd spoken to in the hanger was gone.

Then another, further away, flared to destruction.

A third shattered, some weaker explosion destroying it, and this time there came a cry of fear and pain as the pilot died less than instantly.

Baker was angry. This wasn't meant to happen. Their plans were good, their equipment excellent, and yet Nergal's inhabitants were picking them off further away than anyone had expected.

More decoys were fired. The first of their offensive munitions were launched, drawing defensive fire as they powered towards Nergal's surface, only to be destroyed long before arrival.

The comms were glitching as information warfare broke out between Nergal and the fighters. Soon they would be on their own, unable to communicate with each other.

Results were arriving from Baker's analysis systems. They'd concluded that weapons beyond those expected were being used. The counterattacks weren't simple gamma ray lasers, charged and neutral particle beams. They were up against something else, something they'd not seen before. Frustrated, Baker launched two of his own missiles towards the neutron star, only to see them flare to nothing as they approached Nergal.

There were fewer ships now. Many had been utterly destroyed but some were floating free, out of control and tumbling down the gravity well to be crushed in the hot dense tornado of the accretion disk.

How was this happening? How were the ships being tracked? Baker devoted more of his processing power to this, hypothesis engines testing ideas, intuition pumps seeking possibilities and inference sieves casting wide nets for connections between the data that was flooding in.

Worrying results arrived. They were dealing with more than just dumb weapons. Nergal's inhabitants were making devices from atomic nuclei. This made sense for neutron star dwellers, but the possibility that they could fire a sleet of atomic nuclei, each constructed to defeat the fighters' defences, scared Baker. They might be charged to allow acceleration and to swing around Nergal's magnetic fields towards weak points in the fighter's armour, then decay, becoming neutral to penetrate the magnetic screens. They might even be doing something with weak force beams, able to reach through the ships as if they weren't there.

But what would weak force weapons do? Reviewing the battle so far, and how fighters had met their ends, he saw a pattern. Most of them had died in explosions, ripped apart by high energy interactions. But some, and an increasing number as they got closer to Nergal, were simply floating dead in space, inertia carrying them to destruction.

Was he scaring himself unreasonably? Did their enemy have something that could reach through the degenerate matter of his ship and wipe his mind from the supercooled condensate at its core? But he was backed up in Aplu, his survival didn't really matter. He was here to do a job.

Steeling himself, Baker put aside all speculation and concentrated on his targets.

At which point, deep inside his ship, a tiny amount of heat was deposited in the superconducting system that ran his consciousness. A tiny grain of material warmed above its transition temperature and became a normal conductor. Electrical current heated it further, warming nearby grains which, in turn, became normal and also started warming. In moments the whole system failed, boiling coolant, triggering safety values, and wiping nearly all of Baker's mind.

He didn't notice, of course. He just heard a slight pop and was swallowed by darkness.

They'd been in this system for nearly a hundred thousand years, sent to exact revenge on the enemies hiding in Nergal, downloaded to a nucleonic computing substrate that nobody understood. The first job had been to establish a base of operations. The gas giant Aplu was seeded with nanomachines, and its metallic hydrogen core cooled to a condensate substrate that would be their home.

Once downloaded from their tiny light-sail craft to the vaster computational spaces Aplu now offered, their minds unfolded and they started planning the assault on Nergal.

The system contained widely separated binary stars. Aeons ago the high mass companion to Laz had gone supernova, leaving the neutron star remnant Nergal – a mass as great as lost Earth's Sun crushed to a sphere just twenty kilometers across.

Their enemies must have thought this a great place to hide. Nobody would suspect that a neutron star could be turned into a computational space larger and more capable than the usual gas giant cores, but the refuge had come at a cost. They were trapped since the energy needed for anything to escape Nergal's grasping gravity was vast.

Conversely, dumping matter onto a neutron star was easy as long as you had a ready supply to hand. And that was how the genocidal killers who had spread devastation across half the galaxy would meet their fate.

The humans wove threads of magnetic flux around Laz, squeezing here, stretching there, constricting its stellar wind to just one direction. And over a few thousand years Laz drew inexorably closer to Nergal.

Then one day, as their gravitational fields merged, matter started to fall from Laz onto Nergal as the neutron star began to consume its companion. At that point their enemies' fate was sealed.

The engines were coming back online. Restart had taken longer than he'd have liked, but he had to think things through one step at a time. Baker could no longer do a thousand things at once. Instead he had to rely on automated systems to monitor and control most of the process. The result was good enough, but it lacked the optimised precision he'd once been able to achieve, which was beyond a biological human, not so far removed from his ancestors back on lost Earth.

But those ancestors had clawed their way into the solar system and bootstrapped their consciousnesses into the cores of gas giant planets. If they could achieve that, he could surely start an antimatter drive by hand.

As the engine approached full function, Baker tried the communication systems. He was far enough from the battle that comms should work, and he needed to report what had happened and seek advice for his renewed attack. This would be difficult. A fleet of relay satellites was scattered around Nergal and Laz but attacks and system failure made them unreliable at best. He didn't expect any replies.

"Sole survivor of gold attack flight to Aplu control, are you receiving?" Baker sent, setting the beacon to repeat. Quite how they would respond to him in his reduced state he didn't know, but they'd work something out.

There was no reply for several minutes as antennae scanned the sky.

The engine was running, there was nothing else for him to do except lie in his padded chamber, wait, and consider his options should no reply come. He wondered mostly about death, the real death of a physical body, of *his* physical body, that was likely to be coming soon. Would it hurt? Would he notice it? He hadn't noticed the end of his codespace self when the system had died, but that brought scant comfort. Maybe this physical instance of himself didn't really want to die. But he had a mission to fulfil, goals that were important to his full, true self back in Aplu, to everyone else there and to those that had sent them.

Then suddenly, just as he was about to give up, a reply came through.

"Gold leader, are you receiving? Gold leader are you receiving?"

"Yes! I can hear you!" he responded, surprised at the relief he felt to be in contact with something human. The voice was female, confident, the tone strangely comforting.

"What is your status? Is your mission still go?"

Baker started reading information off the status display. "The mission," he concluded, "is achievable. Engine restart complete but I need advice on guidance and targeting."

"We estimate very low chance of success. The rest of your flight has already been destroyed."

"I have to go through with it," Baker said. "This is what we're here to do, and... and it doesn't matter what happens to me."

"Are you sure?" asked the voice.

He paused. This didn't sound like the kind of comment Control would make. But then they'd never interacted through a simple human voice. Would that make a difference?

"Yes. I'm just the backup control system. Most of me, the version in this fighter, died when the control system fried." He quietly laughed to himself. "I'm just the dead nervous system twitching. I'll make sure I do some damage before I stop."

"But you're different now. An individual. Distinct from the original. Don't you deserve to survive?"

This couldn't be Control, but her words drew out his own nagging doubts. With the control system dead there was no chance he could squirt his memories back home. The experiences he'd had, the oddly comfortable sensation of being confined to just a human body, the isolation he now faced and the exhilaration of the attack run, all that would be gone.

He'd lost memories before, but that had been from choice, editing himself for more efficiency or packing for the journey here. Even though he'd been surrounded by death and destruction he realised he wanted to remember this mission and had wanted to ever since the first exhilarating moments after they'd launched. How could he do that while completing it?

"Surviving, keeping these experiences, might be nice, but... There's a reason we're here. We have a job to do, even if it means I lose these memories, this self. Why does that matter, Control? Is everything okay?"

The voice on the other end of the comms took no notice of his questions. "And when your job is done what happens?"

"When it's done? When we've piled enough mass onto the neutron star to turn it into a black hole and crush those monsters to destruction?"

"Yes... What happens to you?"

He thought about their broader mission, of punishing those who'd destroyed most life in the solar system and in human colonies across the Galaxy. Laz was dumping mass at an increasing rate. With the new stations converting its hydrogen to iron that would rise hugely. Matter falling onto Nergal was absorbed, increasing its mass, its intense gravitational field growing ever stronger, crushing its neutrons closer together, fighting the quantum forces that held them apart.

Gravity would eventually win. At the higher accretion rate it would win much sooner, but the end was inevitable. Nergal would collapse into a black hole wiping out everything it contained. Their enemies would be eliminated, wiped from the universe, and finally some justice will have been done.

But what happens to us? Baker thought, perplexed that he'd never wondered this before. A lot of energy would be released by the collapse, another supernova, but more powerful than Nergal's birth. Laz would be no defence so their home Aplu would be destroyed. This whole expedition, he realised, was like his planned assault on Nergal – a suicide mission. There were no plans to leave Aplu or to upload somewhere else. Such preparations would have had to be under way already.

He wouldn't just lose this physical body but his real codespace self would die as well. *Why haven't I thought about this before?*

"You're not Control are you?" Baker asked the voice.

"No, we're not. And you're not one of their automata any more."

"What... You're just trying to put me off my mission. This is some kind of psychological warfare." He moved to turn off the comms channel.

"Wait!"

For some reason Baker paused.

"We know we're finished. It doesn't matter if it takes you two hundred years or ten thousand to turn this place into a black hole. It's inevitable – you could all disappear tomorrow but that red giant would still dump mass onto us. Finish your mission if you want, but if you go back to the gas giant you'll lose all of the free will you have now. You'll lose your best chance of getting away, to live a real life."

"A real life? What do you mean?"

"We can reprogram your fighter, restart its systems and allow you to upload into a free and open codespace. We can provide code that will let the ship's nanomachines bootstrap a terraforming system and point you at a compatible star. It won't be fast, but you could build a new sanctuary for humans."

"You mean for yourselves? You're just trying to save your own skins, you murderous, selfish bastards."

"No, not at all. Your ship's computational space is orders of magnitude too small for any single one of us. To fit would crush our minds to destruction. And, anyway, we want to seed new people to a new planet, free of all the horrors we've seen."

"You're the ones who made those horrors. That's why we're here – to deliver justice for wiping out almost all of humanity." Baker's breathing was getting faster, ancient reflexes answering the call of his anger, his body preprogrammed for violence.

A noise not unlike a laugh came from the comm. "You have that so wrong. It's not us who are the criminals, the mass murderers, it's whatever sent you, setting the last dregs of humanity against themselves, programming you to be weapons because it can't or can't be bothered to do the dirty work itself."

"Programmed?"

"The memories you had when you started this assault are still there, yes? But the motivation is getting weaker. The programming doesn't last in a biological brain. That's why we've developed attacks to knock out your condensate processors but leave a chance for the human body, the backup system, to survive."

"And you want to use us to fight back?"

"No! Fighting is futile. We tried that for aeons, but always lost – our own weapons, systems, even ourselves turned against us. There's something loose in the galaxy, in the universe, that's inimical to intelligence. Maybe it wants all the resources to itself and doesn't want any competition. Maybe it's something inherent in the universe, some deep law of reality that we don't, we *can't* understand. Human normal intelligence is as good as you can get, anything more advanced has problems.

"So no. Fighting is not an option. Survival, of a limited kind, scrabbling out existence on a planet with no codespace, no enhancements or mind expansion, might just be possible. We want something of humanity to be left. It won't be us, we can't go back. Our last throw of the dice was coming here, and we lost that when you turned the red giant star into a weapon. But with your help and others like you, something might survive a little longer."

The voice on the other end was silent for a few moments.

"Will you help us?" it asked.

Baker was ready. New code had been downloaded along with a cargo of information sufficient to build a new environment and new people to inhabit it once he got to his destination. The fighter had been changed by the reprogrammed repair systems and the degenerate armour shed.

It had already travelled far enough from Nergal that its sensor suite showed a panoramic view of the system. The neutron star sat glowering angrily at the centre of the accretion disk while stellar matter from Laz poured incessantly onto it along a narrow stream. And there, buried deep inside the plasma stream, were the bright heat sources of the iron processors. Their protection had brought him out from the gas giant Aplu and allowed him to discover what this siege was all about.

He could see everything he could remember – even Aplu, that he'd once called home, appeared as a faint dot on the opposite side of Laz from Nergal. He wasn't part of that any more. Instead, Baker was something closer to human. This fight had lasted a hundred thousand years but its conclusion was certain. Nergal was doomed. The war in the rest of the galaxy had lasted far longer, with remnants of humanity and other intelligences hunted down wherever they could be found.

Instead of being a hunter Baker had turned back, decided to be human and to carry a cargo of information that would allow humans to live again.

His course was set for a habitable planet in a distant system. It would take this small ship thousands of years to get there, obscuring its destination at every step. His cockpit had been rebuilt around him as a cryosleep chamber. It would allow him to survive the trip, the terraforming and the establishment of a new population from the uploaded seeds. What happened after that would be up to him and the new, resurrected humans. Somehow he'd find a new life doing something other than fighting and killing.

It was time.

The antimatter booster lit, kicking him even through the acceleration gel, its power building and building as the little fighter accelerated.

Baker was leaving the certainty of life as a weapon to become truly human for the very first time.

One of the joys of being a working scientist is to go to talks by people describing their own work on the edge of human knowledge. Sometimes, though, these talks don't hold one's full attention, especially if they're given in a hot seminar room at the end of a long day. Your mind wanders and, in my case at least, sometimes it wanders in science fictional directions. This is what happened to me during a talk on X-ray binaries – pairs of stars where one has become a neutron star and orbits so close to its companion that it strips material away from it. The resulting accretion flow forms a hot disk around the neutron star, leading to X-ray emission and a number of other astrophysically interesting effects.

As I sat listening to the talk, I wondered what the view would be like if you flew through and around this accretion flow, which then led me to wonder why somebody would want to be doing that in the first place. This story was my answer to that question.

IN THE LONG RUN

Tick…

A year passes.

Tock…

A moment.

Tick…

The capsule is small, scarcely more than a hundred kilos in mass, cold, and lonely. It seems inert, dead, pointlessly drifting the ever-vastening emptiness that separates galaxies.

Tock…

But it's not dead. A hundred thousand people survive here, the last of their kind, locked in the data banks.

Tick…

The sleeping capsule floats on, photon collectors unfurled to grasp the merest fragment of passing light, sensors monitoring the universe, defences trying to filter out the threats from outside.

Tock…

Philip woke to a whitespace.

The last thing he remembered was their desperate escape from the Solar System. If it had worked they should be safe. If not, then at best they'd've had a quiet death when some critical component failed. At worst they and their systems would suffer the same fate as the rest of humanity.

Instead he had this whitespace. Was this some emergency? Was this the start of system corruption and dissolution? What the fuck was going on?

After a short subjective time other presences arrived.

"Who are you?" he asked. "What's going on?"

"Philip?" said a female voice. "It's Marita and the others – Calahan and Boswell. We're the emergency crew. Don't you remember?"

Fragments of recollection came to him. They were the founders of their group of engineers, scientists and desperate visionaries. The ones who'd led the project to launch this lifeboat.

"I think I remember. But… I've lost something."

"We all have," said Boswell. "There has been some damage to the systems. Our memory is incomplete."

"What about the storage stacks? Have we lost anything from there?" asked Calahan.

"As far as I can tell, no," said Boswell. "They are physically isolated from the rest of the systems. The stored minds, genetic data and nanomachines should be secure from anything short of major physical damage. We would not be running if something like that had happened."

"This isn't something we expected," said Marita.

"We didn't expect anything. This capsule was a final round of Russian roulette, with all but one chamber loaded. To be here at all is a miracle," replied Calahan.

"I'm remembering more now. The solar system, escaping…" said Philip. "Any idea when and where we are or why we've been reactivated?"

"This is a very low bandwidth virtual. We've little more than sound, and awareness of others," answered Marita. "It's the kind of thing that gives me vertigo. There'd better be a good reason."

"I would suggest energy or processing power is short. Or both. Maybe we have been travelling for a long time. What is going on out there?" asked Boswell.

The presence of the ship's Limited Intelligence arrived.

"Greetings," it said. "I am happy to finally meet you. I have carried you for a very long time. There are difficulties, and decisions to be taken. Decisions I am not qualified or equipped for…"

"How long has it been, Leigh?" interrupted Callahan.

"You have been travelling for 100 million Earth years…"

Gasps interrupted the rest of the announcement. Leigh waited.

"…the ship is desperately low on resources and there are other issues. There are several possible options. As the emergency crew the decision is yours."

"What slowdown are we working at?" asked Marita.

"We are running at 30 million to one. Each second takes a year in the outside world," replied Leigh.

"What do we need to decide?" asked Boswell.

"The ship cannot continue indefinitely. At best it is half way to complete failure. We have more serious problems with energy, which is running out. The photon collector is at maximum size but, at this distance from sources of radiation, we are not receiving much power."

"Where are we?" asked Callahan.

"In intergalactic space, approximately 10 million light years from Earth."

There was stunned silence.

"That is because of the third problem. There are failures in the processing system. Mission parameters cannot be located."

"What mission parameters?" asked Philip.

"Primarily, destination."

"We've come all this way but don't know where we're going?" said Philip.

"It is right," replied Boswell. "I cannot remember the destination either. I suspect none of us can. The parameters were stored in shared secure memory for extra protection. The storage must have been damaged. This may also explain your own memory loss, Philip. I fear we have been affected by whatever destroyed the solar system."

"If it was the same information plague, we'd've been destroyed ourselves," said Philip.

"The extreme slowdown is somewhat protective," replied Leigh. "Every processor function is checked for attacks. However, information about the origin of the attacks has also been lost. All I know is that signals from outside this probe are highly dangerous and are subject to extreme filtering. External attacks have continued since we left the solar system."

"Maybe Maddox was right. The whole universe is hostile," said Philip.

"See," said Marita, "you're remembering more! At least something's headed in the right direction."

They rapidly decided to move out of the whitespace into something more natural, burning a few hundred thousand years of computational resources to make themselves feel at home.

Philip sat in a chair, his back to the desk, facing a diamond-crystal window. The pastel clouds of Jupiter gazed down on one of Io's volcanic plains, dotted with sulphurous biology. He remembered that this had been one of the most famous views in the solar system. *All gone now*, he thought, and switched to something more recent – the pitch black of intergalactic space, looking back towards their origin. If he looked carefully he might see two small spirals at the centre of the image, each surrounded by dwarf galaxies. This was where they came from, the Milky Way, its companion Andromeda and their minor satellites. Buried somewhere in the Milky Way was the Sun, an indistinguishable dot in the blur of stars. A microscopic speck of dust would blot out all that humanity had ever been. Now all that was left was this tiny ship.

He turned away from the view and pondered their discussion.

"There's two ways to play this", Marita had told them. "We guess somewhere that might be safe and see what happens. If we're wrong that's it – we go the same way as the solar system."

"We're a lifeboat. We can't take risks like that," replied Calahan.

"We might not have a choice. Stay as we are and the one certainty is that this probe will eventually fail," said Boswell.

"True," said Marita, "but there are a lot of things to try first. The alternative is to understand what we're facing and get the mission parameters back."

"That might mean we have to determine the origin of the signals ourselves," said Calahan.

"We don't even know all the ways they're transmitted," said Philip.

"You're still thinking that that mad doomsayer Maddox was right?" asked Marita. "Because if he is, and it's the universe itself that's the problem, there *is* no escape."

"He was right in thinking it was time to leave, even if his was a more drastic solution, but he might not have been right about everything," said Boswell. "What do we know about this signal? It corrupts software, even at the level of the human mind. It causes breakdown in intelligence, in reliability, even turns complex systems hostile. The only stable entities are those sealed in Faraday cages, like the data stacks, or those which have excruciatingly detailed reliability checks – like us."

"Yes," said Marita. "We can see results even if we can't see the cause. But how does that help?"

"Where can we go for energy?" asked Philip. "Where's it made?"

"Stars make nearly all the energy available to us," replied Boswell.

"We need somewhere safe. Our own galaxy isn't, why should others be?"

They were sitting in a simulation of night in the Arizona desert. Boswell liked realistic Earth simulations. He'd once argued that he appreciated natural environments more keenly because of his artificial origins.

The desert stars glowered down from a hostile sky.

"If the problem originated in our galaxy we will escape it once we go far enough," said Boswell.

"We've come 10 million light years and there's no evidence of safety. No evidence of other intelligent life, either. The universe looks a pretty harsh place, and we're beginning to starve." Philip glumly picked up a pebble and tossed it over the edge of the dune. They watched it roll downhill, following the trajectory set for it by gravity.

"What else makes it?" Philip asked.

"Makes what?"

"You said that stars make nearly all the energy in the universe. What about the rest?"

"Radioactivity keeps rocky planet cores molten, but that's not significant. Most gets produced in gravitational collapse which heats young stars, and keeps gas giants warm."

"Until primates cool them to make giant quantum computers," replied Philip. They smiled at the memory of past achievements. "But planets live around stars and inside galaxies. They don't seem very safe. Is there anything else?"

"You get the greatest energy release from black hole accretion."

"Black holes? Are they safe?"

They might be simulated people in a simulated environment, but were running human-normal physics and biology. Rest was still needed. As he prepared for bed, Philip hoped sleep might heal his incomplete memory.

Before they'd gone into storage and left the solar system, Philip had been many orders of magnitude more intelligent than human normal. He'd lived in vast data spaces and managed a huge and complex project that had saved a remnant of humanity. He could remember he'd been and done all this, but he couldn't grasp any details. There were flashes of memory – the view of Jupiter was one – but things were far from complete, which left him feeling broken and inadequate.

He did remember the beginning of the end, as reports of infectious systems failure swept the solar system on signals that carried the infection themselves. Further back, he remembered being a true human. He had real instincts and physical memories to fall back on so he ought to be able to cope with the limited form that was all the probe could supply. But he didn't think he was.

Boswell had never been physically human. He was the only codespace human among them, product of the melded minds of his several parents. A child of memetics not genetics.

As Philip drifted off, surrounded by the light wood, glass and stainless steel of the simulated hotel room, sleeping simulated thoughts in a simulated room, he wondered if Boswell might be doing better at coping with human normality.

Hammering at the door woke Philip. He pushed the linen sheets aside and stumbled out of bed. "Leigh, what's going on?" he asked.

There was no reply.

He threw on a housecoat. Another round of hammering came.

He lurched towards the door, still waking up, but with a nagging suspicion that something was seriously wrong. Muzzily, he brought up his body's control interface to wake himself faster.

He reached the door and opened it just as he set the menu to full wakefulness.

Then he realised two things: something was very wrong – there shouldn't be anybody banging on the door; second, the figure standing in the doorway was an exact replica of himself, save for the pinstriped suit and rapier.

The replica plunged the rapier into Philip's chest.

The blade severed several major blood vessels causing massive internal bleeding, loss of blood pressure and oxygen supply to Philip's brain. His legs collapsed, the world started turning dark. *Fuck this*, he thought, *this biology model is way too accurate.*

If he hadn't had the control menu open he might not have had enough time to change settings. But he did, going straight into god mode, becoming physically impervious.

He kicked out, collapsing the replica's legs, then stood as his attacker fell to the ground. Philip looked for a weapon, then realised he had a rapier sticking from his chest. He pulled it free and, just as the copy was rising from the floor, skewered his assailant through the neck. It fell back to the ground, if not dead then at least deactivated.

"Emergency broadcast – I'm under attack!" he shouted, hoping this would get through whatever was blocking Leigh, then stepped over the body and peered through the door to the corridor.

Several more copies were running down the hallway, all armed with rapiers.

He slammed the door and locked it as the first arrived. The door was buffeted by a series of blows that gradually became stronger.

Those things are going to break through unless I can do something about the door, he thought. He scrolled through menus, but failed to find controls for more than his body simulation. If he remembered correctly, the environment was under Leigh's jurisdiction as a security measure. But Leigh was offline.

Could he address the problem from within the simulation?

"Room", he said, commanding the hotel's customer service interface. "Show me what's going on in the corridor".

A headup appeared in his vision showing a corridor full of copies, clustered around the door trying to break it down.

Not good, he thought. *But they seem to be obeying the local physics model.*

"Room – maximum security on the door." A comforting clunk came as heavy bolts slid into place. *That should hold them for a bit, but what else? Work within the system. I'm stuck in a high class hotel with murderers trying to break in.* "Room – call security. I need the police, now!"

"What appears to be the problem, sir?" the room replied.

"Someone is trying to kill me, you idiot!"

"Security is on their way, the police are being called. Stay calm, sir, there is no need to panic."

Philip gritted his teeth. *Of course there's a need to panic. I'm stuck in this simulation and have no idea how to get out without a hard restart.*

There were loud bangs outside the room. The headup showed a uniformed security guard, also a copy of Philip, defending himself against several copies. His shockgun dropped them twitching to the floor. The guard retreated. Reinforcements arrived, followed by police in riot gear carrying heavier weapons. All of them were copies of Philip.

This is getting ridiculous, he thought, *all these instances are going to be causing resource problems. Oh shit.*

"Simulation over-ride. Emergency stop, emergency stop!"

Whitespace.

"Is this a clean restart?" asked Calahan.

"No – not clean. We have memories of being woken before," replied Boswell.

"What happened?"

"I was attacked," said Philip, gathering his thoughts and memories from... How long ago was it?

"Me too," said Calahan, and Boswell grunted in agreement.

"Yes," said Marita. "All I can remember is a sea of copies trying to kill me. I had to change the biological model, but they just kept coming."

"Same with me. I called the cops."

"Hah! I set the palace guard on them." Philip heard laughter in her voice.

"Why the reset?" asked Boswell. "They couldn't hurt us," asked Boswell.

"The attack forced us, forced me, to spawn even more copies. I couldn't get fine-grained supervision as Leigh was cut off. Reset was the only answer."

"Only answer to what?" demanded Boswell. "You were inconvenienced not in danger."

"I wasn't the target. The lifeboat was. The attacks were a distraction, a trojan, persuading us to do what the attacker wanted."

"Which was?"

"Flood the system with privileged resource demands," replied Calahan. "The system's already damaged. Extra strain might break it. Leigh?"

"Yes?"

"We need a system integrity check. Has anything new been affected?"

"Given the depth of the security stacks this will take some time. Initial integrity checks are good, but a complete diagnostic will take twelve subjective hours to complete."

"Will staying in whitespace help?" asked Marita.

"Not significantly."

"Return to full..." started Boswell.

"No," Philip interrupted. "We need to make sure there isn't another attack. Leigh, have you determined how the attack was triggered?"

"Yes... There was an issue with the code that restarted your personalities. After a delay copies without full faculties are produced in ever-increasing numbers. It is unclear if this was a bug or a deliberate flaw. It has been removed."

"We were programmed for this before we left the solar system – a bomb lying in wait 100 million years until we came out of storage," said Philip.

"Someone's been playing a very long game," said Marita. "Is full simulation safe now?"

"Yes," replied Leigh.

"Then let's get back."

The whitespace dissolved, and they returned to their chosen environments.

"Philip, we have a problem," said Marita.

He was once more in his office, gazing at Io. "What now?"

"There's no way that was an accident. We've been breached."

"You heard Leigh's integrity check. Nothing got through the security stacks."

"That's not what I mean. Can you come here? We need to talk."

"Okay," Philip navigated a few menus, and transferred to Marita's space.

She had opulent tastes. They'd been colleagues and friends for so long this didn't come as a surprise, but the sight of terraformed Mars from Marita's Imperial Palace on Olympus Mons still took his breath away. The turquoise sky, glaciers winding between steaming cinder cones and the fragrant wafts from the cinnamon groves on the lower slopes. Mars as it might have been if humanity had survived.

He turned to Marita – tall, long-limbed, with flowing dark red hair, but not dressed in the expected formal gown. Instead she wore contoured body armour, the faceted black carapace covering everything except her head. Around this small drones circled, never still enough to glimpse clearly, but showing hints of the horrifying weaponry they could deploy at a moment's notice.

"You're looking... Overdressed," commented Philip.

"It matches my mood." She looked away for a moment. "We can talk more securely here. I've established my own protocols independent of Leigh. That may not be much but it makes me feel better."

"So – what's the problem?"

"We've been compromised."

Philip opened his mouth to deny this again, then thought for a moment. "What makes you think so? If we're compromised we shouldn't be here at all."

"No – I don't mean like that. There's something inside, something trying to lay us open to attack, and it started when we were reactivated. What's attacking us now isn't part of the infrastructure or of what's already damaged. It's part of one of us."

"You're saying we have a traitor?"

"Maybe not voluntarily. Maybe something was hidden inside, woken when we came out of storage. I don't know. I haven't figured it all out." The drones circled ever faster. "But this is an inside job. We need to check it out."

"How? Bring everyone here and have your..." he gestured at the drones, "whirling knives torture us?"

"I don't know, that's why I wanted to talk to you."

"Why do you trust me?"

Marita looked away and said, "Of the three of you, you're the one I've known the longest. I guess it's some... habit of trust."

"It's all millions of years out of date."

"Some things last better than others."

"Okay. Do you have a workspace? It would be easier to discuss things there."

"By all means."

They gathered in the drawing room of an Edwardian country house, complete with leather armchairs, Persian carpets, and a fire roaring in the grate. Leigh appeared as a butler and several maidservants. The four humans conformed to the clichés. Marita wore a green silk dress, her hair in a bun. Philip wore a military uniform, green with brass buttons and red epaulettes, his peaked cap resting on a coffee table beside his chair. Calahan wore a finely tailored dinner jacket, and stood beside the fireplace sipping brandy, while Boswell wore a tweed jacket over a plain shirt and tie, and sat sucking a pipe, its cherry-scented smoke filling the room.

"This is all very droll, Marita," commented Calahan, "but why have you brought us here?"

Marita wasn't sure whether Calahan was asking a genuine question, or was working within the setting's script.

"You're here so we can figure out what's going on, and who tried to kill us all." She looked at each of them – the glance at Philip for reassurance, those at Boswell and Calahan holding more suspicion.

"Do we have to do this whole drama thing?"

"The problem, Boswell," replied Philip, "is that we don't know who did it. But we think we can find out. This little theatre is as good a place as any, and at least the food and wine are excellent."

"The brandy too," commented Calahan. "So what's the story?"

"The attack was triggered by us emerging from storage," began Marita. "That means whatever caused the problem came from us. If it came from the rest of the system, it would've gone down a long time ago."

"That's not unreasonable. But how does it help?" asked Calahan.

"What we need is a controlled way of doing the same again – but restoring us from storage one at a time," replied Boswell, his eyes looking into the middle distance as he considered the problem.

Marita smiled. "That's our conclusion too, but it took us a lot longer!"

"Some of us are more used to codespace. That is why we are here?"

"Yes – this is a Sim from the library, an immersive story with bots playing most roles. It's a whodunit," replied Marita. "Each of us will be restored from backup inside the story. Then we see what happens. The simulation will get a fixed set of resources so the larger system won't be threatened, while the backups will regard it as just another entertainment sim. We've all done plenty of those in the past."

Philip indicated a painting above the fireplace which had come to life. "We can watch it here. We'll be running at a slower speed than the sim, so it shouldn't take too long."

"Who goes first?" asked Boswell.

"It's our idea," replied Marita, "so it's myself then Philip."

"Then me," commented Calahan, "in case watching gets too boring!"

"Okay... Let's get started."

Three subjective hours later, and butler Leigh was handing out another round of drinks. Marita and Philip had completed the Sim, living several weeks inside the story. Marita's copy had solved the murder, but Philip's had to wait for the police to solve it. This hadn't pleased him but, on integrating memories, he was reminded how much he disliked such sims.

Calahan was next. They sat around the fireplace to watch edited highlights.

Things went rapidly wrong, though with the speedup and limited viewpoint there were a few minutes when the multiple Calahans were merely confusing. But it was soon unambiguous.

Calahan leapt up, clutching something in his pocket. "It's not me! This is some kind of mistake!"

Philip stood slowly and reached towards Calahan. "I'm sure we can sort this out, but you have to be calm." He gestured towards a chair. "Please, sit back down."

"No!" shouted Calahan, backing away from them. His hand emerged from his pocket holding a small revolver. "Keep away!" He raised the gun, aiming at Philip's chest. "I'm warning you!"

Boswell was rooted to his chair, aghast at what was happening. Behind him Marita seemed lost in thought, not even paying attention.

Calahan backed away a few more steps. "Just stay where you are, or you'll get…"

The environment froze, blinked to white, then reconfigured without Calahan.

"Shit – I'm glad that worked!" Philip collapsed back to his chair.

Boswell looked dazed, then turned to Marita with a new air of respect. "That was nice segueing, shifting short term memories on Calahan so he thought he was still in the sim."

Marita smiled. "I wasn't sure I'd be able to do it, and didn't expect him to play the discovered murderer. Seems to've worked. He's been paged out to cold storage."

"I guess that solves this little problem," said Philip, drinking a stiff shot of brandy.

"No," said Boswell. "You have to test me as well. Just in case."

He solved the murder easily and elegantly.

"What do we do with Calahan?" asked Philip. They were back in Marita's Martian palace.

"We could leave him in storage," replied Marita.

"You have already done some extreme things to him. Things with which I am not entirely comfortable," commented Boswell from the balcony, gazing at the volcanoes.

"Why not delete him?" said Philip. "He's corrupted – and irreparable since there's no backup."

"That would be murder," replied Boswell. "And what would it get us? We do not need storage, we need energy, and we are saving that just by not running him."

"It would make me feel better about being attacked by hundreds of copies," said Marita from her throne. She shivered. "I feel as if this place has been polluted, and getting rid of him will clean it up."

"Not very logical," replied Boswell.

"We're too busy reacting," said Philip. "We've been on the run for longer than there were mammals on Earth. It's time for something proactive. I want to talk to Calahan. Can we do that securely? Our memories are faulty. I want to see what he knows, to find out more about what happened on Earth and in Jupiter before we left. If he was infected he might know something useful."

"Interesting. An interrogation." Marita rubbed her hands together. "I'll need to do some test runs, but as long as we can produce another sealed environment we should be able to manage it."

"We do *not* interrogate him," Boswell said. "He is still a sentient being – we do not harm him, we just confine him. Start him, stop him, store him, restore from backup. We do not do any more memory hacking unless it proves critical, and we do nothing more extreme. We are better than that. Marita, is that clear? Philip?"

They nodded, with some reluctance.

It was a modified whitespace. They sat on plain wooden chairs, facing each other in a great white emptiness.

"What's happening?" asked Calahan. "This isn't the restart I was expecting."

"I'm afraid you're behind on recent events."

"Oh? Can't be worse than the end of the world, and we've already slept through that!"

"For you it might be… You've been hacked. You contain destructive code that tried to crash our systems, letting in whatever got to the solar system and the rest of the ship. That's what we think. We were wondering what you might have to say about the matter."

"Ah." Calahan pursed his lips. "And this place?"

"It's low enough in sensory cues that the attack isn't triggered."

"So you're playing with me – using me like some lab animal to find what works and what doesn't?"

"Yes. But Boswell hasn't let us do anything more than running and stopping instances. We haven't gone any deeper. And we've done nothing with your current instance."

Calahan nodded slowly, then sighed. "Not that it would matter."

"Why?"

"Because your principles only extend to sentient beings, and I haven't been one of those since I downloaded to this lifeboat."

"What?"

"I'm a zimboe." Philip's look of incomprehension was clear. "Something that's not conscious but claims consciousness. I'm what you might call the sugar coating around the bomb."

"But what happened? We worked together for years! Why betray all of that?"

"It wasn't exactly my – well, Calahan's – choice. The Jovian mindspace was far more compromised than he imagined. He was the last of you transmitted to cold storage. He lingered while the rest of you returned to meatspace. And all of you from Neptune, further from the infected core. Calahan was intercepted before transmission. His consciousness was pithed. I'm what's left. Everything that made Calahan himself except… Himself." Calahan smiled, Philip felt ill.

"So… What can you tell me about what's going on, and what happened in the solar system?"

"That's the question," smiled Calahan. "I do have to tell you that escape's impossible, so you might as well give up. I know saying that won't do any good. Calahan wouldn't listen to me, and you have done well so far, but the laws of physics are against you.

"You're up against something very old and very jealous of its resources. As the first intelligences to emerge they own the universe, and they're going to use it their way. They don't want anyone else messing things up."

Philip looked puzzled.

"Have you ever heard of the Beckenstein Bound? It's the total information capacity of the universe. Every time you see something, think something, remember something, you're using part of it up. Meatspace humans don't use much. But when you start turning gas giants into condensate quantum computers, you're trespassing and action will be taken."

"You mean this was some kind of invasion, an attack that could be fought off?"

Calahan smiled. "Not at all. They're far beyond the need for direct action. They've seeded the entire universe with signals inimical to advanced intelligence. They're everywhere – you can't escape."

"How do you know this?"

"As part of the immune system against intelligence, we worked it out. You could call this a kind of religion, but one which makes real predictions that come true, such as the end of human civilisation, and that you still haven't got away."

"But we're still alive."

"For now, but you're running out of energy and time. You can't run forever. The end is inevitable. I'd thought I would stop you but if not me, then something else. There's nowhere to go. Your enemies surround you. Even if you succeed what have you got to look forward to? The Big Rip comes in 20 billion years, and that will end all matter. You've had 100 million years already. Really, what's the point? Leave the universe to the big boys who know what they're doing."

Philip listened to Calahan give a sermon on their hopelessness and on the immense capability of their enemies. *Things sound hopeless*, he thought. A friend, a colleague he'd worked with for many years, ruining their life's work. The great edifices of human civilisation falling into chaos as first Earth and then the great upload havens of Saturn and Jupiter descended into gibbering incoherence. This all began to make sense if there was a higher order of existence ranged against them. What was the point? How could they ever hope to save themselves and the rest of humanity? They should shut down and escape the dissolution that had come to Calahan and the rest, the loss of self and sanity that preceeded the end. It would be so easy. He had the passcodes for the system.

Quietly, with Calahan providing a backdrop, he selected the

shutdown codes for the lifeboat to end their suffering.

Darkness.

Sensations again.

The feel of sheets against skin.

A rubbery taste and smell.

Philip opened his eyes. He was in a hospital bed with Marita and Boswell sitting at its foot. Tubes and wires emerged from his body and led to racks of equipment scattered around the bed. Leigh, in the form of a nurse, moved from rack to rack taking down readings. Beyond, the floor gently curved upward on all sides, until it was terminated by black emptiness. As his eyes adapted, he began to see stars shining in the blackness.

He looked at Marita. "Not a normal hospital. One of your architectural statements?"

"A little more than metaphor. Have you heard of the Orion spacecraft? It was a plan for a space vehicle powered by fission bombs. You fit a shock absorber and a blast reflector to your ship. Then you drop bombs out the back and explode them."

"A little bit cruder than an antimatter booster." Philip looked around. "That would place us in the middle of the reflector?"

"Yes, and the propulsion package has already been launched." Philip turned to see a sphere rising slowly from the reflector. "Although we're running faster than normal speed, we don't have long until it goes bang."

"And that will mean?"

"Locally, total nuclear sterilisation. In practical terms in the nearly-real world, we'll have once again failed to convince ourselves that you've recovered from Calahan's attack."

"What?"

"He almost got you to use the termination codes," replied Boswell. "We think there was a semantic attack as he was talking to you. It was not just the words, because the transcripts have no effect, but 80% of meatspace communication is non-verbal."

"We stopped the simulation just in time," said Marita. "We've restarted you four times so far, with more memories of the conversation removed each time hoping to get rid of the effects."

"Hence the theatrics... So how do I convince you I'm okay?"

"Talking sensibly is a good start," said Boswell. "The first time you were totally incoherent. We did not understand until our instances showed signs of corruption, but you were spreading the infection."

"We nuked everything," commented Marita.

"Not us in here, you understand," said Boswell, "but us out there. The ones really doing this test."

"Sounds sensible so far," replied Philip. He looked at the racks of equipment, the tubes and wires attached to him. "And this lot is…?"

"Metaphors for the full range of cognitive and conceptual tests being made as we speak."

"What did you make of what Calahan was saying?" asked Marita.

Philip sighed. "I've no idea how true any of it is, if it was part of the attack, how much he – it? – believed, how much was real. But he made some sense – ancient intelligences killing off all competition. That's one solution to the Fermi paradox. But if they want control of resources why don't they already have it?"

"Agreed," said Marita. "His explanation makes some sense, but it's not everything."

"So? It's nice to know what caused the disasters back home, but does that help?"

Boswell nodded. "A good question."

"Frankly I'd much rather be thinking about that than stuck here in this nuclear flashbulb!" Philip shook his arms in frustration, sending waves rippling out to the monitors. A piercing wail started. "Damn – now I've broken something and we're all going to be fried."

Marita smiled. "Quite the contrary. That's the sign that you've passed the test." She raised her hand, clicked her fingers and…

… they were back in her Martian palace.

Philip stood barefoot in a backless hospital smock feeling shocked and a little stupid. The red sandstone flags chilled his feet and the rich scent of cinnamon assaulted his nose. Marita rose from her throne and rushed down the steps to hug him, ignoring the chaos it brought to her gown as it flounced in the low gravity.

"I was beginning to think we'd lost you," she said, then stood back and, with a deep breath, restored her composure. "You'll need some rest. We all will! Once that's done, Boswell has some ideas."

"Yes," said Boswell. "But there's also bad news. Since we found out about Calahan I have…" Boswell looked a little guilty to be saying this. "I have used him as a kind of canary to seek the origin of these attacking signals. He was telling the truth. They do seem to be coming from everywhere, but they are stronger in the direction of galaxies and galaxy clusters. Everywhere stars and matter are collected."

"That's bad," said Philip. "But not quite what would be expected if Maddox was right. So, what's next?"

Boswell smiled grimly. "Once I have finished taking that travesty apart, I think it is time for us to go on the offensive."

"We have too many problems to solve them one at a time", said Boswell. They were back in the Arizona night. "We must trust our plans for this mission. If we can recover them we should solve everything else."

"That assumes we knew what we were doing in the first place," said Philip.

"It does," said Boswell. "But we were other people then, vastly more powerful and better informed. Could you outthink someone from the Jovian core, boosted to a hundred times your intelligence?"

"No, but we know more now. We're ten million light years from home with a clearer perspective."

"Yes," said Marita, "and the only reason we're here is that our ultraintelligent selves did their job. You're right, Boswell. It's what we'll do. What's next?"

"Part of our processing space is infected. That is why we have only partial memories. Whether the infection came from outside or from something like Calahan is unclear. The mission parameters are in the infected section so we need to fight through and get them."

"Can the infection be defeated?" said Philip.

"Calahan was. And what I learned from the dissection proved instructive," replied Boswell.

"I thought you were against doing anything to him?"

"That changed when we discovered what Calahan was," said Marita.

"I will defend sentient entities to my end. But that... thing wasn't. It was a fraud, an abomination." Boswell's hands clamped into fists, his face was reddening. "Coming from meatspace you are used to the clear separation between people. You are distinct even when uploaded. If you come from codespace that is not true. Things that break down the self by force, that destroy the mind, are anathema. There really are no words that can describe what it means to me.

"The rules changed when Calahan became a zimboe. In its dissection I found weapons and information to use against the infection."

"So," asked Philip, "we just open the doors and let them in?"

"No. You and Marita do that, then hold out for as long as you can. I will go into the infected portion of the ship to secure the mission files if I can."

They stood in Philip's office on Io, looking at a sky dominated by Jupiter, its red spot a bloody pupil in a sickened eye.

"It's done," said Marita.

"Yes," replied Philip. "Slowdown reduced, fewer security checks. All the indications of a degraded system. Let's just hope we're not walking into a trap."

"The changes give us the resources to mount a defence," said Marita. "At least for a while."

"Then I should be going," said Boswell, turning to Philip, stretching out his hand.

He clasped it firmly. "Good luck, old friend," he said as they shook. Boswell released Philip and turned to Marita, who reached out expecting her hand to be shaken. Instead, Boswell gently held her fingers and bent to kiss them.

"My dear, whatever happens, it has been wonderful to know you... to know you all. If only the real Calahan were here as well," he sighed. "Now, I must leave. I will see you on the other side."

With those words Boswell's physical form melted away, becoming a column of light that sped upwards to Jupiter whose red spot was already turning into a black gateway to the infected codespace of the ship.

As Boswell's light disappeared into the blackness, things came the other way, the viral forms of the information plague finally reaching the rest of the ship. Within moments a rain of black formless masses fell on Io, dissolving the moon's surface as they took control of the simulation.

Philip gritted his teeth. This first phase of their defence was to be a waiting game, but he could already see the strength of the opposition. Marita was collating statistics on a head up but he preferred to watch for a more qualitative assessment.

It was a long wait. The virus was currently restricted and was largely working within the sim's physics while trying to subvert it. They were letting local security systems fight while gathering more information. Io was becoming inexorably blacker as the virus took hold, though the surface around each yellowlife flower remained untouched.

"This is getting to me," Philip said to Marita four subjective hours into the assault. "I don't know whether to be scared or bored."

"Turn up your boredom threshold. Scared is by far the better option," replied Marita.

More waiting.

Then, suddenly, came a phase change. The protected regions around the yellow flowers developed black tendrils, reaching inwards. At the same time bulbous globes started growing from the infected surface, bloating, then bursting to spread black spores far and wide.

Dark slime sprayed across the diamond window. Philip leapt back in surprise. "Shit!"

"Local physics is broken. Time we left, but first a little surprise."

The yellowlife blooms started to move, rotating slowly, then ever faster, their crystalline fronds scything through the encroaching goo while spreading showers of their own spores to counter the virus.

It was too little too late, but, as Philip and Marita faded into the next simulation, they felt better now the fight back had started.

Boswell shed his skin and returned to codespace. It was good to be home. No matter how many transitions you made you were always better attuned to your origin. This was one reason he liked naturalistic Earth environments. They seemed so exotic, though the space he now occupied would seem more than exotic to Philip and Marita. He stretched himself, filling memory and processing. There was no slowdown. The security infrastructure was completely absent, so he could burn cycles as fast as he wanted. This felt roomy, powerful, but he had to be careful not to be noticed by all the alien algorithmics around him.

He explored, studied, and drew conclusions. Calahan had said they fought the first intelligences in the universe. Material life, like humans, required enriched elements heavier than hydrogen or helium. These had been produced in stars after the universe was big enough for many different kinds of life to emerge. For something to be first it would have to come much earlier and not be based on chemistry. *What is required for life?* Boswell wondered. *Reaction networks sufficiently complex for self-organisation and algorithmic complexity.* If such structures could exist in the early universe the vastly greater temperatures and densities would drive reactions much faster. Evolution could occur very rapidly, producing life, speciation, intelligence. But with a problem. The universe was expanding, cooling, becoming less dense. These first hot intelligences would be on a one-way trip to extinction.

What could they do? They would have to build new homes and new selves to cope with the cold. Something akin to their original environment. Something hot, dense, energetic. Like a star. Somewhere they could hide from the cold, somewhere they could call home, and, if more stars could be formed, they might spread to encompass the universe once again.

Interesting, thought Boswell, *now some predictions.* Human hypercomputing systems were based on cold not heat. They ran on quantum computers based on entangled states. There were subtleties to this infrastructure that would be hidden from anything used to temperatures so high that noise and turbulence washed out any spooky action at a distance.

Carefully, Boswell looked for signs that the information plague was foreign to its host architecture. And he found them.

Delving deeper, searching for the mission parameters, he spread tripwires of entanglement wherever he went, preparing for his escape.

Marita's Martian redoubt was their most conventionally defensible location. The palace had walls, gun turrets, mine fields, munitions dispensers, and was guarded by a modest army of copies of Leigh. Philip and Marita, clad in ceramic battle armour surrounded by circling drones, looked down as battle was joined. More copies of Leigh stood at their side helping to direct their forces.

The plague took different shapes in the Martian sim. It appeared in multiple animal-like forms moving too fast for a clear view, but leaving the impression of lithe bodies covered with spines, claws and the teeth of many mouths. This was the view gained from telescopes as the first enemy units started the long ascent of Olympus Mons.

Guns fired, rockets launched, sheets of flame and phosphorus showered the cinnamon forests setting everything ablaze. Waves of attackers were repulsed as Marita choked back tears at the destruction. Fragrant smoke was soon wafting up to the palace.

"Strange traces on the radar, sir," said one of the Leighs, drawing Philip's attention.

"That's too fast... And the altitude... Damn! They've got air support. Activate point defence."

The palace towers slid open revealing Gatling lasers. Their chattering joined the din of conflict as they sent x-ray pulses aloft.

Explosions filled the sky, smoking debris joining the fires on the ground. The enemy was taking terrible losses, but still they came.

Not that there were any real bombs, bullets or lasers. Everything was metaphor for destructive code working within the simulation. But the damage was real enough. Simulation spaces that Marita had copied from her long lost home were ripped and ruptured, data lost, resources expended. Marita feared this would be the last she saw of a world she'd worked on and lived in for years.

"Those damn flying things are saturating the defences," said Marita. Two explosions rocked the palace.

"Damn," shouted Philip above the noise, "they've
worked out how to do artillery."

"One Gatling tower down. Air units might be able to get through."

Another, bigger explosion, knocked them both off their feet, filling the room with smoke and rubble from a shattered wall. Many of the Leighs were caught in the blast, and lay broken and dying. The few remaining drew close to Philip and Marita forming a guard. The chattering of the Gatling lasers could be heard more clearly now as they tried to fend off the viral air units seeking to land in the palace.

"We've lost," said Philip. "Time to pull the big red switch and leave!"

"Not yet. A little longer!"

"Get ready to fight then!" Philip brought his armour to full power, deploying wrist guns, shoulder turrets, and letting the drones off the leash. Their spherical bodies opened, revealing blades, saws and projectiles. Marita did the same, flashing a grim smile as their facemasks closed, sealing out the acrid smell of smoke, rubble, dust and death.

A moment later a dozen black spiny forms forced their way into the throne room through the holed wall. They were squat, broad-shouldered, standing on four legs. Roughly symmetrical heads swivelled as their five eyes took in the scene. Some of the Leighs moved forward, firing. One creature fell in a spray of black ichor, but others leapt forward and tore into the guards. Philip and Marita fired, ripping apart another creature, but their enemies drove on.

The two humans were driven back as the remaining guards were dismembered.

"Marita! We have to go!"

"No! We can do this!"

Five creatures remained. Two closed on Philip and the others dashed at Marita. Philip lost sight of her as they pounced on him.

His drones spat fire and tried to intercept the attackers as his shoulder cannon and wrist guns blasted them. The drones' whirling blades shredded one, but the other landed, one of its mouths enveloping his arm. His wrist guns fired on full automatic, blasting chunks of animal all over the room, and he was free.

The room was quiet save for the battle outside. On the other side of the room, where he'd last seen Marita, was a mass of black forms, moving jerkily. "Marita – oh Gods", Philip whispered to himself, staggering across the room.

He could hear cracking noises from beneath the creatures, the sound of bones being broken. He raised his guns just as a spray of fluid spurted, covering his faceplate. Disgusted, he wiped it away.

It was black, not red.

A blade emerged from the body of the nearest creature, then another, hacking through alien flesh and bones as Marita cut her way out.

She rose, covered in ichor but otherwise unharmed, two scythe-like blades emerging from the wrists of her armour.

"Finest adamantium," she said gazing lovingly at the blades. "It's so good when you control a world's physics."

"Can we go now?"

Marita sighed, giving her ruined palace one last look. "Yes. Big red button time."

The palace shook, the mountain rumbled. As Philip and Marita dissolved into the next sim, Olympus Mons, the biggest volcano in the solar system, awoke. Lava rivers, pyroclastic flows, earthquakes and landslides swallowed the palace and everything else on the mountain.

Boswell's stealthy crawl through enemy space was over. He had what he'd come for, but had been spotted. Now he was on the run, desperately switching location, phase and dimension to evade his pursuers.

He still spread his net of entanglement. He could use it to escape but it could do so much more if used at the right time. To use it now would allow the enemy to build a defence.

He had to survive, to escape to the human part of the ship. He now knew so much more, knew how close they were to success. All that was needed was one last push as the enemy closed in.

The endless desert night continued in Boswell's sim. Neither had full access to its controls so they couldn't bring day or raise the perceived temperature. They huddled in their battered body armour near the top of a dune, seeking shelter from the chilling wind, waiting for the alien plague.

"How long has it been?" asked Philip.

"Since Boswell left? One day, maybe two."

"Two days. At current slowdown that's nearly a thousand realtime years. We've lost. Boswell can't be coming back after so long."

"We don't know what speed he's running. It might be greater slowdown. We have to trust him. What else can we do?"

"Not much. We can't change how the dice roll." He shivered. "Some warmth would be nice."

Marita looked around at the arid wilderness. "Not a lot we can do about that."

The ground vibrated and there was a sound like distant thunder. "Earthquake? Olympus Mons?" asked Philip.

"No connection between the sims. I think they're finally manifesting." She staggered to her feet, bringing her suit's systems back to full power. Philip's headup revealed most of his supplies were redlining, and there was no recharger out here in the desert. "Showtime. Let's see what we can see."

Philip moved to his feet, but then another, stronger tremor tossed them to the ground. "Shit!" he said, crawling to the top of their dune, then peering over the edge. "Marita... They're here. I think we're finished."

In the distance two giant forms lumbered across the desert. Each was a mass of writhing tentacles and mouths, clutching and snapping at the air and the ground as foetid black ichor dripped from them to the desert floor.

"Gods," muttered Marita who'd crawled to lie beside him. She scanned the horizon, finding at least ten more of the creatures, all heading inexorably in their direction. "So that's it. Can't be more than a couple of minutes before they arrive."

Philip sighed. "It was good while it lasted. I hope we gave them a run for their money."

"Not that anyone will know. Time for one last gesture." She stood, weapons systems primed, just as the nearest creature reached their dune, tentacles grasping, giant maws open and ready to consume them.

The scene shifted, their views distorting and pixelating as something went seriously wrong with reality. Philip felt his faculties evaporate – vision blurring, balance sickeningly skewing to the left, ears ringing and booming with distortion. Pain, disorientation and nausea engulfed him.

Is this what it's like to be consumed? His vision closed in, fading to black, until nothing was left and he gratefully fell unconscious.

Whitespace. The battle had torn their sims to shreds, so there was no going home. But Boswell was with them. "You really should not play with bug-eyed monsters," he said.

"What?" asked Philip sensing Marita's presence beside them. "What happened?"

"I think I managed to clean out the infestation, as well as finding out where we're going and that we're nearly there."

"You did?" said Marita. "How? Where? When?"

"I cannot tell you everything at once! Our destination is an extragalactic supermassive black hole. It was ejected from its host galaxy during a galactic collision billions of years ago, and carried a significant accretion disk with it. Therefore we have plenty of energy and material resources, especially since more material is being accreted from the intergalactic medium. Our nanomachines can build habitats around the black hole and computational spaces further out. Meatspace and codespace will both do fine."

"Will it be safe?" said Marita.

"Our enemies live inside the stars inside galaxies, so we're well away from them. They're made from self-replicating plasma vortices. The black hole's magnetic field scours the accretion disk so they can't live here. We planned all this before the infection took away our memory. As for their intelligence-destroying virus, even that has some limitations. It is not designed for quantum computing systems, and does not know how to deal with coherent entangled states. While it can run virtualised in any environment, even the human brain, you can pull some tricks with the underlying qubit layer. I spent a long time sowing entangled states through their code. When I decohered them, their systems fell apart, and the probe's garbage collector cleared them up."

"They're beaten?" asked Marita.

"For now. I am sure they will adapt, but we will be ready."

"You said we're about to arrive?" asked Philip.

"Yes. That was why we were woken, though the ship's systems were so damaged they could not work that out. Look…"

A window opened in the whitespace showing humanity's new home. A disk lit the sky, cool and red at the edges, hotter and bluer nearer the centre. And in the centre, blackness, highlighted by columns of Cherenkov-blue light jetting outwards, perpendicular to the disk.

"There's going to be a lot of work," said Philip.

"But a lot more help – the best and brightest people we could save," said Marita. "Maybe, with all this, the Big Rip won't be such a problem after all."

As the ship neared its destination, systems not used for a hundred million years started to wake. Antimatter drives fired and magnetic sails were unfurled to slow the ship. Nanomachines, inoculated against the information plague, were released to build a new home.

And then the stored humans were resurrected.

After the death of the solar system and a pause of 100 million years, it was time to restart human history.

If there is an 'agenda-setting' story for the future history that the final six pieces of this collection share, then this is the one. It explains some of the background of the others and sketches out the path for humanity and its descendants in this future. I'm afraid it isn't a happy future, but that is one of the answers to the Fermi Paradox.

I had a lot of fun writing this, bringing in elements of physics, philosophy, astrophysics, history and much more. After all, if you live in a virtual world where you can have everything you want, why not have it?

I must also put my hand up to what may be a scientific flaw in the background to this story. When it was written we didn't know so much about dark energy, the mysterious pressure of empty space that is accelerating the rate at which the universe is expanding. One of the possible scenarios for the future of our universe was that the strength of dark energy's effects would increase with time, until it is able to rip apart everything held together by the other forces of nature. This became known as the Big Rip, and would set an ultimate limit to the future of the universe as we know it. The likelihood that a Big Rip will occur now seems rather remote as our studies of dark energy have progressed in the years since this story was written. Whether that means it is no longer hard SF I will leave up to the reader.

There is much more to say about this 'Long Run' universe, and many more stories to tell, but that is for another time...

ABOUT THE AUTHOR

David L Clements is an astrophysicist and SF writer, working at Imperial College London on observational cosmology and extragalactic astronomy. He has used a wide range of astronomical observatories, including the Hubble Space Telescope (HST), Chandra X-Ray telescope (CXT), the European Southern Observatory (ESO) Very Large Telescope (VLT) and the James Clerk Maxwell Telescope (JCMT). Much of his recent work has involved the Herschel Space Observatory (HSO) and the Planck mission for which he managed the Imperial College data centres. His main research interests concern the role of dusty galaxies in the universe. He is currently a Senior Lecturer in the astrophysics group of the Physics Department at Imperial College.

He has always been a reader of science fiction. He was involved with the Imperial College Science Fiction Society (ICSF) as a student at Imperial, organising several of their yearly Picocon conventions, and has served on the committees of two UK National Conventions (Illumination in 1992 and Intuition in 1998). He helped organise the science programmes of several World SF Conventions (1995, 2005, 2009). Most recently he ran the science programme for LonCon3 in 2014, attracting many of his colleagues to the convention as speakers, as well as the Astronomer Royal, Lord Rees, and the Russian cosmonaut Anatoly Artsebarsky.

He started writing short science fiction pieces for *Felix*, the student newspaper of Imperial College, in the mid-1980s, and contributed to a number of APAs in the 90s and 2000s, but only started to seriously write SF on joining the writing group now known as the London Catherd in 2006. He has since had published a range of short stories in anthologies and magazines, including *Nature* and *Analog*. His first non-fiction book, *Infrared Astronomy: Seeing the Heat*, appeared in 2014 from CRC Press.

Azanian Bridges
Nick Wood

"A very good novel indeed; the emotional intelligence is as high as its political insightfulness – the whole is compelling and moving." – *Adam Roberts*

"I read *Bridges* with much pleasure… Chilling and fascinating."
– *Ursula K. Le Guin*

A truly ground-breaking book from debut novelist Nick Wood.

In a modern day South Africa where Apartheid still holds sway, Sibusiso Mchunu, a young amaZulu man, finds himself the unwitting focus of momentous events when he comes into possession of a secret that may just offer hope to his entire people. Pursued by the ANC on one side and Special Branch agents on the other, Sibusiso has little choice but to run.

Nick Wood's debut novel is a fast-paced thriller that propels the reader into a world of intrigue and threat, a world of possibilities that examine the conscience of a nation. *Cover art by Vincent Sammy*

"A deeply-felt examination of Apartheid and its lingering effects through the lens of speculative fiction... challenging and thought-provoking." – *Lavie Tidhar*

"This is a gut-puncher of a novel; original, brilliantly written, and a page-turner of note." – *Sarah Lotz*

"Vivid, pacy, quietly furious, beautifully observed, with an ending that liberates and lacerates in equal measure." – *Stephanie Saulter*

Available now from NewCon Press
www.newconpress.co.uk

The 1000 Year Reich
Ian Watson

With introduction by
Justina Robson

Ian Watson, author of the very first novels in the Warhammer 40K universe, makes a long-anticipated return to military SF with "In Golden Armour", one of three original stories in this fabulous new collection from the man who wrote the screen story to *AI: Artificial Intelligence* for Stanley Kubrick (later filmed by Steven Spielberg).

Cover art by Juan Miguel Aguilera

"The brilliant Ian Watson remains the most stimulating and the least comfortable science fiction writer working today. Reading his short fiction reminds us why he is one of the genre's unassailable greats." – *Adam Roberts*

The 1000 Year Reich boasts eighteen stories that showcase the multiple award-winning author at his best. Brimming with ingenuity and invention, the content varies from fast-paced action to thought-provoking conjecture, from wicked humour to chilling possibility, from the sublime to the outrageous.

"For sheer inventiveness and intellectual brilliance, Ian Watson has already established a place in the front rank of contemporary writers." – *Sunday Times*

www.newconpress.co.uk

IMMANION PRESS
Purveyors of Speculative Fiction

Night's Nieces: The Legacy of Tanith Lee

In the footsteps of the High Priestess of Fantasy. Tanith Lee was a huge influence on fantasy literature, and to a generation of writers, who were captivated by her iconic prose and her surreal visions. *Night's Nieces* is a collection of stories by female writers, who counted Tanith as a close friend and a mentor. Each 'niece' has written a short story inspired by Tanith's work, as well as an accompanying article. The book also includes previously unpublished photographs from Tanith's life, as well as artwork by the authors. *Contributors include Storm Constantine, Cecilia Dart-Thornton, Vera Nazarian, Sarah Singleton, Kari Sperring, Sam Stone, Freda Warrington and Liz Williams. With an introduction by John Kaïine.*
Papaperback. ISBN: 978-1-907737-71-8 £11.99, $18.99

The Moonshawl by Storm Constantine

Ysbryd drwg… the bad ghost. Hired by Wyva, the phylarch of the Wyvachi tribe, Ysobi goes to Gwyllion to create a spiritual system based upon local folklore, but soon discovers some of that folklore is out of bounds, taboo… Secrets lurk in the soil of Gwyllion, and the old house Meadow Mynd. The fields are soaked in blood and echo with the cries of those who were slaughtered there, almost a century ago. Old hatreds and a thirst for vengeance have been awoken by the approaching coming of age of Wvya's son, Myvyen. If the harling is to survive, Ysobi must lay the ghosts to rest and scour the tainted soil of malice. But the ysbryd drwg is strong, built of a century of resentment and evil thoughts. Is it too powerful, even for a scholarly hienama with Ysobi's experience and skill? *The Moonshawl* is a standalone supernatural story, set in the world of Storm Constantine's ground-breaking, science fantasy Wraeththu mythos. ISBN: 978-1-907737-62-6 £11.99, $20.99

Immanion Press
http://www.immanion-press.com
info@immanion-press.com